Escape and Evasion

CHRISTOPHER WAKLING

FABER & FABER

First published in 2018
by Faber & Faber Ltd
Bloomsbury House
74–77 Great Russell Street
London WC1B 3DA

Typeset by Faber & Faber Ltd
Printed and bound by CPI Group (UK) Ltd, Croydon CR0 4YY

A CIP record for this book
is available from the British Library

ISBN 978-0-571-23925-2

FSC
www.fsc.org
MIX
Paper from
responsible sources
FSC® C020471

2 4 6 8 10 9 7 5 3 1

For Gita, Lucas and Zoë

So, decision time.

Press the button.

Just press it.

Joseph Ashcroft, Big Beast at Airdeen Clore, digs his fingernails into the leather inlay of his Square Mile desk. He feels lightheaded, giddy. No hurry. It's a big step, after all.

He takes a breath. Looks away from the screen. Looks instead at the photographs on his filing cabinet. There's Lara, his beautiful daughter, upside down in the little silver frame, dangling from a swing, hair scraping the wood chips. Remember that park? The one with the coffee stand and the squirrel. It stole Zac's ice-cream cone while he, Joseph Ashcroft, fielded a call from Boston. Cheeky bastard squirrel! And in the next picture there's his wonderful son, Zac, very young and bright orange in his little NASA suit. He loved that outfit so much when he was small. Naomi didn't, though. 'A bit Guantanamo,' she said. Possibly she was right. It wouldn't be the first time, would it? Naomi. *Naomi and Lara and Zac* . . .

Jesus, he's overheating. The little red dot up by the ceiling reckons it controls the temperature in the room, but . . . Joseph runs a finger round the rim of his Jermyn Street collar and blinks at the 'Enter' key.

Press it.

One keystroke and we're done here.

The screen is indifferent, backlit, daring him not to do it.

Bar a fortune, he has nothing much to lose.

The kids – his excellent kids! – are already ring-fenced by their mother. He could insist, but she has a way of insisting harder. And anyway, despite all her cod-psychological ultimatums – post-traumatic stress disorder, please – he still loves Naomi. Her straight black oil-slick hair. The concentrating face she has when choosing gifts. And the way she walks, as if off to build a wall. These thoughts of Naomi send a deep regret-pang, painful as chilblains, right through him.

His finger is hovering over the bent arrow key.

Press the bastard.

Get it done.

But he can't.

Not yet.

Because a shape has appeared in the doorway.

It's Rafiq, one of the senior juniors. At what, eleven twenty on a Tuesday evening, still here. Of course he is. Because here, at revered investment bank Airdeen Clore, it's up – meaning here the whole time, beavering away money-wise – or out.

'Joseph.'

'Rafiq.'

'Anything need doing for tomorrow that you can think of?'

'No. I'd just touch base with Zuckerman and Hong Kong early doors. Hold hands. Dot stuff, et cetera.'

'Sure. We're sorted with all that.'

So competent.

'Night.'

'Night.'

'Night, then.'

'You take care, Joseph.'

The way Rafiq does a mock salute, then pushes his hand through his hair. He's what, twenty-nine? The team's star player. A star folding into a black hole tomorrow if . . . no, *when*. Regret-pang number two: imagine the effort poor Rafiq put into getting here. All those exams, the revision at his parents' kitchen table in Solihull, dinner plates cleared to one side, a television on a sideboard showing the regional news or some such. Joseph bets Rafiq's mum makes good food. *Pakora*, possibly. He imagines Rafiq's mother rolling the little balls of vegetable and spice full of love while her thirteen-year-old son rivets the maths into his top-set book. All for . . .

Just press it.

What's the worst that can happen?

Well, other than the inevitable police manhunt, there's . . .

Lancaster.

Head of Airdeen Clore's security team on the one hand, old friend on the other.

Joseph thinks of a shark's fin slicing through the water. In Zanzibar he and Naomi swam with turtles. They sort of fly underwater, pulsing kindness. Lancaster, by comparison, is uncompromising as a hammerhead. Still, Joseph is prepared for him, pretty much, has a plan, of sorts.

To prove it he gets up from his seat, unlocks the big filing cabinet, retrieves an envelope containing ten thousand pounds in cash, sits it in the middle of his desk. Not a great deal of money, peanuts in the Big Beast scheme of things, but *his* money, withdrawn from his current account. It's enough to get by on. They'll freeze all his assets as soon as they work out what's happened, and that will hardly take them long, but this cash will see him through.

He looks at the door, longing to be out of it. There's just the small matter of pushing the button first. Beneath the 'Enter' key, with its bevelled edges, lies an intricacy of springs. Joseph takes a deep breath. Grips the ___.

The what?

He's gripping it, for God's sake.

The ___.

Desk.

That does it.

That being the word hole.

So what if he filled it quickly?

The damn gaps and slips have been getting worse and worse.

Has to be a sign.

Is one!

The screen has gone black, but it comes to life instantly as he pulls the keyboard close.

There, now, it needs to be done.

He knows so, because he's thought of little else for months.

So get on with it.

He does.

With one quick tap he changes everything.

2

That's that, then. One in the eye for the Man. A round-house punch, administered by . . . the Man! – Joseph Ash-croft. He leans back in his chair and spins in it, a full seven hundred and twenty degrees, feeling what? Munificence? No, something more like relief. Plus, admit it, fear. A shivering down below. Well, that's only natural. It's a big old dollop of the bank's assets he's liberated, after all. Had to be. As Dad always said, if you're going to do something, do it properly, meaning use the right tool for the job and give it all you've got.

Dad.

Mum.

He misses them.

What would the old boy make of this, then?

'You're a disappointment to us, son.'

No, no, no: except yes.

Joseph hasn't much time. Still, he allows himself a moment, shoots his cuffs, stares at his watch. The unflustered sweep of its second hand. Brushed steel, diamond glass. Marvellously Swiss. Well, you have to look the part. Or had to, at least.

Ha.

He's done it.

A hundred thousand lives – give or take – made marginally easier.

His own . . . quietly undone.

On the computer screen it's just numbers.

There's no tidal wave ripping through the palm trees, no shuddering of buildings upon their foundations, no sweeping curtain of fire.

Numbers don't make much noise on their own. But what he's done will be seismic in its own terms. Money is shivering through the system, digits flickering like wind through the forest canopy. The same cleverness Joseph made use of to mask the bank's position – when necessary – will now compound its problem. The money was already tethered offshore. He's just unmoored it, sent it swirling into a hundred thousand unsuspecting accounts. $20,120.14 here, $14,306.98 there, $7,449.08 there. A mere $576.77 here. But $209,990.65 there.

Random strangers.

These people – or those like them – were not persons for whom the bank generally went in to bat.

Beached, sidelined, stymied, whatever, they were in need of a helping hand.

And what did Airdeen Clore do, down the corridor, at its sharp end? What any self-respecting bank would. Took that neediness and forced the punters to buy it back in the shape of unserviceable loans and inflated premiums.

So what? That's the system. There to be played. Win, don't whinge! Re the losers: who cares?

Him.

Joseph Ashcroft, that's who.
He didn't, but now he does.
At least it looks that way.

3

Best get going. But before he does Joseph takes the kids' photographs off the filing cabinet. It feels wrong leaving them marooned here. There's a problem, though: the silver frames are too bulky. He removes the photos and slips them inside his briefcase. It's more of a satchel, really, a gift (well chosen, as ever) from Naomi way back when she was still holding out for him to change his mind, bank-wise. 'You're what, now, some corporate big shot?' A bit tattered, but the leather looks good that way. He adds the envelope containing the cash to the satchel as well. It nestles next to another, slimmer one, addressed to him at home.

St Thomas' Hospital's logo in the top corner.

Joseph's not quite managed to open that envelope yet, but he will.

Soon.

He puts on his coat and strides into the corridor. There's no light switch to extinguish: sensors do all that. He doesn't even need to swipe his security card for the lift these days. It just knows he's him automatically. Look at those cameras, high in the corners. Lancaster will watch all this in black and white tomorrow morning. Wind the footage back a bit. There he is, at a quarter to midnight, leaving the office. Nothing unusual in that. Except there is.

Goodnight, Joseph.

The lift door sucks back. It's empty. In he gets. His heart is revving in his chest. It takes a hell of a time to reach the ground floor, this lift. Almost like it's toying with him, on an intentional go-slow. Joseph keeps his eyes on the crack between the two doors.

Icecaps shrink, tectonic plates shift, planets realign.

Finally the doors part, revealing the lobby.

Super calmly, as if gliding on a rail, Joseph crosses the marble foyer of the bank. He nods goodnight to the grave-yard shift receptionist, even manages a smile for the security guy on the front door. And he keeps on going, out of the building, down the front steps, into the London night.

Now what?

Take some steps.

Ordinarily – or at least sometimes – there'd be a driver waiting, but not today. Joseph strolls down Gresham Street, jinks into a narrow lane and pulls out his Blackberry. Ejects the SIM card, bends it in half.

Why?

Because it feels right.

As does dropping the lot through a drain grate. There's no splash that he can hear but something oily shifts down below. He straightens and sets off at a brisk pace in the direction of King's Cross. Not because of the train station there, despite its handy Eurotunnel link, because that's not the plan.

What is the plan again?

He's headed for a small hotel he knows, having used it

9

once for a meeting with a Cypriot investor back in 2011. So, not well enough to be known there, making it a good place to lie low.

Lying low.

That'll take him back.

To where?

Northern Ireland in 1993, or was it '94? Either way, staking out that farmhouse in the snow was a lot tougher than this will be. His first real soldiering, more or less, snooping around in search of the IRA. No soft sheets, then. Just a ditch full of slush. Remember that robin teetering along the barbed wire? He'd hoped it would perch on his gun barrel but it never did.

In going to ground like this isn't he deserting his children, his wife, his family, the very thing he wants back?

No, because Naomi's sidelined him already, so it's not his fault, it's hers, except that possibly she was justified in suggesting he leave.

Either which way, this grand act, while an important kick in the teeth for the bank, plus a helping hand for the deserving poor, may in fact help her see who he is again.

4

The concierge at the hotel is what, twenty-five? He has a long fringe, and peeps out from under it like a child, at odds with his having to be a grown-up, as the job of concierge requires.

He reminds Joseph of somebody. Uncanny resemblance to . . .

Who?

He can't think, not until safely in his suite upstairs. Puts it down to feeling so jumpy, what with the crime of the century and everything.

Joseph unlaces his handmade shoes (the chap in the shop convinced him they'd last a lifetime, properly looked after) and pairs them at the foot of the bed. Then it comes to him. The policeman, back in 1991, the one the store detective turned him over to down at the station.

For this theft isn't Joseph's first crime.

He started pretty small: the incident with the books. Very shameful. Good books, though: *Nineteen Eighty-Four* and *The Secret Diary of Adrian Mole*. He'd stolen them for a dare. Regretted it first, read them second, and buried them in the garden under the conifer hedge third. Out of sight, but not out of mind. His mother's face, when he confessed. Dad's, too. Deep creases in his brow.

'Son, we are disappointed in you.'

They made him tell the bookshop lady, who told the police ('shop policy, my hands are tied!'), who went through the motions. Formal caution. The folks hadn't banked on that, had they? Wished they hadn't pressed the point, possibly. After all, he'd turned himself in.

Well, he vowed, he wouldn't make that mistake again.

And he hadn't. Not with the light bulb when he was a student. Mind you, he hadn't needed to then. Damn store detective. But at least they – Mum and Dad – never found out about it. He, forty-four-year-old Joseph Ashcroft, Big Beast at revered finance house Airdeen Clore, having just robbed his own bank of $1.34 billion, is still mighty pleased his mother and father never found out a store detective stopped him for pocketing a £1.49 light bulb in 1991.

There were mitigating circumstances. It was Boxing Day or thereabouts. His parents had people coming round. And his mum needed a light bulb. 'Don't forget!' she'd said, lending him the keys to her Ford Fiesta. Yet the queue in the department store was just so boringly long. It snaked all the way back into the Turkish rugs. So he'd returned the album – *Live Rust* – his reason for going to town in the first place – to the Y shelf. But somehow the light bulb found its way into his coat pocket en route to the exit.

Filial duty.

Not an excuse fit for the store detective.

He was a small man with strong hands, and he stank of aftershave.

'So you forgot to pay for it, did you?'

'I must have.'

'Well, that's a shame.'

'I'll pay for it now.'

'I'm afraid it's a bit late for that.'

Sanctimonious prick.

It was all Neil Young's fault. *Live Rust*. He bought the album later in HMV. But that day was all about the light bulb, the one he'd, er, forgotten to pay for. The policeman – that's who the concierge brought to mind – was only a couple of years older than Joseph, but pretended he was about a hundred and ten. What have we here, then? He made Joseph turn out his pockets. Car keys, beer mat with Tanya's number on it, plus wallet, in which: £70. Money his dad had given him for Christmas, but he wasn't about to tell the baby-faced desk sergeant that.

'One light bulb, price one pound forty-nine,' the policeman said. 'Yet you had all this money on you?'

'As I say, I forgot.'

'Not very bright, was it?'

He didn't intend it as a joke, or realise that it was one, in fact. Not a flicker.

'Occupation?'

'Student.'

'I see. Whereabouts?'

'Cambridge.' The word sounded ridiculous, as if he'd laid a truffle on the desk. 'Studying what?'

'English literature.'

The police-boy filled out another section, his handwriting comically neat and slow, and looked up from under his fringe.

'So, English literature,' he said eventually. 'I suppose that will be good for telling stories and suchlike.'

The colour rose in Joseph's cheeks. 'I suppose,' he said.

'Well, this is all good material,' the policeman said, looking round the room. Joseph looked too, saw posters of syringes and crashed cars, plastic chairs bolted to the lino-covered floor, and a door with safety-mesh glass.

'Promise me one thing,' the policeman said.

Joseph waited.

'That if you ever choose to write about this, you leave me out of it!' He grinned.

'I promise,' Joseph said.

Promises, eh. He'd kept that one. Not that it mattered. Where might the policeman be now? Had he risen through the ranks, become the head of something or other police-wise? Possibly. Could he even be the man for the job? Track that thieving bastard Ashcroft down! He's got form. The light bulb, et cetera. No. Not with handwriting like that. They don't put you in charge of anything serious if you can't join up your 'w's, 'v's, 'm's, and 'n's. Police, detectives and so forth: not Joseph's biggest worry anyway. Swim forward hammerhead Lancaster. Sharks can smell blood half an ocean away. When he picks up the scent he won't let go.

With that cheery thought Joseph takes off his suit, selects a hanger from the wardrobe, ___s it up.

___s?

What's the word?

Damn, these tiny holes, gaps, blanks. He's sure they're getting worse. The same happened to Dad, an early symptom of

14

the bastard disease, but that's just a coincidence, because it has to be.

Hangs.

That's what hangers are for. His suit looks lonely in the wardrobe, though, doomed. Joseph sticks it on the back of the door instead. There's a hook for the job. Naked, the smell of himself rises up. Best take a shower. Why not a bath, in fact? Look at all the little bottles of conditioner and whatnot. Always used to stash such miniatures in his washbag to take home for the kids after work trips abroad. Another pang. Lara loves having her own bubble bath. Joseph pauses, then tips it beneath the hot tap. Cue froth. The little bathroom fills up with steam. Baths are a homely thing: at boarding school and in the army it was always showers. Run the thing hot, just bearable to step into, sit down in, and lean back. A moment or two passes. It's quiet in here, but not quiet enough. Slide beneath the surface. The water zips itself shut over Joseph's face. He opens his eyes, sees nothing but the blankness of bubbles on the surface. It's like lying in a snowdrift except that it's not. Why not? Because it's hot.

Up next: bed.

You'd think it would be hard to sleep, with the world about to hunt him down, et cetera, but as Joseph climbs in he enjoys a long, lion-on-the-savannah-style yawn. That has nothing to do with the Egyptian cotton sheets, either. He closes his eyes and sees numbers.

Very soothing.

It's not night everywhere.

Some people are just getting up. Complete strangers, buttering their toast, pouring out cereal, or eating whatever they eat for breakfast in St Petersburg, Cape Town, Kolkata, wherever it is in fact morning just now: in for a pleasant surprise.

No, the right word isn't pleasant; it's transformative.

Some of them may try to give the money back, but he's generated too much electronic mist for that. Him and the bedroom-based boy-genius in Milton Keynes. They bounced the takings through enough offshore shell company accounts – it took some doing – from the Bahamas to the Caymans to Beijing to Switzerland and back again, to make sure they forgot where they came from.

Wondrous technology.

Joseph: masterful un-maker of universe.

The sheets smell so clean.

Let them come.

Lancaster too, why not?

Let him.

Come.

5

He opens one eye.

It's six fourteen.

He feels: less gung-ho.

He checks the news channels but the story hasn't broken. They'll be putting two and two together to make $1.34 billion at the bank, but nobody's after him yet.

He goes down for breakfast at seven thirty. Checks out the other guests as he takes his scat. There's a Japanese couple at the next table, each wearing a set of headphones. Across from them sits a man in a golfing sweater and yellow corduroy trousers. The only other people in the room are three suits intent upon an open laptop.

Nobody pays any attention to Joseph.

He orders smoked haddock and poached eggs on toast, follows it up with a bowl of porridge, plus orange juice and black coffee. Always had an appetite on him before an exercise, operation, or the close of a deal. Unnerved everyone else, the amount he could put away when they were puking with nerves. No reason to doubt he'll find lunch later, but this morning feels like the run-up to time in the field.

A driver and car could well be waiting beneath the plane trees in Cleveland Square, but he's not there, he's here.

Thankfully, nobody is waiting outside the hotel. He needs to sort out some new kit, so heads towards Oxford Street and John Lewis. Office workers with their heads down, late for work; a cyclist mounting the kerb to skirt a rubbish truck; fogged-up bus windows; a queue in a coffee shop: normality is stunning.

And here he is, amongst the department store's first customers.

What does he need? He doesn't exactly know, but sets off to find it. Naomi used to help him clothes-wise. She stopped offering after he came home with his first made-to-measure suit. She rolled her eyes when he explained, but deep down she must have known he was right.

For everything off-the-peg, there's the internet. Underwear, gym kit, condoms, ski helmets: all delivered straight to the office. So it's strange to pick up packs of boxer shorts, socks and T-shirts in an actual shop. He needs some jeans. A couple of shirts. This hoodie. That coat. Another shirt. He doesn't want to be doing much laundry, so a couple of these other ones can't hurt. And a pair of boots, too. Takes the lot towards the changing room to be told there's a six-item limit. This flummoxes him for a moment. The shop assistant, homely, fissures in her makeup, offers to hold the extra items for him.

The confusion must show in his face.

'Just shout and I'll hand them in.'

So there he is, undressed in the mirror, curtain drawn, suit on the chair. Flecks of grey show in his chest hair and he's thickened around the middle, no doubt about it. He sucks in and tenses up to see muscles shift beneath. The lighting in this cubicle makes his hair look thin.

'Okay in there?'

'Yes, thank you. If you could . . .'

He hands the shirts through the curtain. Fingers with plum-coloured nails offer him jeans in return. It's oddly intimate. He catches sight of the shop assistant's watch. Ten fifteen. Here he is in his underwear in the cubicle of a department store off Oxford Street, bathed in mood music, trying on clothes offered up by a manicured hand, and meanwhile, just a couple of miles away, within Airdeen Clore's fortress walls, proper end-is-nigh wailing. Yes, by now it will be rippling through all of the bank's fourteen floors. The crisis team will try to contain things but they'll fail. Everyone – the board, traders, analysts, deal teams, secretaries, caterers, cleaners – will know by lunchtime.

Excellent.

He gathers his soon-to-be new clothes into a pile, thinking about the number 1.34 billion. It's a big, handsome number. Still, 1.5 trillion dwarfs it, and that's how many dollars the richest 0.001 per cent will shift offshore this year. Roughly 5 per cent of annual global output. Meanwhile, some 25 per cent of the world's population will live on less in the same period. Joseph knows these stats because knowing them is slash was part of his job. Whereas giving a shit about them wasn't, because such shit-giving was definitely up to some-body else. He wished them well, but his job was to help make the money in the first place. He'd told Naomi this many times. Normally she put her fingers in her ears before he finished.

Well, she'd surely listen now, right?

Because now, having done something pretty massive, he definitely cares, poor people-wise.

Doesn't he?

6

Joseph picks out a leather holdall in the luggage concession and convinces the younger, prettier shop assistant on the till to pack his new things directly into it. No point in putting a bag in a bag. He pays cash for the lot because he has to, doesn't he, but a man kitting himself out so thoroughly and paying for it all in used notes is a bit suspicious, isn't it? Joseph hears himself explaining that he's visiting London, that the airline has lost his luggage, all the while thinking: just shut up. She tells him that the same thing happened to her on her trip to Lanzarote last spring, how annoying it was, she totally sympathises, what with her having to borrow her friend's bikini for the first two days.

'But you've got some lovely new stuff here.'

'Yes.'

'I know it's not the same, though. Your own things are important.'

'No. I mean yes.'

'They'll catch up with you eventually,' she says. 'Mine did anyway.'

He nods and thanks her, thinking: they?

If he's going to keep himself hidden – that being the plan, if you can call it a plan – he's got to avoid drawing unnecessary attention to himself.

He did in fact consider dashing straight from the office to the Eurotunnel with his real passport, but they'd check it, and even if he had made it through before the bank alerted the authorities he would have left electronic breadcrumbs for whoever to follow.

Whoever: Lancaster.

So the plan is to hide close. In the city, for as long as possible. Thenceforth to the countryside. Last long enough in the field and they'll slacken the search, won't they? Possibly. And, in the meantime, news-speaking, in terms of what he's done sinking in, well, Naomi will have a chance to see he tried.

Tried what?

To redress things, balance-wise.

There may even be an opportunity to see the kids – his beautiful kids – before.

Before what?

The end.

Don't be melodramatic.

We all wind up there sooner or later. The trick, he's long thought, is to be the one who gets to say when.

7

Joseph walks back to the hotel. Surely he should take a circuitous route? He does. Finds a phone shop on the way and buys a pay-as-you-go smartphone from a teenager with a beard. Spots a chemist as well, and ducks inside to buy the basics. Arm & Hammer toothpaste, always. A new razor, shaving gel rather than foam, because that's what Naomi got for him. He also buys a set of hair clippers and a crepe bandage.

The concierge is out from behind the reception desk in the foyer, positioning a massive vase of flowers. They look like lilies. Yes, those ones with the orange bits in the middle. Careful, it's a bugger to get that pollen off cloth. Remember at the wedding? And yes, the concierge has got some on his shirt, poor bloke. Joseph watches him set the vase down and stand back. Presumably he gets to use the hotel laundry? Still, it probably won't come out. The lilies smell a bit cloying. They are open-mouthed, predatory. Joseph doesn't point out the stain. He offers the concierge a stick of chewing gum instead, then takes the stairs two at a time. Got to shift that midriff somehow.

He hangs the little 'Do Not Disturb' sign on his door, locks it from within, and drags the chest of drawers a couple of feet to the left, so that it sits nicely under the door handle.

Overkill, no doubt, but better safe than worry. *Sorry*. Time to check the television. There's a lightness in his stomach as he turns it on and scrolls through to the news channels. But the story still hasn't broken: there's no mention of the bank, either there or – once he's struggled with the wifi code – online. Share price intact. Nobody declaring any windfalls.

Hmm: that's almost a let-down.

No, no, no, give it time.

He can't undo what he's done. Nobody can.

That thought hits home and he's suddenly very tired. It's an odd – and old – reaction. Ever since school, nervous dread has made him fall asleep. For most people it does the opposite. Makes them alert. But maybe for him the sleep impulse is some kind of defence mechanism.

Anyway, the dread-sleep first hit him when he was about twelve, with a three-month stretch of boarding school loom-ing ahead like three years, and the hype and aggravation of twenty other boys not yet asleep in the same big room, that first-day-of-term nervous buzz, the panic rising, the false bonhomie, nobody able to settle, nobody except him, because his response was to shut his eyes and switch himself off, completely, just like that.

Wake up, Joe!

Impossible: Joe's not home.

He's done it time and again since, too. Lying in that ditch on the Derry milk farm. As soon as it was his turn to get some kip: wham, lights out. Ditto in that breakout room in Houston, waiting to negotiate the refinancing of a drilling company worth tens of millions, with the terms already horribly set against them. Job on the line. Funny to think of that now. Still, then, he'd simply lowered his head to the cool tabletop and . . . slept. Now he does the same. Mutes the television, lies back on the queen-sized bed, lets the mattress take his weight, and within seconds he's in a half-state, free-falling.

8

They serve a mean club sandwich in the hotel. Joseph orders three over the next day. They come with a sort of mustardy mayonnaise: it sets the thing alight. Must keep fed up. For no particular reason, he collects the little toothpicks they use to stab the sandwiches together. Puts them in his new washbag. Imagine getting one of those things stuck in the roof of your mouth. There's a trick with toothpicks his father once showed him. Something to do with making a rectangle within a square. Possibly it was matchsticks . . .

It's quite boring, this waiting, but wait is what he does, wait and watch, monitoring the television and the news sites on his phone screen.

When will they break the story?

Not yet.

Frankly that's pretty impressive. Holding off this long. Well done Cooper, Hemmel, Toole-Jones and the back-room boys. But even they can't whitewash the thing indefinitely. Sooner or later the numbers will give. They always do.

Joseph paces his hotel room, which is actually two rooms, substantial en-suite included, knowing how it will play out. There'll be an unexplained dip in projected profits first, followed by an immediate share price wobble, and then the full crash. As soon as that's inevitable they'll give the jackknifing truck of the bank a rogue driver: him!

Which headshot will they use?

The most recent one, off the website, probably, taken by that Czech woman with the suspiciously big lips. You'd think trying to make other people look good all day would create some insight. She was all right, though, understood that he wanted to angle his head to the right, so as to hide the neck scar. It's what, twenty-one years old, good and faded now, though it still goes a bit livid in cold weather. She took a passable photo in the end. It showed him at his authoritative-but-approachable best. Hint of a smile eye-wise, jaw nice and firm. And his hair – well cut, still sandy – looked positively vigorous in that light. He'd visited the barber especially. 'Your hair is good,' the photographer had said. Actually, yes, she was a nice woman, bee-stung bits aside.

And her work will soon be popping up everywhere, Hydra-style!

Might as well take precautionary measures now, he thinks, and retreats to the bathroom. The clippers are fully charged. He sets them going, leans forward over the sink and eases the blades through his fringe up over the top of his head, but the clean swathe-stripe he's hoping for doesn't quite materialise. It takes two or three passes to clear a fire-track front to back. Bit more chiselling, temple to temple, forward and back, and yes, he's pulling a convict into the mirror. That or an ageing squaddie. He keeps going until his scalp is all stubble. When he turns the clippers off the vibrating doesn't stop immediately. It's somehow worked its way into his skull. Bzzzzz. A head full of ___.

___?

Oh, please.

Bees.

Thank you.

His face looks sort of lopsided now. And wow, his ears. Do they keep growing with age, or is that noses? Two days of unshaven beard runs raggedly into his sideburns.

He scowls.

Naomi always hated it when he left stubble in the sink after shaving. Iron filings. Evidence, in fact. He swills water right round the rim to catch all the cuttings. Down the plughole they go. Let the hot water run a while, just to be sure. And now, pack the clippers into the new bag. Ditto old good suit and brogues. He sets aside some of the new clothes while he's at it. Time to get dressed in civvies. On go the jeans, a plain T-shirt and the charcoal hoodie. Nondescript. In this light the blue of his new jacket looks a bit purple. Oh well. He puts that on, too. Might as well finish the job off, he thinks, and takes the crepe bandage from his washbag. So soft, crepe. Silent. He unspools a length of bandage and carefully wraps it diagonally across his head. Like that. Yes. It covers his left eye and ear. He uses the tiny scissors in the hotel sewing kit to cut off the flappy bit of bandage and tucks the end in under the tightness at the back of his head. Tape would be good, but this will have to do.

He looks nothing like himself.

The first thing anyone will notice is this big slice of white.

The bits of face either side of the bandage, shorn of hair, bristling with new beard, look nothing much like the Czech woman's photo of him now.

Good job.

He reaches to unwrap himself but his fingers stop short of the bandage. Feels odd: sort of calm and ready and jittery all at the same time. Something's telling him to go through with it straight away. Waiting equals risk. The bloke downstairs, well, he could in theory see the news when Joseph does. He might put two and two together and make $1.34 billion himself. Why not scoot now? Check in at the next place in disguise. Come to think of it, right this moment downstairs they might well be wondering why he hasn't left his room in two days. That's a bit suspicious, isn't it? What's he doing up there? Hiding? Let's go and see.

9

Pausing before the door, Joseph hears a noise. It sounds like a squeaking wheel. Yes, somebody is pushing a trolley down the corridor. They want to put a bit of WD40 on that. Lovely smell, WD40. He remembers the time he went for a swim in the sea off Morte Point, forgetting his car key was in his pocket, and wanted to blame Naomi because she'd suggested he go in.

'You were a bit insistent: where was the rush?'

'Really?'

The RAC man rescued them then by dropping the water-logged key in a little pot of WD40.

Said squeaking halts for a moment. Then it starts up again, grows louder, and seems to stop just outside his door. Joseph stays very still. Thinks of the farmer, if that's what he was, taking a piss a few feet beyond the snow-filled ditch. Joseph held his nerve then and holds it now: in time the squeaking moves on. He shuts his eyes and listens to it go. A white dot, shrinking to nothing, like on Dad's old TV, the one in his study.

Time to leave the capsule if you dare.

He pulls the chest of drawers back into position, careful to align the little feet with their original dents in the carpet, and takes one last look around the room. Nothing to see here. All square. He cracks the door and peers out into the corridor. Again, nothing. Just the sigh of the lift doors shutting. If the lift has gone, it can't return for a moment or two, meaning now's the moment. He shoulders his bag and heads for the stars.

Christ: *stairs*.

Drops down them two at a time, slows before hitting the lobby, cuts across that with his head bent, ready to shift gear if a 'Can I help you, sir?' comes from any angle. Which it doesn't. Because fact is, he's not the centre of the universe, at least not yet. But boy those lilies still smell wrong. Possibly a heightened slash distorted sense of smell is one of the symptoms. Can he not remember because not remembering stuff is also a free gift, part of the package? He doesn't know. He slips past the flowers, out into the street, his one eye blinking double time in the sunlight.

Joseph cuts south, ducks into a Tube station, Holborn it is, and woah, there's a bit of a crowd. Something wrong with the line. He waits. Having a driver and car at your disposal twenty-four seven takes the sting out of London. Ah, Cleveland Square, the big silver Merc tight to the kerb. And the espresso machine on the melamine kitchen surface, the Bang & Olufsen entertainment system, the picture of an otter Lara drew at London Zoo, hung in the brushed-steel frame. History. He can't squeeze on to the first train that arrives, makes the next, and of course it's rammed. The suits in his walk-in wardrobe have more room.

Christ, Joseph's chin is pretty much resting on this short bloke's head.

He grips his holdall tight.

The chap to his right has a magnificent red beard, part pirate, part landscape gardener. Smells of tea tree oil, though. Left-leaning sociologists generally had beards in the 1980s. By contrast, Dad looked like Cary Grant. Though there was the pipe, to be fair, and those little tools for shoving the tobacco into it. All that paraphernalia was more true to academic type. Or was it? Either way, Dad resisted typecasting: when they were packing food parcels for the miners Dad insisted on including those little tins of Gentleman's Relish.

Joseph 'excuse me's onto the platform at Liverpool Street, works his way to a less crammed westbound Circle Line train and surfaces at Baker Street, not far from where he started out. Hide close. Exhaust fumes hang in the canyon of the Marylebone Road; the traffic burbles to itself. He's headed for Dorset Square. Walks a quick circuit of the nearby streets and chooses a pompous little hotel whose glossy black front door is framed with overstuffed hanging baskets, brass plaques and rating stars.

This'll do.

The woman behind the desk glances up and clocks his bandaged eye. Does an obvious double take and immediately looks down at her screen. Tiny thing, but still, it suggests what Joseph has long known, or suspected, or at least hoped, namely: most people are in fact nice.

Even the ones who apparently aren't.

Bankers, say.

Anyway, this woman here, insensitive double take aside, is clearly good at heart. He asks her about room availability and the rate card and she answers in a very bright sorry-about-that-it-won't-happen-again voice. Even so, she has to look up again sooner or later.

'I had an accident at work,' he hears himself say when she does.

'Oh.'

'Working a lathe without goggles. A chip of metal hit me in the eye.'

The woman winces and puts her hand to her mouth.

'It's not too painful now,' he reassures her.

Her hand comes away.

'And anyway, the eye doctor reckons it will mend in time. They have this new procedure.'

'Ah. Moorfields,' she says, gesturing with her thumb. Not, in fact, in the direction of the renowned eye hospital, but that doesn't matter. Seed planted.

'Yes. I'm up for tests.'

She's pleased to hear this. Cue big smile. Unprofessional half-stare well behind us now, forgotten. She shows him to his exorbitant little room. Noticing the cost, now, is he? So he should be. It's not just pricey, this hotel, but shonky, too. They've cut the place up with thin partition walls. Later that day a couple check into the room next to his, have farmyard sex, head out, and return an hour and a half later in the middle of an argument. He turns up the television but the chat shows and dance-offs can't compete with the spite broadcast next door. The man keeps shouting, 'That's what you always say!' and the woman repeats, 'Because I'm fucking right!' on a loop.

Naomi: the angrier she got with him the more quietly she spoke. Late home again: murmuring regret. And that time she found out about the intern: woollen violence.

Silence.

Woollen silence.

Not a tactic favoured by this pair. Eventually someone down the corridor bangs on the wall, but that only works to quieten the noise for a few moments and soon one of the hotel staff is appealing to the couple in the hall. What does it matter: attention focused elsewhere has to be a good

34

thing, right? Of course. But his room feels claustrophobic now. That claw-footed bath in the corner on its little island of tiles: it's an absurd waste of space! He lifts the blind. Dark outside. And still no news on the television – or internet. Making this a miraculous cover-up, spearheaded by Lancaster, no doubt.

Suddenly he's got to get out.

The bandage is in place. It's his shield. He takes a walk across Regent's Park, up onto Primrose Hill, nobody paying him any attention at all. Wow, German lager tastes good through one eye. He knocks back a pint in a pub overlooking the park and raises a second to the picture of a fish hung slantwise on the pub wall. We're relaxed here, the slant says. Any angle is fine picture-wise. He agrees. Possibly he's not eaten enough today: the beer feels kickingly strong. No! It's him that's strong! Big Beast? He is now, for sure! They'll be chewing each other's heads off in the bank, even as he considers a final drink. Just in time for last orders. Fair enough. Everybody has to go home some time.

This here bit of the park is nice and dark, though. With the lamp posts all spread out. Look up at the night sky. It's beautiful. Orange sub-glow aside, those are actual stars. Galaxies of them! All up there, making him feel real, as in . . . small. Less Big Beast as was, more speck of nothing. Go easy on yourself, man! It's not just you. We're all tiny.

What must Lara be thinking now? Does she even know? She will soon. She's twelve, not four. You can't just disappear and expect a girl like Lara simply to roll with it. He's not done this sensibly at all. Why didn't he explain? Why doesn't he?

He shouldn't, not now, but yes, he must. He pulls out his new phone and keys in her number.

Ring ring.

Ring ring.

Ring.

Crap. She's not there. But hold on: here she comes. Her own sweet voice. There's no faking it! 'Hello it's me, Lara, or rather my phone so why not leave—'

He listens a moment, cheek to cheek with her – so to speak – through plastic.

Jesus! What is he thinking?

He jabs the call dead, stares at the phone a moment.

But the sound of her voice!

He could well be about to cry.

He doesn't.

Instead he dials again just to hear her sweet mock-worldly voice.

'Hello it's me, Lara . . .'

And again.

'Hello it's me.'

Again.

'Hello.'

And . . .

Each time he hangs up before leaving a message, and each word, each syllable, even the intake of breath before she speaks, well, it's like a mini hit of Lara to him. Realistically hit-like, in fact, because as with hits of everything he's ever tried there's an immediate and horrible law of diminishing returns at work, with each mini hit somehow

37

less effective than the last even as it makes the next one inevitable.

No!

Be strong.

He stops dialling her number and just stands there looking up. There's a mineral taste in his mouth and the cold night air is laced with exhaust fumes. Despite the city glow sucking some of the brightness out of the stars he can in fact recognise one or two shapes he knows: Orion's Belt, the Plough, a smear of Milky Way. They taught him this stuff in the army, but he was never very good at it. Where's the North Star? No idea. And no moon that he can see, either. He swivels on his heel in search of it, steps backwards into the path and starts as he catches sight of something blinking quickly towards him. A cyclist skids to a halt, blowing hard in his face, a skeleton of luminous strips.

'Careful, mate!' the cyclist says.

'Surry.'

The cyclist blinks at him, comes to some sort of not-worth-it decision, kicks a pedal to the top of its arc, and starts off again, strobing to a dot down the path.

Surry?

Sorry.

The guy was right, he should be more careful. Joseph jog-walks back to his hotel, not quite knowing why he's in such a hurry, not until he finds he's already there, sitting on the tartan bedspread, with the photographs of the kids in his lap. A different kind of hit. Lovely photos, great kids, so proud, et cetera, but there's a problem. Something to do with time. Zac kept saying 'basically' when this photo was taken, which was what, eight months ago? 'Basically I'm not a fan of cabbage.' 'Arsenal are basically best.' Yet he'd already stopped saying that the last time Joseph had the kids. A visit to the Tower of London. Two hours was all she allowed. His own fault, of course, but still. Not long enough to do much but notice that Zac's sweet 'basically' tick had gone. Move along, nothing to see here, certainly not 'basically' any more. Just a traitorous picture. Because photos are never quite *now* enough, are they? These ones here don't even show the up-to-date versions of the kids. Which makes them helpful to look at, yes, but also killingly sad.

He climbs into bed.

In it, with the light out, he pushes the photographs under his pillow, fighting back the sorrow. Time, it's a funny old bastard. He drifts, thinking: Mum, poor old Mum, and Dad, funny old . . .

Except when he wasn't, not always.

There was nothing funny about the stunt he pulled on Joseph's fifteenth birthday. Or rather, the day they celebrated it. Not his real birthday because his real birthday was at school, worst luck. In school there might be a large thin square cake and 'Happy Birthday' sung loudly at dinner time, but the cake would taste of wet paper and the singing always had a sort of grating boom to it that said: actually, we don't care. In response to which, you had to pretend not to be bothered. At home the real cake plate came out, the same one for every birthday – Charlie, Joseph, Mum and Dad – every year. It had wavy edges.

So what?

So the wavy-edged plate was out, and there was a big slab of fruitcake on it, and Grandma had just arrived, and that was good because they were waiting for her so they could begin. She was taking her scarf off and hugging Charlie, who was what, eight, and pretending he didn't mind that it wasn't his birthday (good practice for school later, Charlie, keep it up), but couldn't hide his delight at being given an un-birthday present anyway, which Joseph didn't mind because he was now fifteen, not a little kid, and therefore old enough to wait.

All of which was by the by.

Dad had gone to park Grandma's Toyota Cressida, with the little AA and RAC badges stuck in the grille. One minute he was there in the window frame walking down the drive, the next he was gone, because he'd collapsed in the flower-bed. Half in it, actually. When Joseph got to him his torso was in the lavender bushes and his bottom half was kicking at the flint chips on the drive, as if trying to get free.

Joseph called the ambulance himself. Then helped haul Dad indoors and laid him on the long sofa. He'd come to his senses by then, sort of. 'I feel find,' he said. 'Find? *Fine!*' But his eyes rolled back into his head again and his face was the colour of the icing on the big uneaten cake. Mum looked worse. Grandma took her and Charlie into the other room, leaving Joseph to watch Dad blink at the plaster coving and ceiling rose. Held his hand. It was papery, dry to touch. Still, every now and then it squeezed back.

'I'll be home later. Save me a piece of cake,' Dad said.

'Of course.'

'It's just a funny turn.'

'Yes.'

'Don't look so worried.'

'Sorry.'

'Take care of your mum and Charlie, and yourself. If necessary.'

'What do you mean?' Joseph said, though he knew exactly.

Dad's left leg wouldn't stay still. It seemed a slice of him wanted to tap dance. Joseph fought an urge to pin it down.

When the ambulance finally arrived, Mum rode with Dad in the back, leaving Grandma to look after Joseph and Charlie, who insisted on opening his un-birthday present. Then Grandma suggested Joseph open her gift to him, too. It was a watch, lovely and modern with a metal strap and square face, but sadly schizophrenic: it told the time twice, once with hands sweeping around a pale yellow dial, and once on a little digital screen, and that would have been great, thank you very much, except that Joseph couldn't make the two times coincide exactly. He lay on his bed trying, but the second hand was always off. The counterpane was a Chinese dragon he'd been given when he was ten. No, no matter how much he fiddled with the little bezel and buttons, he couldn't synchronise the analogue and digital halves, not exactly. He gave up eventually, just lay with his hands behind his head listening to the ticking. A fragile sound. Just keep going, it said, keep going.

Keep going.

That's what they're clearly doing at bank HQ, despite him. It's impressive, inspiring even, for now.

Joseph wakes thinking of a bull in the ring, kicking up sawdust, big neck full of lances, doomed. The image urges him on. Him, Joseph Ashcroft, matador on the move. Or is he the bull? Either way, he's incognito. Yes, by eight the following morning he's up and dressed and bandaged and hovering at his door, intent on getting out. He can't spend another day watching television, not with this Regency wallpaper pushing in. Puts the essentials in his old satchel just in case, thinking: get out for a walk, man, take some air.

Mistake.

He first notices the man with the pointy shoes while waiting for his coffee to devolve down the chain of command in Starbucks. Joseph is keeping his one eye down. Spots a pair of dun-coloured winklepicker-type shoes, dagger toes spread in a V, and thinks: clown. The tapered trouser bottoms are part of the problem. Sportsman's stance, though, athletic calves. Joseph can't help himself, lifts his face to take in the proud owner of this ensemble. Sees the man in profile, sharp jaw, narrowed eyes; he must be what, thirty-five, so he should know better.

Elfin barista: 'Anything with that, sir?'

Clown: 'No.'

'A pastry, something from the—'

'No.'

The man glances sideways, catches Joseph's eye, and something flickers in his face as he quickly looks away.

To the barista, more softly: 'No, thank you.'

Joseph's flat white is ready. But he's not. The clown is looking at him again. He can feel it. Thinks about asking the barista to decant his drink into a takeaway cup but resists: don't do anything out of the ordinary, not now. Fights to keep his hand steady as he picks the coffee up. The clown has taken a step closer. Despite the pervasive coffee, Joseph smells his aftershave, a sort of peppery watermelon. He has ordered a flat white to drink in, too. Takes a seat across from Joseph's. Not four feet away. And every time Joseph glances up – he can't help it – the clown seems to do the same.

The coffee tastes metallic.

Should he bolt it down and leave, or wait the guy out?

Opts for the latter.

But . . .

The clown doesn't leave. Just sits there pretending to concentrate on his phone screen, pecking at it now and then with his thumbs.

The phone, of course.

What a complete idiot.

Oh Lara, Lara.

It doesn't matter that he didn't leave her a message, or that Joseph's phone is a new one, meaning she won't recognise the number, or that she hasn't tried calling back. She doesn't have to. Lancaster will have done the legwork without her even knowing. He has ways and means. Of course he does. How could Joseph have imagined otherwise? Thinking about it now, he's sure: Lancaster will have had Naomi tapped; why not Lara too? So he must have traced Joseph's phone to the hotel, where it sat pulsing 'I'm here, come and find me!' on his bedside table all night.

Next step: have this clown chap stake the place out.

What a tool he's been!

Joseph is sure, now, that the clown followed him into the cafe. He has metal tips on his heels, look. Tap, tap, tap: Joseph heard something like that on the pavement behind him. And the clown isn't about to leave now, either: he's queuing for another coffee, waiting there patiently while the elf sorts his order, as if to say: don't mind me mate, I've got all day.

Joseph pulls the traitorous phone from his jacket pocket and places it on the seat beside him. Takes a deep breath. Quick, now, while the clown is waiting for his refill. Go!

Joseph slips out from behind his table and into the street. Six or seven shopfronts blur past, and another – selling soap, or possibly candles, given the smell – outside which he pauses – he can't help it – to look back.

Blatant as a sheepdog! Hustling after him with his take-out cup as if to say: here I am, on your trail.

Trail? *Tail*?

Never mind: run!

14

A delivery truck is pulling to the kerb, its air brakes blowing like a whale, and before it rocks to a dead halt, Joseph steps across its path towards a double-decker facing the other way. He jogs around the square back end of the bus and jumps aboard. It's just about full. The only empty seat is up near the front, next to a young girl in a knitted hat. Joseph shrinks low beside her. She's playing a game on her screen, swiping at it as though conducting some sort of orchestra for ants, but the earplugs up under that hat can't be playing the soundtrack to the game because she's speaking to somebody as she plays.

'I know it's just a toaster,' she says.

Joseph thinks: I don't have a ticket. Oyster. Need to swipe before . . .

'But it's yours!' she goes on.

Never mind that, did the clown see him board the bus?

'He's a bastard!'

The bus pulls off.

Too slowly: it's barely making headway in the traffic.

Joseph leans forward in his seat to check out the shoppers on the pavement.

He half stands, leans to look over the knitted head. The bus is moving faster now, but that could still be him in the distance quickstepping through the crowd?

He has a hand on the seat back in front of the girl and he's craning to see better but he can't quite make—

'For fuck's sake! Get away from me!' The girl's knitted head bobs from side to side indignantly. 'Piss off, you pervert!'

She's talking to him. Shouting. Instantly he's up out of his seat, hands raised, backing down the aisle, all the way to the rear step with its yellow pole, people turning to look at him as he goes, damn them all, and he's swinging out low onto the pavement before the bus has even come to its next stop. Because he won't be expecting that, will he, 'that' being jumping off just after the bus has rounded the first corner!

Joseph darts into a shop. There's an escalator to his right. He takes the moving stairs two at a time and arrives in menswear. All the clothes are hanging on mannequins with tiny heads. Why so small? No idea. And why are they all leaning backwards? In reality they'd fall over, unless they had something to lean on, like the girl on the bus, who had a window to press her knitted hat against, recoiling, from him, Joseph Ashcroft!

Possibly it was the bandage that did it.

The bandage.

Joseph ducks down between two rows of duffel coats, as if to retie a shoelace, and swiftly unwraps his face. There. He hadn't realised how much the bandage affected his hearing: now he can enjoy the offensively mild rap music bleeding through the shop's sound system. The bundle of crepe is warm in his hands. He rams it beneath the flap of his satchel. What next? Well, this shelf here is full of baseball caps. One size fits all. Joseph picks a hat at random and looks for a 'Pay Here' sign. Glances over the racks of duffel coats as he goes. There's no sign of anybody watching. The assistant has asymmetric hair, wears a chequered shirt rolled to his tattooed elbows, and handles the hat like it's some sort of holy relic. Would Joseph like him to put it in a bag?

'No.'

'It's no trouble.'

'No thanks.'

'You're sure?'

'Yes.'

Joseph puts the hat on his head. Is the assistant smirking? It doesn't matter. Joseph thanks him and sets off for the escalator, still scanning the shop, but more confidently now. The girl on the bus was helpful in a way. By forcing him to jump straight off again, she helped him give the clown the slap.

Slip.

Whatever: he can't go back to the hotel again, which is a shame, because all that new stuff he bought is still there. Clothes, clippers, whatnot. Well, they can have it. He'll buy more. So why's he worried? It takes a second before he realises: the kids' photographs. He checks his satchel, sees the envelope containing his cash, the unopened letter from St Thomas' Hospital (ignore it!), his passport, but no photographs, because . . . they're still slotted under his pillow.

Is he a complete idiot?

It seems, sadly, so.

15

There's no use wallowing in it. He pulls the cap down as he exits the shop, turns north and heads in the direction of Hampstead, but does not stop there, no, because an urge to put distance between himself and his stupidity pushes him on up towards Highgate, Archway and Crouch End beyond. His hoodie is heavy with sweat by the time he stops jog-walking. It's a long time since he's run off a treadmill: the pavement feels hard underfoot, and his bag strap has cut into his shoulder with all the bouncing. Still, he's safe, nobody followed him, and there's a park bench here to rest on. He sits down, takes off the cap, runs his hand over the damp sharpness of his shorn head, breathes deeply and watches a couple of pigeons bobbing about together next to the bin. One of them has a sort of club foot. My, that's depressing.

Dad.

He didn't just have a funny turn. The doctors swiftly ruled out a stroke and heart attack, but the good news stopped there. Real cause of flowerbed dive? A vicious disease called Huntington's chorea. We all get something in the end. But Dad, for all his old-man-pipe-smoking, was just forty-two. Huntington's chorea is a neurodegenerative disease, meaning it attacks nerves. Cue personality warpage and crippled movement. Normally strikes in mid-life, which is somewhere between thirty-five and forty-five. So he got away lightly. No, no, no. Early signs include depression, egocentrism and aggression. Ah. That explains . . .

Nothing.

As the illness progresses, it torches the victim's capacity to think straight, plan and remember, as well as speak, chew and swallow. Yikes. The lines go down between the brain and the muscles, co-ordination un-ordains itself: roll on spasmodic dancing, jerking, writhing. Seizures, like the one Dad had, take the floor. Still, there must be hope? Sort of. Huntington's can be kept at bay with drugs for a while, but, very sorry, there's no cure. In the 1980s life expectancy from diagnosis to death was in the region of ten years. Sharp-end sideshows include pneumonia, heart attack, or, er, suicide. Whichever!

Dad explained all this, without quite managing to explain any of it, as he drove Joseph home after a month of school. He pulled into a roadside Happy Eater. The car windows fogged up a bit but you could still see out. Joseph stared hard at the large plastic dinosaur slide planted next to the car park. Better to look at that – or anything – than Dad's face. Dad, who kept one hand on the steering wheel and the other on the gear stick, even though they weren't going any-where for the time being. Papery knuckles, wedding band.

'Are you dying?' Joseph asked.

'What? No!'

'But you're really sick?'

'I'm—'

'That's what you're trying to tell me, isn't it.'

Dad pulled the Granada back onto the road and accelerated hard. Hedgerows and trees swam backwards past them: Joseph couldn't focus on any one branch or leaf for long enough to stop the blurring.

'I didn't even know I had anything wrong with me at all until my dodgy episode,' Dad said. 'And anyway I'm on the medicine now . . . Jesus! Get out of the way!'

They'd come upon a tractor. It was dragging a vicious-looking contraption whose raised tines were on a level with the windscreen.

Another week would pass before Joseph returned to school and sat on his own in the library, the windows black and shiny at the end of the long oak table, the medical text-book's stark facts splayed between his elbows, and only then would his worst fears be confirmed. For now there was still hope that Dad really was angry with the tractor, which passed a gateway without pulling over, making Dad rev the big Ford's engine, drifting them to within a few feet of those rusty old spikes, and hit the steering wheel with an open palm. Which wasn't out of character: for a committed pacifist he got pretty angry from time to time. But the growl he followed up with lacked heart. He shook his head and smiled at Joseph.

'Man to man,' Dad said.

Joseph nodded.

'We're all at it, trying, one way or another.'

'Trying what?'

'Christ,' Dad said. 'That's not what I meant to say.'

Joseph stared at his father's knuckles again. The skin across them looked as if it would tear easily. That Christmas he would buy his Dad a pair of leather driving gloves. For now he just nodded again.

'Don't you worry,' Dad went on, letting the car drift back from the tractor. 'I'll soldier on.'

16

Soldiering on. That's the job now. And Joseph, what with having been a real soldier, well, he is the man for that job. Except: what is the job exactly? Can't go back to the hotel because they, meaning Lancaster, will have it staked out. Possibly has the kids' photos in his own bag already. Joseph takes a deep breath. He won't, you know, *do* anything to them, will he? No! Though ruthless, Lancaster was as offended by civilian casualties as the rest of them. Possibly he'll have the house watched for a bit. No more.

What's this, then? A newsagent. Complete with fruit stand displaying grey bananas and dusty apples set out on some sort of AstroTurf mat. Next to it, a plastic tower full of newspapers. A quick look at the headlines beneath the scratched Perspex lids reveals they're mostly to do with a climate change summit, plus a capsized Indonesian ferry. Pause for a moment, double-checking. Surely, by now?

But no.

Joseph pulls his cap low and takes a random red top plus the *Financial Times* to the till. As he's paying, a shrieking noise starts up outside. But it's just a car alarm, or rather a silver-haired man struggling with his four-by-four on the double yellows. Still, the Turkish guy behind the counter finds Joseph's flinching amusing, until Joseph looks straight at him. Whereupon: nothing. Great! It's him, Joseph Ashcroft, unrecognised. He strolls back to the park bench with the club-footed pigeon, now departed, to have a read, knowing that if the news *had* broken it would have been in size forty font on the front of both papers, which it's not, making it unsurprising he doesn't find the story tucked inside the pink business pages, let alone on tabloid page three. He should have bought some of that fruit. Didn't, though, so has nothing to eat while he sits there imagining how the story would have – or will – run in the *Sun*. Something like this, he thinks.

WHAT A TOTAL BANKER!

Joe Ashcroft is not the same as rogue traders of the past. They made bets, lost them, and then lost bigger bets trying to cover up their losses.

That's how likeable Watford lad Nick Leeson took down Barings in 1995. His duff trades cost the venerable London bank a whopping £860 million.

It's also how crafty Frenchman Jérôme Kerviel left Société Générale with a £3.6 billion hole in its side in 2011.

Somehow the French bank's bosses managed to patch things up and sail on. The fate of Airdeen Clore – like Barings before it – is not so sure.

Ashcroft *was* one of the bosses. And he hasn't tried to hide anything about his crime. Except, that is, the money he 'allegedly' stole.

A staggering $1.34 billion has disappeared. Insiders suspect it's hidden offshore. Red-faced colleagues in the bank's inner circle are scratching their heads. Some of which, we can expect, will have to roll.

So far all fingers are pointing one way, in Ashcroft's direction. 'I'm convinced he acted alone,' said Peter Strummer, chief executive of corporate and investment banking at Airdeen's.

A huge manhunt is underway. UK police and the bank's private security are working around the clock to track Ashcroft. He has not been seen since Tuesday night.

Interpol are also on the case. They may not know where the money has ended up, but if the cash is offshore we suggest they start by looking for the crooked banker under a palm tree, somewhere nice and warm.

He sits on the park bench for a fair while, imagining alternative versions of the article, eventually noticing that it has begun to rain, not heavily, a gauze of tiny droplets which drift softly in the air and cling to his sweatshirt. He's shivering lightly. He walks back in amongst the shops, spots an army surplus store which sells camping and outdoor gear, and is about to buy a replacement jacket – the sort of nondescript black North Face parka you see all the cameramen wearing in those behind-the-scenes National Geographic films – when something else catches his eye.

He leaves the shop encased in a neon-yellow padded anorak with luminous strips on the back and arms, a road-worker intent on ripping up the central reservation.

17

This job, then.

It starts south of the river, in Stockwell, he knows that much.

With Charlie.

Charlie?

Yes, Charlie!

Who else can he trust, blood being thicker than water, et cetera?

There's no point in arriving at his brother's school before three twenty, and Joseph's keen to avoid public transport, it being so very public, so he decides to walk, as in retrace his steps to and beyond the centre of town, which does make coming north in the first place a bit questionable, but no, possibly it was helpful re throwing them off the scent, meaning he's not lost the cunning that's seen him triumph so far in life's many theatres, such as of 'war' and 'high finance'.

He turns up his big yellow collar and strikes out for Vauxhall Bridge. This eventually takes him through Whitehall, et cetera, the very corridors of power. Somewhere in amongst these great grey cakes of stone, with their mullioned, spotless windows, oil-black railings, and many surveillance cameras, there will, undoubtedly, be a meeting in progress to discuss 'the situation'. A worried politician or two, angry civil servants, conniving lawyers for all sides, of course, plus representatives from the bank. They'll be doing the old chastened-yet-defiant double act.

'We regret this situation.'

'But it's not our fault, not exactly.'

'No accounting for such a rotten egg.'

'Yes, we had systems in place, and yes, they were adequate.'

'But no, we didn't expect one of our own to breach them.'

'Be that as it may, we are where we are.'

'Respectfully, we need your help, to shore things up, for the wider good.'

'Or else.'

Ha!

He's pitched them right into it, hasn't he?

From the bridge he can see the Houses of Parliament fronting the Thames. The rain has thickened. It falls in veils. A tourist boat drifts past, the pre-recorded guide's pronouncements rising up in snatches. A camera flashes pointlessly within the glass-encased upper deck and the boat moves on. As should he. He heads for the Wandsworth Road.

Two o'clock. Joseph has made good time, and he's hungry, so he looks for somewhere to wait and eat. Here's a likely greasy spoon. Its windows offer him his reflection as he takes his seat. Stubble and shorn head, plus eye-stabbing coat. The satchel looks a little out of place. He stows it beneath the Formica table, bolted emphatically to the linoleum. Every conceivable combination of eggs, bacon, sausage, mushroom, beans, tomatoes, toast, chips, tea, coffee and fruit juice is listed on the menu. Also, strangely, moussaka. He ignores that and, rudderless before the other options, orders an all-day breakfast special, which seems to include everything, heaped in a sort of pyramid two handspans wide, plus a cup of tea served with the bag afloat it in, leaking brownly. He starts at the window end of the plate and eats his way east, thinking about Charlie.

He and Joseph are made of the same stuff, but life has carved them into different shapes.

This egg is good.

The seven-year age gap split them from the outset, and Dad's illness stretched the ties further.

The fried tomatoes are hotter than the centre of the sun.

Mum kept Charlie at home. Joseph finished boarding school and went to Cambridge. At twenty-one he joined the army. Charlie was fourteen and wrote a song about it called 'Idiot Hymn'.

Pretty good that: hymn, him.

The teabag bleeds out on the tabletop.

By the time Joseph gave up his commission, Charlie had been a geography teacher for three years. Joseph sold himself to the City, worked hours Charlie laughed about, and rose through the ranks, making it somehow harder and harder for his brother to speak to him normally.

Baked beans on soggy toast: delicious.

'It's an Alfa Romeo, Charlie.'

'Wow, that's great; you must be really . . . pleased.'

Charlie helped organise the Occupy movement and became an inner-city deputy head. Along the way he fathered twin girls, to whose mother he is still married. Joseph forks up another mouthful of bacon and remembers that he spent three hours at Charlie's house last Boxing Day, during which time his brother didn't really meet his eye, possibly because he hadn't called for nigh on a year before that. Still, he never forgets the girls' birthdays. He even offered to buy them a pony one year, though Charlie ('of course, we'll just tether it in the park') refused the gift.

Joseph pushes his plate away. Surreptitiously, he takes his notebook from his bag. Tears out a sheet of paper and starts to jot down a list. Of what? Items necessary, of course. He can't very well order them himself, can he? He has no way of getting online safely, no means of paying electronically, and nowhere to take delivery. Plus he can't just go marching into the sort of shop that sells all this and buy it himself because, well, Lancaster. He'll have those sorts of shops watched for big orders, or at least he could have, which amounts to the same thing: namely, not a risk Joseph can take. Charlie, though. With all his Outward Bound expertise, Duke of Edinburgh and so forth, yes he's the man for this. After all, the same blood flows in their veins, doesn't it?

Well, sort of. Meaning: hopefully.

18

Huntington's disease is hereditary. If one of your parents has it, you get to roll the dice, too. Actually, it's more of a coin flip. Fifty per cent chance. Heads you win, tails you lose.

Joseph worked that out in the school library, the big book spread between his elbows, the smell of polish gentle and smooth as the wood of that long oak table with its reading lamps and their orange glow. Beside him, a black window. He was fifteen. Apart from the creaking of the heating pipes the room was quiet. He ran his fingers over the spread page and sat very still indeed, utterly certain: those words were not about him. They just weren't. He felt it with his whole body, emphatically, as if he'd just lowered himself into a hot bath. Lucky escape. He snapped the book shut.

In fact, to begin with, the disease didn't seem to apply to Dad either. They just carried on as normal. Joseph was away at school. He wasn't very good at Spanish, and he didn't make the under-sixteen football second eleven, which was disappointing. He thought about that, and he thought about Dad for a bit, and then he thought for longer about Peter Osborne, who was in the year above him, and who had an unfortunate high-pitched laugh, and heard Joseph mocking him for it as they stood in line for lunch, so decided to prove himself by punching him in the back of the head. Boom. Joseph saw actual stars. And Dad was ill, and yet wasn't; he seemed fine at half-term. Whatever this thing he had was didn't make much difference, and it's tough for a teenage boy to think of other people even when they're in the same room, much less five weeks and a hundred and twenty miles away. They'd find a cure. Dad said so. And, don't admit this thought, but there it is anyway: Dad was Dad, not him.

They didn't bring it up until after Christmas, which until then went just fine. Dad carved the turkey with the electric knife, and Joseph didn't bury anything stolen under the conifer hedge, and they all watched the *Only Fools and Horses* Christmas special together, and that made Mum laugh so much she had to wipe her eyes. Charlie got a petrol-driven remote-controlled car from Santa. Joseph showed him how to drive it round the car park, great figures of eight, timed with the digital half of his watch.

Then one evening, after they'd put Charlie to bed, Mum asked Joseph to come through to the front room. Dad was already there, in his chair, legs crossed.

'Sit down, son,' he said.

He did, next to a bowl of olives Mum had placed on a little table. As if he was a guest.

'So. Enjoyable Christmas? Good one, yes? Charlie certainly likes that car.'

Joseph nodded.

'Which is good, isn't it. And you're having fun too. Which is important.'

'What's going on?'

'Eh? Ah. Well.'

Dad looked round the room for the words.

'This wretched Huntington's. It's . . .'

He took a sip of wine and put the glass down carefully, then knotted his fingers together over his tummy. He was wearing a Christmas sweater. Not him at all.

'. . . It's, well, we're obviously concerned about you and Charlie.'

Joseph picked up an olive.

'There's this test,' Dad went on, quietly. 'A simple thing they can do, which shows up the problem gene, as in whether you've got it, or not. It's one hundred per cent accurate, this test. They take some blood. And I, we, well, we're obviously concerned, so we took Charlie to the hospital and . . .'

Joseph shifted uncomfortably in his chair. He couldn't believe it, that he hadn't thought of Charlie before. This was about 50 per cent chances, and since Joseph knew, for certain, that it wasn't him . . . The smell of the petrol, the buzz-roar of that excellent and therefore expensive radio-controlled car. They'd had him tested. The salty olive taste was thick in his throat. Poor Charlie. He was just eight.

'And the great thing,' Mum said, her voice high and bright, 'is that he got the all-clear. Which is, well, obviously wonderful! A huge relief.'

'Of course. That's brilliant.' Joseph fought to control his face. It wanted to give up tears, crumple, laugh, for Charlie, who he, Joseph, loved, loved, loved. He'd never felt it before this moment, not really, the deep hard ache of actual . . . Charlie! Doomed for a moment, then not. Just Charlie again!

'Which leaves us with you,' said Dad, his fingers still in a knot.

Wow, the way he phrased that, or said it, or something, well, it blanked out the warm love feeling with instant resentment. Not for Charlie, no. For stupid Dad with his bastard genes. No, no, no: poor Dad! But they'd done this test thing without letting him, Joseph, know. While he was away at school getting punched in the back of the head. Meaning he was now playing catch-up. Meaning everything he was feeling was somehow out of date, thin, phoney.

'That's such good news about Charlie,' Joseph said. It even sounded hollow. And it was all their fault.

Dad leaned back in his chair to tell the ceiling. 'Yes, and we've booked you in for the test, too.'

'Tomorrow,' said Mum. 'First thing. That way we'll get the results before next Wednesday, before you're back off to school.' She paused. 'There was good news with Charlie.' She took a breath. 'I just know it will also be good news for you.'

Joseph was still looking at his father. Now he followed his gaze, took in the ceiling, white, lined with a crack-covering patterned wallpaper. The repeated crenulations were a maze. If Charlie was safe, did that make it more or less likely that he would be okay, too? No. Separate coin tosses. Mum knew that, surely. He did anyway. Charlie's result changed nothing.

'Joe?'

'Yes,' he said. There was no way out up above, but when he looked back at his parents' hopeful worried faces, it

seemed he did have a choice of sorts. He felt himself deciding. 'I'm sure you're right,' he told them. 'There's nothing to
worry about with me, either. That's what I felt when I read
up on the disease. That's what I feel now.'

'I feel it, too,' said Dad. 'And by next Wednesday we'll
know for sure.'

'Which will be a real relief!' said Mum.

'No.'

Cue: long pause.

'Joe?'

'I don't need to take a test.'

Dad's fingers squirmed over each other. 'For us to be sure,
you do.'

'It's my decision, though, isn't it?'

'Well. I suppose . . . we thought it best for Charlie, though.
So we also, naturally, think—'

'But I'm not Charlie,' he said.

'Joseph?'

'No.'

19

Joseph heads for his brother's school slash academy, mindful that he mustn't be seen. The first children are trickling from the gates. He carries on past them in search of the staff car park, trying to look as if he's on official luminous business, checking the signage, drainage, parking bays. There, behind the barrier, over by the low breeze block wall. Charlie's Vauxhall people carrier. Definitely his: look at that bumper sticker. It's a Christian fish, only this one has sprouted feet and the word 'Darwin' across its middle. Ah, Charlie. Where are you?

Annoyingly, late.

Fifty minutes!

During which time Joseph has to make himself scarce but near, one eye on the car, one on everybody else, meaning the staff and parents and children who drift about on their academy business. Thankfully nobody seems to pay him any attention at all. Still, it's stressful. By the time Charlie appears, freighted with books but bouncily striding across the car park all the same – triathlons! – Joseph's first urge is to ask him where the hell he's been.

But he doesn't. He sort of skulks into view instead. Charlie blips the central locking, opens a rear door and slings his bag onto the back seat. Then he jumps in and drags the car through a three-point turn, heading for the barrier gate. As the swing arm lifts, Joseph realises that his brother hasn't noticed him standing there. He's just, going. No, no, no. Before the car pulls forward again Joseph steps to its side and raps on the passenger window. Charlie does a confused double take. What? Who? No time to explain. Joseph hooks open a back door and jumps in among the child seats.

'It's me,' he says.

Charlie cranes his head round and there is actual fear in his eyes.

'Me, Joe!'

Charlie's head bobs back on his neck. 'It's a Friday afternoon,' he says.

'So what? Let's go!'

'I have to pick the girls up from nursery.'

'Please, just get us moving.'

The car doesn't move. Something in the set line of Charlie's mouth makes him the exact person he was aged fourteen, ten, four. He's fighting to keep himself from smiling, pleased to have the upper hand in a situation he doesn't understand. Christ, how infuriating!

'Towards the nursery, then. I'll explain on the way.'

20

Charlie puts the car into gear and eases into the afternoon traffic. His forehead, in the rear-view mirror, stays creased. What have we here, then? it says. Best go super carefully. Joseph has seen that expression before, too. Many times. For instance: here's Charlie at primary school, way out ahead in the egg and spoon race. Slow and steady, with a safe pair of hands, equals: win.

The longer Joseph waits to talk the harder it is to start. He owes it to Charlie to be honest, but what he, Charlie, doesn't hear, can't be got out of him, can it? Can't hurt him, either. Him and Libby, plus the girls. Joseph has a certain responsibility to them. Meaning he must keep them out of it as far as possible. Why, then, is he in the back of his brother's car at all? Hear that crunching? It's the sound of Joseph's own logic cracking its knuckles.

The hot-air blower is on, and this high-vis coat is heavy. Joseph struggles out of it. Every now and then Charlie glances at him in the mirror. Waiting patiently. They drive in thickening silence. There's a carabiner attached to a length of nylon rope amongst the kiddie detritus in the footwell. Joseph picks it up and turns it over and over, opening and shutting its sprung jaw. Charlie leads Outward Bound courses at school, climbs in his spare time, owns three different kinds of bicycle, and wedges a ton of kit into his roof box for the family camping trip each summer. Outdoorsy! But not military, no. Hated the whole army thing when Joseph was in it, ditto the City when he started with that. Anything Joseph, in fact, was not Charlie. But still, still, the thick stuff. Blood!

'I could use some help,' says Joseph.

'What happened to your hair?'

Joseph runs a hand over the stubble-sharpness.

'And the beard?'

He shrugs.

A pause, then: 'Why aren't you at work?'

'Well, circumstances have . . .'

Another pause. 'Have they given you the—'

'What? No!'

'Good.'

'Things are going well. It's just . . . I need your help to pull something off.'

'My help?'

'Yes.'

Joseph pauses again as Charlie negotiates a mini roundabout. Nice and gently. It's mesmerising, his driving style. Joseph sits back and looks at London's suburbs scrolling past. Here we are at Richmond Park already. How did that happen?

That means they're not far from Norbiton, where Charlie and Libby live, with the girls of course: happy family. And presumably the nursery is near there, too. Making it important that he, Joseph, gets on with it. Before they arrive. It's just hard to begin.

68

'Do you mind pulling over,' Joseph says.

Charlie checks the mirror. 'Why?'

'So we can talk.'

'I'm kind of late.'

'Can't Libby step in?'

'No! If you'd rung . . .'

Nevertheless, he brings the Vauxhall to a halt at the side of the road. Good old Charlie. It really is a grey day. Those deer in the distance look like they're made of concrete.

'Well?' says Charlie.

'Yes, of course. I should have rung. Life's been a bit hectic.'

'Is this to do with Naomi?'

'No, no change there.'

'I'm sorry.'

He's still looking at Joseph in the rear-view mirror. See those new crows' feet round his eyes, plus grey in his hair. Irrelevant. He's the kid brother. Always will be. Born wise, anyway, Charlie. A man with a plan. Whereas Joseph always seemed to be reacting to things. Not now, though. Now he's taken control.

Hold on, what about the unopened St Thomas' letter?

Stop it.

But that's the point: 'it' won't be stopped. He'll have to confront the news one day.

Not now, though.

'She called Libby, actually,' Charlie goes on. 'Said she hadn't heard from you for a while, wondered if—'

'You mustn't tell her you've seen me.'

Charlie swivels in his seat. 'Why not?'

'Just don't.'

'If you say so.'

That's a teacher's stare all right. Deputy heads are the hard men in the school hierarchy, aren't they? Enforcers. Tuck that shirt in, young man. Or possibly, these days, something more to do with sexting, or a knife. Little Charlie. Eyeballing him, Joseph Ashcroft, Big Square Mile Beast. As was. Think! People like being asked for advice, rather than a favour. Can't remember who taught him that but it's stood him well before, so why not here?

'I've got this project,' Joseph begins. 'It's, like, a . . . team building thing. And I was wondering whether you'd give me some help choosing kit.'

'A project?'

'You know, camping gear, a sleeping bag, cooking stuff.'

'You jumped me in the car park for this?'

'It's important.'

'Are you sure you're all right, Joe?'

'I will be if you help.'

'Back up a bit. What are you on about?'

What Joseph really wants to do is explain the whole thing, because Charlie will listen, Charlie will understand, Charlie will even approve. You've gone and done what, Joe? Jesus. Wow. You're an actual hero.

But he can't tell him.

So instead he says: 'It's sort of an away day, but longer. Like an away week. We have to fend for ourselves, camp out, live off the land. There'll be tasks, feats of endurance and so forth. Generally I'll have to make do.'

The crows' feet deepen when Charlie smiles. 'They really are a bunch of wankers, aren't they.'

'Here.' Joseph fishes out the list he made in the cafe and offers it to his brother. 'I've jotted down some thoughts. It's just a start. You organise these sorts of things. Check if there's anything I've forgotten.'

It's more a squint of incomprehension than a smile now. Very slowly Charlie says, 'Look, you should come round to the house. We'd like to see you. All of you. From what Libby said I'm sure Naomi would agree to that. Come for dinner, bring the family, and we can discuss this . . . camping trip.'

Joseph shakes his head.

'Right now, Joe, I'd say you could do with getting some rest.'

The hum of traffic through the park underscores the quiet. Something ancient is working itself out. He's Charlie, they're in his car, he's calling the shots. And yet he's not. Because Joseph is Joe, and you can't reverse birth order. One of those deer has moved closer. It's gouging listlessly at the grey earth beneath those trees. More big bushes really. Silence can be an effective tool. Whose silence is this, though? It's his, Joseph's, and it's growing. The deer lifts its head. They're all neck, deer. Joseph can look at it for as long as this takes.

'Anyway,' Charlie says eventually, 'you were in the army. Surely you'd know better than me what you'd need for wild camping, or whatever.'

A concession! He's thinking about it. Joseph waves the objection away. 'That was ages ago. You know what's what now. I'll come to dinner soon. I'd love to. But this is important.

I need this stuff. I wouldn't be asking you to get it for me if I didn't have to.'

'Get it for you?'

'Yeah, look.' Joseph places some banknotes on the passenger seat, more than enough to buy all that he could possibly need. 'Use this. And treat the girls with the change.'

Charlie tries to hand the money back. 'What's wrong with you buying it yourself?'

'I . . . can't. Please, just order everything on that list and anything else you can think of and pay for whichever delivery option is fastest and leave it in the back of the car for me to collect at school,' says Joseph in a rush.

'You want me to leave my car unlocked, full of shopping bags, in central London? Come to the house!'

'Please.'

'Joe.'

'You're late, and I'm sorry. I'll make it up to you.' Joseph reaches forward to run his hand over the back of his brother's head. The warmth of it. Charlie rolls his shoulders and dips away. Joseph opens the door.

'Thank you,' he says, climbing out.

'Wait,' says Charlie.

Joseph pauses.

'I don't need all this.' Charlie thrusts the banknotes back at Joseph again.

'Keep it,' says Joseph, thinking: that word 'all' is excellent! Because it means he's going to get the kit for him, doesn't it?

'This is too much.'

'Come on, I'm asking a favour getting you to sort the kit for me; the least I can do is pay.'

When the twins were born Libby nearly died from preeclampsia and the doctors kept her in hospital for two weeks. The woman in the next bed had given birth to a dead baby and couldn't stop crying. Charlie wouldn't let him pay for a private room, even then. But this is different: he's asking a favour. Joseph pushes Charlie's hand back through the window and turns away.

'I'm worried about you, Joe.'

'No need. Just sort me the stuff, please.'

'I'll get it, I'll get it, but—'

'Thank you.'

They look at one another, but it's painful, easier not to. Focus on that big bird flapping sideways out of the stand of trees over there instead. The wind has got up. Yet that's the sound of Charlie turning the key in the ignition. The car pulls off. Joseph watches it go. Ah, Charlie, he thinks. I love you. It's only as the Vauxhall turns out of sight that nervousness undermines the warm glow.

He's highly visible – fluorescent – here amongst the deer. Better make tracks.

He sets off south, out, out of the park, and down an arterial road flanked by suburban villains.

Villas.

Ha.

Ha ha.

That's actually a funny one.

But Christ, what he'd give for it to stop.

21

If – no – when Charlie orders the stuff it will still take a day or two to turn up, meaning Joseph needs to lie low somewhere until then. In Kingston he passes a Travelodge. That'll do. Bland being the word here, he takes off his bright coat, turns it inside out, and tucks it under his arm before entering. The man behind the desk has a very high forehead. He makes Joseph think of battle re-enactments.

There's something strange about the room Joseph ends up in. What is it? The chequered bedspread! It's exactly the same as the one Naomi bought for spare bedroom number three. Ah, spare room three. Joseph did his time in there before he left. The attempts to make up, also featuring the counterpane, plus I-still-love-you sex, the chequers rumpled on the floor. And straightening the room afterwards, pulling the throw tight over the duvet together. Two people working together can make a bed much faster than one person. Joseph runs his hand over the plum-coloured squares. To make a bed with someone you love is as intimate, in its own way, as anything that you might have done together in it the night before. Something twists inside him. This is like their spare bedspread, but it's not theirs. Travelodge is a massive chain. How many more just like it are spread over cheap mattresses up and down the country?

Joseph takes a scalding shower and lies back on the bed, steaming. He blinks at the ceiling for a while, resisting the temptation to check the TV news. Instead, he opens the drawer in the bedside cabinet. Yes, a plastic-covered Gideon Bible, stiff-spined, never read. He cracks it at random.

PROVERBS 13

A wise son heareth his father's instructions: but a scorner heareth not rebuke.

² A man shall eat good by the fruit of his mouth: but the soul of transgressors shall eat violence.

³ Those who guard their lips preserve their lives: but those who speak rashly will come to ruin.

⁴ The soul of the sluggard desireth and hath nothing: but the soul of the diligent shall be made fat.

⁵ A righteous man hateth lying: but the wicked man is loathsome and cometh to shame.

⁶ Righteousness keepeth him that is upright in the way: but the wickednesses overthrow the sinner.

⁷ There is that maketh himself rich, yet hath nothing: there is that maketh himself poor, yet hath great riches.

⁸ The ransom of a man's life are his riches: but the poor heareth not rebuke.

Didn't have to read for long to hit something relevant, did he? And yet the certainty of these verses is a bit off-putting. Reminds him of Square Mile chutzpah. Say it confidently enough and others will believe. Because bullshit baffles brains. Which kind of puts a damper on verse three. Also: 'the wicked man is loathsome and cometh to shame': bollocks does he! Joseph rereads verse seven a couple of times, smiling to himself: 'rich, yet hath nothing . . . poor, yet hath great riches.' It doesn't really feel that way, not lying naked on a Travelodge counterpane, but if you say so.

He's tired.

Bugger the news for now.

He shuts his eyes.

22

Seven times a week for twelve straight years.

God in metronomic doses.

Why?

Just because.

Joseph thinks of vitamins, cod liver oil, and times tables. It was necessary. Not at home, no, apart from the odd carol service in the Christmas holidays, for Mum's sake, but at school, where it was part of the . . . what's the new word? . . . yes: ethos.

Formative years.

Top them all up with a daily shot of God.

Ha.

Formative? Well, yes, in theory. Joseph was as ripe for indoctrination as any eight-, eleven-, fourteen-year-old. And like the rest of them, he sat through a service a day for all those years. Making the sheer toothlessness of the regime all the more remarkable. Let's face it, beyond a propensity, when running away, scared half to death of himself, to marvel at the complimentary Bible, all those thousands of hours spent listening and singing and kneeling and praying seem to have slipped from him as completely as honey off a hot spoon.

Our father, who –

I vow to thee –

God be with –

And did those feet in ancient –

Marching on to war –

The school chaplain had a pink face and fine blonde hair. He was young, despite the ageless Sunday flowing robes. What else? Well, he sang in a loud voice and spoke with a soft one, which seemed a ploy, disingenuous.

After the incident with the stolen books Joseph was given an appointment to see him. This was called pastoral care. There was a page on it in the school prospectus. Phoney and cloying! But the chaplain, it seemed, as he opened the stippled-glass front door and ushered Joseph into his study, was in earnest, for he'd put out tea and biscuits on a spindly modern coffee table, and now set off to fetch a jug of milk. Joseph took in the book-lined walls. Heavyweight tomes on practical ethics and comparative religion above the desk, but also big books on photography and art on that shelf there, Robert Mapplethorpe next to the Marquis de Sade, and that wall to the right seemed full of modern fiction. Was that an actual copy of *The Secret Diary of Adrian Mole* on the desk? Ha, it was, and the chaplain caught Joseph looking at it on his return.

'Just doing my homework,' he said with a smile.

Joseph felt himself redden.

'So,' said the chaplain, waving away the remark with one hand and pouring the tea with the other, 'what's all this about, then?'

Joseph took a breath to answer, but the chaplain cut him off.

'Actually, scratch that. I can guess. You were showing off. But you actually wanted the books too. Right?'

'I suppose.'

'And it's not some cry for help?'

'No.'

'Good.' He offered Joseph a biscuit and went on. 'I was arrested once, you know, for public disorder. I chained myself to a railing at university. There was a point to it, I think.'

Joseph nodded. 'I'm not going to do it again. You don't need to tell me—'

'I wasn't going to. But thanks for reminding me. Don't! What I was going to say is that you are free to borrow my books. Here.' He leaned forward in his Scandinavian arm-chair and handed Joseph a copy George Orwell's *Down and Out in Paris and London*. 'If you liked *Nineteen Eighty-Four* I imagine you've already read *Animal Farm*, and this is his next most important work.'

Joseph studied the cover. A fingerless glove. A cup of tea. Something rose up inside him, making it hard to speak. The chaplain's sharp-creased trousers had risen up, too, reveal-ing turquoise socks. He crossed and uncrossed his ankles and told Joseph he'd look forward to hearing his thoughts on the book.

And fifteen months later, when Mum suggested Joseph get confirmed – for form's sake, and weakly, as Dad didn't agree – he sat in the same room and drank tea from the same china tea service while the chaplain, in orange socks this time, made space for him to confess that he didn't think he really believed in God.

'I know what you mean,' the chaplain said.

'Really?'

'Best to wait, if that's the case.'

For what, he didn't say.

But, before Joseph left, he did lend him a copy of Robert Musil's *The Man Without Qualities*, together with a book of poems by somebody called the Earl of Rochester, neither of which Joseph read.

23

For forty-eight hours Joseph stays put in his Travelodge room, listening to his beard grow. It's itchy. What he'd give for those books now, the Bible being a bit, well, biblical, after a while.

There's the cheap television screen in the corner, with the little remote control here on the bedside table, and yet he's determined to abstain from them. That way he wins. Because, so what if Lancaster's contained the story? The reporting of it is irrelevant, as compared with the deed itself.

The bank is a shot elephant. Sooner or later, come what may, it will go mad in the bush, trampling guarantors and investors and insurers underfoot, while the deserving multitude bless their anonymous luck. Focus on that, on them.

On day three, after he's spent another forty minutes staring at the picture of the cows on the wall, noting again the painter's cheap trick of underscoring shadows with a dusky pink edge, he hears the hotel cleaner tap solicitously on the door and ask whether now might be a convenient time for her to give the room a once-over. It occurs to Joseph that staying put any longer might arouse its own suspicion. Since nobody else has come knocking yet it might be fair to assume that he's in the clear for now, making it tempting and in fact sensible to take a walk, before he goes entirely nuts.

He heads out.

To church!

Not, he thinks, on purpose, but after wandering Kingston's dormitory side streets for half an hour, time spent with his collar up and his head down, glancing over his shoulder every two hundred yards, every twenty, every two, he decides he's had enough and, when a church presents itself to him, its studded oak front door ajar, he ducks through the latch gate, makes his way along the brick path, and slips inside.

Look at these flowers in the entrance, tall displays of something purple spiked with pampas grass. Somebody must have got married here at the weekend. Which was when? He's lost track of the days. At Charlie's wedding Joseph was an usher. For half an hour before the service he stood next to a similar man-sized flower display, itself artfully placed in front of a space heater. It was a cold day. Joseph was charged with the job of distributing flyers to the blue-skinned guests, whereas Charlie had chosen that Patrick bloke, his old friend from school, as his best man. Didn't mind at the time, but somehow it stings now, what with the smell of disappointment coming from yesterday's flower display.

The church is silent, and nobody else is inside it, not that Joseph can see, at least. He waits for a moment in the quiet, then pulls the big door shut and takes a seat to one side of a stone pillar. Good view of the entrance from here. He shuts his eyes all the same. As a sanctuary, a refuge, the church feels almost as good as his Travelodge. It's more public, but the two places share something of the same anonymity.

Welcome, one and all.

The stained glass is modern. Replaced after the war,

possibly. Gone are the dark reds, blues and greens of the school chapel; here they favour big panes of less dramatic, pastel colours, which sadly give the church a watery vibe. This is a C of E set-up, for sure. No need to confess, just take a seat, we're brimstone-free.

What would he do if a confession was on offer today? It would be tempting to reveal all, here, wouldn't it. But why? Something to do with a rich man trying to get through the eye of a needle. On a camel. That, and feeding the five thousand. Giving away the bank's money is a pretty goddamn Christian act when you think about it. So confessing to it would be more like boasting than saying sorry. Forgive me, Father, for I'm a bit like Jesus. You can't say that! But think about it, there are similarities. What with the plan and so forth. Off into the wilderness. Doubt Jesus had a sleeping bag, though. Will there be locusts to eat?

Just: no, no, no.

Because the fact is, there's enough other stuff to confess, but really it's Naomi and the kids he needs forgiveness from, not a stranger in a booth.

He leans back against the wooden pew, which creaks. Lifting his face to the vaulted ceiling he shuts his eyes again, and . . . old habits being hard to break . . . falls asleep.

When he awakes there's somebody else in the church. A woman, wearing a pink parka with the hood up. He almost bolts when he sees her. But she's paying Joseph no attention at all, just walking to the front of the church with a lumpy carrier bag hanging from each arm. Those bags look heavy. She sort of waddles up the aisle with them and does a little curtsy, then dog-legs off to one side. Joseph cranes forward to see her take tins from the bags and set them on the side table. Vegetables follow. Now she's coming back down the aisle. He notices that she's wearing odd sandals. There's something sincere about the whole ensemble, the whole act. She walks past him to the rear of the church and he hears her sit down. This is his clue to leave.

Cue.

He stands up.

A strange urge propels him.

Instead of going straight to the oak door, he's drawn towards the little table on which the pink woman left her offering.

Why? To check what she put there, besides leeks and red cabbage?

Look: a can of minestrone soup, a four-pack of skipjack tuna tins, and two tubs of custard powder.

His hands seem to have a mind of their own.

They're opening up his satchel.

Is he about to slip one of these tins inside?

No!

Quite the opposite, in fact.

He pulls out his cash-filled envelope, takes a few of the remaining notes from it, and puts them on the table.

Takes a step away, then thinks: no.

Reaches for the notes again and slips them into his pocket.

Stands the envelope – containing almost all he has left – between the tuna and the soup.

Breathes out – thinks: take that, Jesus! – and beats a retreat.

24

At the end of his first year at Cambridge, Joseph returned home for the university holidays and, on letting himself in through the back door with the key kept under the tomato pot in the greenhouse, discovered that the house wasn't empty after all: his father was there, too, dead in his armchair.

His first thought was that the old man was asleep with his mouth open and his head canted to one side; he'd have a stiff neck when he woke up. Joseph hadn't seen him look like that before, but that was one of the disease's nasty clevernesses: it threw up new indignities with a cruel persistence. This slack-jawed slumping was probably one of them. There being no giveaway smell, no waxy pallor, no preternatural stillness in the room, Joseph coughed. When that didn't work, he drew a breath to say something loud, but before whatever he would have said materialised he noticed the empty pill jars standing in a neat row on the coffee table to one side of his father's armchair. They were ranked next to a framed photograph of Joseph, Charlie, Mum and Dad on a camping holiday in Norfolk. And what was that, between the pills and the photo? An envelope.

Joseph picked up the photograph. That was a windy week. An elm came down on top of a caravan in the next field, slicing off one tin-can wall. Luckily whoever the caravan belonged to wasn't inside it at the time. You could see their pyjamas, still folded, on the floor. Normally this photo hung above the piano in the hall. The picture hook was still there, horribly naked. Joseph set the frame back in place on the wall and returned to his father's side. He hadn't moved. Of course he hadn't. That obviousness didn't make the fact he hadn't any less shocking, though, did it? Joseph put his nose to his dad's cheek and stayed put like that for a while. When he stood back up, he saw he'd wet the old man's collar with his tears.

He took a step back. The envelope wasn't addressed to anyone. It wasn't sealed either. Joseph untucked the flap and slid the letter out and the first thing he noticed was that Dad's handwriting, rakishly elegant for as long as he could remember, had taken on a stunted and clotted look, and somehow Joseph found himself resenting his father for the change. That wasn't right! He shivered with shame as he read.

I have to keep a step ahead. This will, I know, be harder for you than it is for me. Please understand. I want to spare you. Spare myself. I'm so sorry. I love you ill. Arthur/Dad.

Ill?
No, no, no: an ill-formed 'a'.
Damn, damn disease.
The words were all up at the top of the page and the acre of white space beneath them made Joseph sure his father

had begun hoping he'd come up with something more to say. Not that he needed to. The dark blotch on his collar was already fading. This cramped handwriting was not Dad. Joseph folded the note back into the envelope and put it in his pocket. Then he gathered up the pill bottles and sunk them in the wheelie bin out by the car port beneath a jumble of empty food containers and last weekend's newspapers. He stood there for a while. A blackbird was pecking for worms in the flowerbed. This fence running along the boundary line: he'd helped his father creosote it when he was what, twelve or thirteen? Before the diagnosis, at any rate. A lifetime – or a life sentence – ago: the wooden panels already needed treating again. Later that week Joseph would buy the stain and redo the job with Charlie, who was now thirteen himself. But the job in hand was to check on Dad again and, with the cordless phone pressed to one ear, explain to the family doctor that they'd like him to come to the house as soon as he could. In his chair, Joseph told him. And yes, it looked as if he had passed away peacefully.

25

En route back to the Travelodge (home!) Joseph succumbs and buys an armful of papers to read in his room. He lays them out on the now-taut bedspread and feels a pang of disappointment. There's still nothing about the bank, or him, on the front pages. Or, damnit, among the stories that follow.

What's going on?

Back in 2008, as the crash was happening, Airdeen's did what all the other banks did and refused to revalue their collapsing subprime vehicles for as long as possible. Joseph knows how brazen they were then, because he was down the corridor from the guys who did the work. But this is different. It's not a fund value deteriorating. He's liberated cold cash. Keeping this hidden is a new fraudulent low, even for them. But that's not what's bothering Joseph. Not really. What he can't work out is why they don't think it's in their best interests to confess immediately and point the finger at him.

He sleeps on this.

And wakes feeling lightheaded, purposeless; even the yellow coat folded across the back of that armchair looks deflated.

There's only one thing for it: he needs to see if Charlie has done what he said he'd do.

So let's tidy this place up. Put the papers in the bin, set the Bible in its drawer and the furniture back in place. And head out again, into what looks like a nice warm day. Because it is! The walk back to Charlie's school takes him nearly three hours. He arrives in a sweat at just gone two o'clock. The sun is bright in the staff car park, pouring down onto the windscreens, cutting a fishnet of shadows from the chain-link fence. Look at that woman there, bent over on the pavement, scraping dog mess into a plastic bag. Well done! Joseph walks past her and returns when she's gone.

The car is there, at least, down the far end of the lot, parked next to the wall.

Joseph strolls towards it, thinking: look entitled.

That's it, just walk on up to it, peer in the big boot window.

Stupid name, 'Zafira': more belly dancer than utility vehicle.

What's that hump there in the back, though, covered with a picnic blanket?

Promising, that's what.

Joseph checks quickly across the car roof to make sure nobody's about, then tries the door. Locked. Ditto tailgate. But there's something in there for him, he's sure of it. What else could it be beneath that bulge? Does Charlie expect him to break in? Smash a window? No idea, but it's possible.

As he's casting around for a suitable rock a siren howls.

The noise sends Joseph down on one knee, his heart up into his mouth.

Is this some kind of trap?

He's wondering which direction to bolt in, when the ambulance surges past.

Yes!

The relief spreads through him like a draught of cold water.

An ambulance!

Off it Dopplers.

Great word, that, and right there when he needed it.

Superb!

So, where's a brick, then?

Let's do this thing.

He's still on one knee, which puts his face on a level with the wheel arch, which makes him think to check the top of the tyre, where – bingo – Charlie has balanced his car key. Bloody obvious! Imagine if Joseph had put the back windscreen in.

Joseph pops the boot catch and peels back the tartan rug. Excellent.

Charlie's found him a proper Bergen. Full-sized. Not a camouflaged number, but not some Day-Glo colour either, just a modest, slate grey. And it's heavy! Blimey. What's he put in here? As Joseph drags the backpack towards him he spots the note sticking out of the top pocket.

Joe, you asked for this, so here it is. I want to help you. We all do. When you're done with the back-to-nature stuff please give me a call. Stay safe in the meantime, Charlie.

Ah, Charlie.

How about that.

Did he doubt him?

Of course not.

Charlie!

Joseph hefts the pack out onto the ground, shuts the boot, blips the lock, and returns the key to the top of the wheel. Then he retrieves it again, re-opens the car, and rummages in the door pocket for a pen or pencil, because there's always one there, which there is, because he knew there would be. Pulling out the note again, he spreads it on the car window and writes 'THANK YOU', just like that, in capitals. Then, with the note on the front seat and the car safely locked again he shoulders the pack – blimey, it's been a while – and sets off.

Where to?

Don't worry, he's thought of that, hasn't he?

Oh yes.

26

The rucksack really is pretty heavy.

It takes him back.

He was standing by the pigeonholes in college when he saw it on the floor, an A5 sheet with the words 'University Officer Training Corps' printed across the front in dark green. He picked it up. Nobody he knew had anything to do with the army. He'd never wanted to have anything to do with it himself, either. The flyer said the army paid bursaries of £1,200 a year, but even though Dad's death had left things tight at home it wasn't the money that swayed him. Definitely was something else to do with Dad, though. Before the disease kicked in, Dad had marched against the Falkland Islands conflict and delivered food to the Greenham Common protestors, in his suit. Well, Joseph wasn't him. And six weeks later he would prove it beneath a massive pack crawling up a rain-soaked escarpment in the middle of the night, bits of Wiltshire flint sticking into his elbows and knees, his nose grazing the mud and his pulse banging away in his neck.

They were attacking themselves, or pretending to. He had a wooden-stocked .303 rifle dating approximately from the Somme cradled across the crooks of his leopard-crawling arms, and a sodden cardboard box full of blanks stashed somewhere in his webbing which, since he hadn't done it up properly, had slid round his waist to jab him in the gut. Team Blue – one of the other sections in the platoon – were the enemy for now, and they were out there looking for Joseph and the rest of Team Red, who were doing the same, at least in theory. In fact, Joseph was just trying to keep up with Wegg, a biochemistry student from Hull. He was ahead and to the right. Up under that beret he had alopecia. Apparently he'd been doing this pretend army stuff since he was thirteen. The night before the exercise he'd said he could strip, clean and reassemble his Lee–Enfield without looking, so someone blindfolded him and he did.

Given this competence it seemed a good bet for Joseph to follow him up the ridge. And so it was. They were making progress. It wasn't Wegg's fault that the damn webbing was biting into Joseph's side. He couldn't go on like that, so suggested they lie up in a handy hollow for a moment while he sorted his shit out. Wegg raised no objection, just used the delay to do some pro-fiddling with his rifle.

Joseph's fingers were tingling with cold.

Once he'd adjusted the webbing, he stuck his hands under his armpits and shut his eyes to concentrate on feeling the warmth there.

And when he opened them again he saw Team Blue, bent double, working their way along the ridge, outlined against the night sky.

Ha!

Whoever was leading clearly hadn't been paying attention when Sergeant Illis explained the five 'S's: shape, shadow, shine, spacing and silhouette.

Joseph nudged Wegg. 'Check them out,' he whispered.

Wegg's eyes widened. He held up a gloved hand. Wait for it, wait for it. Now! The hand disappeared and the brambles in front of Joseph burst apart. They may have been firing blanks but the tongues of flame jabbing from their barrels had enough scorch power to burn the leaves. Team Blue were twenty yards away, bolt upright, and very pretend dead when the onslaught stopped. Joseph made out Myers, the geographer from Durham. He was standing with his hands on his hips, saying, 'Fuck that, then.'

Clearly Wegg wanted a friend. Why else would he have given Joseph the credit for conceiving an ambush? But that's what he did at the debrief that morning, fingering the bald path above his ear as he insisted Joseph's decision to lie in wait was astute, not plain lucky. Once a person gets a name for something, even if it's as nebulous as 'tactical nous', the reputation can be hard to shift. Easier, in fact, to have a go at living up to the label. Back in 1982 Joseph's father had gone on opposing the Falklands War long after the army won it. Though he never thought the thought outright himself, it wouldn't have taken a master tactician to work out Joseph's motive for applying for a real commission on leaving the university.

But that's what he did.

With only a 'seems like something useful to do', he swapped ivy-clad quadrangles and exams for square-bashing and kha-ki. Looked up one day to find himself wiping cam-cream along his cheekbones, chin, and the bridge of his nose, 'Nam-style, though in truth it was only Berkshire. The smell of that stuff, not a million miles from the polish they used on their boots and dress shoes, equals Sandhurst. Endless dressing up in the army. Plus cleaning and ironing. And getting filthy again. Yes, the standard hours spent getting kit clean, and many more hours cleaning things that were already pretty spotless before they started. Dust from inside the grille of a radiator. Droplets of water in an otherwise pristine sink. Joseph developed a real interest in mirrored toecaps: just one of the army attributes which later stood him in good stead for the City.

That's when he first met Ben Lancaster, polishing boots.

Lancaster had done something wrong – not aligned his toothbrush with the taps or something – and had to polish the platoon's boots by way of punishment. Joseph held back and saw that Lancaster had been set an impossible task: he had no chance of finishing the job before the 22.00 curfew. Poor kid was working like a bastard at it anyway, ginger head bent low over the task. He didn't even look up when Joseph offered to help, just grunted his thanks. This was 1993. Lancaster had a portable radio. They worked side by side spit-and-polishing boots to a soundtrack of Suede, Radiohead and The KLF, which meant they didn't have to talk much. Still, Joseph learned Lancaster really was as young as he looked: nine months beforehand he'd been sitting his A Levels in a sports hall in Edgbaston. Now here he was at Sandhurst. This boot-polishing punishment was his first slip-up. He didn't make many more. Keen wasn't the word. Here, for example, he somehow polished three boots to every two of Joseph's, no matter how fast Joseph worked. Between them they finished ahead of the deadline.

'What do you need in return, then?' Lancaster asked when they were walking back across the square.

'Nothing,' Joseph said.

'Yeah, right.'

'It's worth it just to spite them.'

'I'd have got them all done in time, I reckon.'

Joseph shrugged.

'But if you think of anything, I owe you.'

'Okay, then.'

27

Joseph lugs the pack through Stockwell across the river and up to Victoria. The bulk of the thing. He feels horribly conspicuous, a rhino among poachers. He hits the station concourse in a hot sweat, but at least there, with the Gatwick Express, et cetera, a big backpack makes sense. Off to see the world! Except that he's not. No way is he going near the airport. They'll still be watching there. Could well be monitoring the train stations, too, though if you think about the clock face of London, from Victoria at 7 round Paddington at 10, Kings Cross at 12, Euston at 1, Liverpool Street at 3, never mind the smaller stations, all disgorging their countless commuters into and out of the city every day, well, that's a hell of a lot of faces to watch, making this a calculated ___.

___?

Bollocks.

___?

Risk.

Joseph buys a train ticket at a self-service machine. Not for the station nearest where he wants to go, because that's the whole point about taking a *calculated risk*: you do your best to minimise the downside. Come to think of it, alongside polished footwear, risk minimisation is another army trait that set him up well for the City.

Shoe-shine plus arse-covering.

He gets himself within sight of the right platform and waits, thinking, for no good reason he can work out at first, about a Terry's chocolate orange. You know, the ones with all the segments. The best way to crack one up entirely is to hit it on one end with a blunt instrument.

Possibly a rolling pin.

That's him, he realises, which makes Airdeen Clore the chocolate orange. Hitting it with a $1.34 billion mallet will split the bank apart, won't it?

Come on everyone, help yourself to a bit.

Crumbs for some, whole slices for others.

Imagine being just a normal punter, relatively poor and so on, and waking up to a swollen bank account, with no idea where the extra money has come from. Some of them will have a go at returning their windfall, no doubt. And no doubt about it, they'll fail. Look all you like, you'll never find out! He bounced that cash through more offshore accounts than there are hairs on Lancaster's head. Still gingerish, after all these years, but cropped shorter than short now, fuzzy as a tennis ball. All it took was a little IT help from that chap in Milton Keynes. At least that's where he said he was.

The clackety-clack local train pulls into the platform. Joseph double-checks the departure board. That's the one. He moves in among the waiting passengers as the train rocks to a stop. Stands in line. Files aboard. Chooses a seat he can stow the rucksack behind and hunkers down.

Smells a bit like cheese-and-onion crisps in here.

Nasty, yet his stomach rumbles.

The train must move off soon.

Infuriatingly, though, it doesn't. It just sits there. Joseph checks his watch and sees the departure time drift by.

Also, out of the corner of his eye, he clocks a moving shape on the platform, coming to a halt just there, right beside his window. Christ. And here's somebody else looming down the aisle.

Instantly he's un-hungry. In fact, his stomach is now a fist. Just keep your head down. But no, try as he might, he can't stop himself from looking. The guy on the platform is in his sixties, dressed in a houndstooth jacket, a country-casual shirt, and a mustard tie. He's taken off his glasses and is wiping his eyes with a thumb and forefinger. When he opens them again he's staring directly at Joseph.

A pane of glass and three feet are all that separate them.

That's a thousand-yard stare.

Slowly the man smiles.

Then he blows Joseph a kiss.

What the—? This must be some kind of Judas-betraying sign! Joseph is up out of his seat, but the way is blocked by the person coming down the aisle. She's a she, which is good, and older, ditto, and big. Steady on with the prejudices. She's plonking herself down in the seat opposite, plus also looking straight through him, at the man, who is smiling at her.

Joseph hadn't realised he'd been holding his breath, not until now, as he lets it out.

The engine judders to life and the old boy pushes his glasses back up his nose. The carriage rocks on its wheels, the brakes release with a hiss, and his head jinks back: did he just do what he thinks he did?

Seems so!

The train finally starts rolling and the woman across the aisle raises her hand to wave at the man, who shrugs at Joseph and winks again.

28

As the train gathers speed Joseph sinks back against the seat and thinks of another kind of winking, the sort he does – or did – with the kids. Lara particularly liked it when she was small. She'd lean in across the big kitchen table and he'd see in her face that she was about to wink or purse her lips funnily, and when she did he'd do the same, making her pull off another type of wink or blink or frown, which he'd copy, too, as fast as possible, and so on, a kind of blink-gurning-tennis that might go on for a full minute and always felt tender and lovely and good.

Naomi found it funny, right up to the end, when she said thirty seconds of flinching didn't count for much in the parenting scheme of things. Well, perhaps it didn't, but . . .

Why did she have to be so right? Even when she cut her hair short on her fortieth birthday, a move he'd said up front was a total mistake, given that it was the same polished black curtain as when he first saw her in that bar, the bob did suit her better, as she said it would.

The train burrows south through the suburbs.

Bridges and billboards ('Paradise Is Just Hours Away!' 'Thirsty? Drench It!') and concrete flyovers and blocks of flats eventually making way for terrace after terrace of bay-windowed two-storey houses in yellow London brick.

For a stretch: back gardens. Look at the sheds, paving slabs, washing lines. An ornamental pond with a plastic heron. And here, with the train clanking along at a cambered crawl, is another trampoline in a net-cage, only this one is jerking to the rhythm of a small boy's listless bouncing.

He looks about Zac's age.

One shoe on, one shoe off.

There's no way he'll ever jump high enough to escape like that.

Put some effort in, small boy!

'Tickets, please.'

Damn, Joseph hadn't expected a conductor. Aren't the ticket barriers all automated these days? She's coming up the carriage from behind him. He ferrets out his ticket. Drops his face towards the window. She'll memorise it anyway. That's her job. Possibly he should have hitchhiked instead.

'Sir.'

He thrusts the ticket up.

'That's the reservation. I need to see the other part as well.'

Her voice is no-nonsense. Maybe she has to get up early. He's not looked at her but he sees her all the same: dark roots and blonde hair and an M&S dressing gown hung on the back of her bedroom door as she buttons her logo-crested shirt. He's digging for the ticket part of the ticket now. Why in God's name can't they print both halves on the same bit of card? There, that must be . . . He pretends to scrutinise it, head still down, while offering the ticket for her to check. Sees bitten nails, a tiny engagement ring, and the worry in his chest turns unaccountably sad.

'Perfect,' she says. 'Have a good trip.'

Manners maketh the man. He looks her straight in the eye (she's actually brunette, and older than her voice) and says, 'Thank you.'

She moves off down the aisle.

But was that sensible, giving her a good look at him and so forth, plus handing her a bit of card with his destination on it?

Possibly: no.

Damnit.

29

The stop short of his station, which of course wasn't the station nearest where he's going anyway, becomes his new destination. He disembarks. That's the word for it. Moving slowly because, Jesus, the weight of the pack. He'll manage. But that's an extra ten miles he's added to the trek ahead, making it what, thirty-five or so in total.

Who cares?

There's no rush.

In fact, he shouldn't start now anyway.

It's the middle of the afternoon. This pack. In broad daylight. Well, it stands out.

Across the road from the station there's a park, complete with children's play area: monkey bars, sandpit no doubt spiked with dog shit, the works. Though the kiddie bit is pretty much deserted he keeps well clear of it, hacks on up to the top of the hill beyond the bandstand instead, where there's a clutch of trees reefed with undergrowth.

Joseph pauses.

Wait till the coast is clear.

Now!

He stashes the pack behind a hawthorn bush.

Then he retreats to the nearest park bench, where he wishes he had a newspaper, or anything to look occupied with.

Just the hours before dusk for company. He settles in to wait.

And the sun does its best to go down.

So slowly!

He keeps one eye on the hawthorn.

A young mother rolls past, texting. Her toddler, blue for a boy, is crumpled in the buggy. He looks as if he's been shot. And she's trailing a dachshund on one of those extending leads. It stops to investigate a bin and the lead spools out. On the dog goes and it spools back in. Up towards the bandstand the dachshund spears left, nose down, at an interested trot. Damn thing is making straight for the bush. Joseph sits forward. It's obvious what's going to happen: at the very least he'll mark the backpack as his own with a cocked leg. But just feet from the bush the lead stretches taut and no, she doesn't seem to be keen on deviating from the path after all and, since it curves away, the taut lead forces the dog to return uncomplainingly to her side.

Bad luck, sausage dog.

Joseph sits back.

He's good at this. Always was. Think of the farmyard, that cold ditch. Yes, waiting is part of his skill set.

To prove it, Joseph waits some more.

And finally, it's darkish, and the park is empty.

But the road is still on and off with traffic, too many headlights sweeping up and down for comfort, so he waits another hour.

Two.

This is easy.

Three.

Somewhat cold. It must be beyond closing time now.
There really can't be anyone sober about.
That'll do.
Joseph collects the pack and moves out.

30

He knows where he's going.

Back at Sandhurst, on that first serious exercise in Brecon, he misread the map with his pen torch, added an extra seven miles to the nineteen he already had to cover, and still made it through the fog and mud and wind to the final checkpoint more or less on time, albeit with shredded feet. But he endured. And he'll endure again now! Never mind the fact he hasn't had to do anything quite as hard since. But so what? He made it over the horseshoe mountains then and despite the concrete mass of the backpack, once he's stepped out of the park in the little commuter town he hauls himself a good three or four miles beyond the mini roundabouts, left right left, although he has to admit it's hard work, possibly because he's forty-four, not twenty-two, and, go on, admit this too: he's not in the most amazing shape.

He's been tracking along the edge of a field, staying close to the overgrown boundary hedge, following the lane that runs the other side of it, ducking down every now and then when cars pass, a boulder then and not a man. But now there's something larger coming down the lane. A truck. The hedge isn't going to be high enough to hide him from it so . . . just look purposeful instead: a rambler going about his normal rambling business of adjusting a bootlace, albeit in the middle of the night, and now the truck has passed and, humph! He straightens up, because it's time to get going again . . . but . . .

Christ.

He's tired.

As in whacked!

Also, now that he's stopped, a bit cold.

The truck rumbles away. For a long while nothing else comes down the lane. Joseph carries on walking. His night vision kicks in. He crosses a stile and finds himself in a field pricked with silvery leaves. Some crop or other coming through. Rows of little plants running up the hill. Very skilful, the way tractor drivers keep the lines straight: he has enough trouble making regular stripes with a lawn mower. Has? *Had.* Over in that top corner the hedge splays out into some sort of copse. He's breathing more evenly now. Listening to the hush. It feels like he's looking for something.

A deer steps out of the little wood, followed by a second, and a third.

Dainty, peaceful, wow.

But not what he was after.

One by one the deer lower their heads to nibble. Joseph watches them for a long minute. Whatever this crop is, they seem to like the shoots. He's pretty hungry himself, he realises, leaning back against the heaviness of his pack. It shifts and creaks and one of the deer looks up and straight away all three are gone.

Still, turns out they were helpful, because straining to see where they've headed he makes out a faint square edge within the copse. Some sort of outbuilding? If the deer came from up there, it must be a quiet spot. He hadn't planned on stopping before the bomb hole, but then again he hadn't planned on adding the extra distance to the walk, so why not lie up for a bit, rest, carry on tomorrow?

No!

Yes!

Don't give in to the thought!

It's not giving in, it's investigating.

He sets off for the little wood. And indeed there is an old barn or shed or something, or at last part of one, set back in the trees. Some broken walls. Not much in the way of a door, or windows, and only half a roof, which suits the sapling growing up through the hole. Joseph pats the tree. He sets his pack down against its smooth trunk and treads around in search of the flattest spot under the half-roof before thinking: hold on.

Do the thing properly.

Recce the place before settling down.

He pulls out and boxes round the wood, checking to see that it truly isn't at the end of somebody's garden.

And once satisfied, he returns and sits down in one corner.

It's 2.15 a.m.

An owl screeches comically loudly nearby.

Christ.

At least he's out of the way here, sheltered, if shivering.

But so tired!

Camel.

Eye of a needle.

He unclips the lid of the backpack and digs down in it for the softness of a sleeping bag. Finds it eventually, still in its plastic cover. Unstraps the bedroll from the bottom of the pack, too. Thank you, Charlie. Joseph fumbles the roll open, drags it out flat. It's self-inflating. Just twist this little knob and it will suck air into itself. How things have come on. Joseph sits on the squashiness to take off his boots. Doesn't bother removing his trousers, just caterpillars himself into the sleeping bag and curls sideways on the mat. Full fifteen years since he last slept outside. Never even took the kids camping. He pulls the pack close to lean against. One day, he thinks, and then: no! Don't go there. So tired. He settles back, shuts his eyes, gives in.

At Airdeen Clore they had a couple of basement rooms fitted out with single beds for people to sleep in, small hours-wise. Joseph never used them, rest being for sissies, not Big Beasts. But he sleeps immediately in the ruined shed. The floor may be an uneven mess of rocks, weeds and God knows what, but he doesn't care; it's not the wedge of brick pressing into his knee that wakes him. The dawn chorus, which goes off like a municipal fire alarm, does that. No joke, the noise is ridiculous, an electro-whistling-trilling insistence that drills him awake after what feels like no time at all. Joseph opens one eye and thinks of the Sunday supplement article he read a while back, which put him straight on birdsong. Turns out they don't all sing every day. Most of the time it's just a bit of practice for the mating season. That's when they all really let rip. Joseph checks his watch. It's four forty-seven on the morning of 4 May. He tries to sit up.

Jesus Christ!

It feels like he's been shot.

He levers himself upright with gritted teeth.

There's cow parsley growing at the open end of the shed-barn-whatever.

Look at the dew on it.

He's thirsty as well as shot to bits.

At least he's warm. Charlie bought him a proper sleeping bag. Joseph decides not to get out of it. He can have a look to see what else Charlie put in the pack by dropping the bag beneath his armpits and sitting snugly inside it. Remember the kids opening their stockings at Christmas?

Stop it.

Just stop it.

Concentrate on this instead. Spread it all out on the ground. What have we here, then?

Long-tipped, waterproof matches, two packs.

A flint and striker, enough to spark four thousand or so fires after the matches run out.

Next, a magnifying glass: it's summer, after all.

Here's a pack of condoms. Why? Because they weigh nothing and can hold a litre of water.

Damn, his mouth is dry.

Water? Purification tablets, at least.

And still with the small stuff: a reel of wire. It will fasten, cut, snare.

Plus a knife, useless for any length of time without a whetstone, which is here too, folded into the leather strop.

Gloves, two pairs, one waterproof, the other warm and thin enough to fit inside the first.

A concertina of two hats as well, one with ear flaps, both lined, neither a match for the balaclava tucked inside.

When Shackleton set off for the South Pole he wore tweed. In the early nineties Joseph's polyester was cut with waxed cotton and Welsh wool. Nowadays it's all layers of merino and Gore-Tex.

Much of what Charlie has bought is still in its plastic packaging. Joseph takes care with the bags. They'll come in handy, as will this roll of bin liners.

Plus clothes. Namely, two base layer tops, two sets of long johns, two pairs of double-skinned waterproof trousers, two fleece tops, one neoprene smock, one storm-proof jacket, a bundle of woollen socks, four pairs of boxer shorts . . .

All of it: black.

Ha.

He'll look like the Milk Tray Man.

Never mind me, Naomi. I'm just here to deliver the chocolates.

Stop that.

There's something marvellous about his kid brother picking him out underwear. Joseph asked for it and Charlie's delivered. Why does he, Joseph, keep thinking about that remote-controlled car? The smell of petrol, the buzzing, Charlie's lopsided smile. It was cold in the car park but they stayed out until it was more or less dark. That's right, Charlie, aim for the apex.

What else?

Elastic bands. Always handy. Plus a chamois towel.

And the bigger stuff is here, too. A set of billycans, plus aluminium kettle. A little Primus stove. Three aerosols of gas. Two sheets of tarpaulin. A hand axe, the back end of which will serve as a hammer, and an aluminium shovel with a collapsible handle, plus a coil of nylon rope.

Back to the small again: a pack of nails, a wire saw, twine. Joseph sets these down on one of the tarpaulins and pulls out the next item, thinking: Charlie, you beauty, you really have outdone yourself, because . . . the water bottle is . . . full.

He unscrews the cap and takes a long cold swig. Christ, that's good. He lets himself drink half of what's there, confident he'll be able to refill the bottle somewhere later.

What a brother. Always thorough. Swallowed Dad's 'never do a thing by halves' edict whole. He's filled one of the pockets with Tracker bars. Joseph didn't even ask for these. And what's this? Kendal Mint Cake! He hasn't tasted that in twenty years!

Still good, though.

Minty.

Ha.

Lastly, in the bottom compartment, here's . . . a heavy-duty tarp. Dark green. Result.

No, there's something else in the side pocket as well. Small and hard, in a case. A little pair of binoculars. The case is leather. It looks expensive. Spread out like this before him, the whole lot says: so valuable! Charlie certainly spent the cash; in fact what Joseph gave him may not have been enough. Possibly Joseph should have diverted a lump of the $1.34 billion Charlie's way. But no, if he'd started doing that where would he have stopped? Robin Hood didn't put gold coins, jewels and whatnot aside for Little John and Friar Tuck, did he? Actually, who's to say? Just because it's not in the story doesn't mean . . .

Oh, just stop.

Joseph pops the flap on the leather case and sees there's something in it alongside the binoculars. Folded small and tight: a piece of paper, two in fact. Joseph wipes his face with his hand, then sits very still indeed. He knows that scribbly handwriting. It's Zac's.

What does he have to say?

Modern-day submariners live beneath the sea for up to eight months at a time. They keep their oxygen in canisters. Have a nice holiday. Love Zac.

Holiday. Charlie.

The second note is from Lara and, ouch, she gets straight to the point.

Whatever Uncle Charlie says is OK, whatever is happening is not OK. Mum is actually worried too. You can't just go off without us. Can you? Don't be ridiculous, Dad! What's going on? Lara x.

32

Joseph stares from one piece of paper to the other and back and forward again. The sun slides up properly. Look, it's pulled a square of blue sky through the open end of the roof.

Christ, the kids.

What is he thinking?

That these letters are unimportant.

Because the one to fear is still in his satchel.

Fear?

For their sake, yes.

That bastard little St Thomas' Hospital crest.

Huntington's is hereditary.

Oh, stop!

Dad's papery knuckles on the steering wheel.

Stop.

The way his face turned slack and fell to one side in—

Just—

Okay, okay.

Joseph diverts himself by going through his new belongings carefully. He checks all the rucksack's pockets as well. But there's no note from 'actually worried' Naomi, is there? No. Did she think what Lara and Zac said was enough? Nothing to add? The familiar silent treatment! He may have deserved it from time to time, but now, well, this is . . . harsh!

What's that?

A tractor grinding up the lane makes the world of other people suddenly real and close. Joseph checks and, wow, the field seemed much bigger in the dark. He retreats to the tumbledown shed again, which in fact might even have been a cottage once, that roof obviously a replacement which itself fell down. Let's put this pack back together, shall we? Properly this time, with the heaviest stuff high up over his shoulders. Put the clothes in the middle. Keep the bottom compartment free for the sleeping bag, which, why not, yes, he climbs back into now. Because it makes sense to lie up here for the day and head out again when it's dark, doesn't it?

It does.

Sleep some more. Safe here.

Joseph pulls his head deeper into the hood of the sleeping bag. Manages to doze for an hour or so but comes to with a smacking realisation: the point is not what the notes say, it's the fact of them at all.

Because, yes, now he thinks about it the problem is all too obvious. Namely: to get the messages Charlie will have been round to see Naomi and the kids. And why's that a problem? Obvious: because of Lancaster. He's already tapped Lara's phone, hasn't he?

We don't know that for . . . but it's likely.

So it's entirely probable he'll have somebody watching the house, too. You know, for anomalies. Such as a visit from Charlie!

The next step, having spotted Charlie's visit, would be to

monitor what he gets up to, out and about, online and so forth.

Hmm, what have we here, then?

A big order for high-end camping kit, that's what. Interesting! Best keep an eye on little Charlie, see what he does with it. Which turns out to be . . . loading something that looks very much like a big rucksack into the boot of his trusty Zafira, plus leaving said people carrier full of goody-stuffed backpack in the staff car park for . . . who have we here, then? . . . Joseph! to retrieve.

Damn, and damn, damnit!

The train of thought rolls on past, its couplings secure.

If they were watching the car when Joseph made the pick-up, they will have followed him. Argh. That old man who blew him a kiss. And the train conductor. Have a good trip! We're right behind you.

Oh, Charlie.

What have you done?

Scattered breadcrumbs, that's what!

Joseph paces about the middle of the ruin running a hand through his splintery hair.

Then again.

Chink of light!

Then again what?

Joseph bangs the side of his head with his palm, trying to knock the thoughts into place . . . possibly Charlie will have used his own head and been a bit superstitious.

No, no, no: *surreptitious*.

Easy mistake.

Means nothing.

Yes it does!

Joseph paces about in the hut. Look at this cow parsley growing in the open door. Snap a sprig of it and watch the juice flow. It's entirely possible to squeeze the sap out of plants, boil it up, and drink it. Though beware gut rot. He has a lurching feeling in his stomach now all right, and it's not hunger. It's that slow-motion car-crash sensation, or possibly falling, in a dream.

Pull yourself together, man.

Charlie runs the Outward Bound stuff for his pupils, doesn't he? Yes! Well, it's credible that he might buy some camping gear and take it in to school, isn't it?

Credible, but . . .

33

Unlikely.

As is this weak attempt to convince himself he's in the clear.

Joseph retreats to the spot where he slept and sits back down in the discarded puddle of his sleeping bag. If they're following him there's not much he can do about it right now, is there?

No.

Later, though.

What?

He shunts himself back into the bag, shuts his eyes and has a go at thinking up a Plan B. Escape and evasion and, what's the word? Subterfuge. He thinks this way and that as the morning turns into the afternoon. Pleasant temperature, he notes. What is he, a weatherman? Look, it's just a nice, late-spring day, with a pine needle and leaf mulch accompaniment. Yes, but he's lying amongst weeds! Nothing wrong with plant life. Joseph picks and chews the sweet shaft of a grass stalk to prove it. But eventually, Plan B, such as it is, heaves back into view.

Ugh.

Might be enough to throw them off the scent, tho—

Then again, might not.

And it's risky, whichever way you cut it.

Very!

Deep breath.

Minutes tick by. Imagine treacle stretching off a spoon. Actually, don't. Eat the Tracker bars instead. And remember waiting in the barracks, wondering which of the two raindrops would make it down the big window first? That one's stopped. Let's try these two. Ten races later, we may as well assemble the lads and ask them to do something equally pointless.

Platoon Commander sounds pretty good, doesn't it?

Twenty-seven men under his command!

But actually?

Well, no: they would have been, if not for Platoon Sergeant Connelly.

He was two years older than Joseph, but he had eight years more army experience, including stints in Operation Banner and in the Gulf. Also: he had a kink in his nose and a corner knocked off one front tooth, which made him look a bit am-dram piratical. Nothing unprofessional about his soldiering, though. He never implied Joseph was green or that his orders were daft. 'Sorted, sir.' 'We're on it.' Or: 'Of course, we've done that already.' And he always had! The lads were one step ahead, thanks to Connelly, which should have made Joseph grateful, but didn't, because it left him with the square root of bugger all to do.

Those first six months.

Jesus!

Apart from five days chasing night-vision versions of

the men around the Black Mountains, and a long weekend sodden in Thetford Forest, he spent most of his time heading off twenty-seven other kinds of boredom. Referred men to the STD clinic, wrote more than one character reference for the local magistrates' court, and explained that no, it wouldn't be possible to stand a man five months' pay to cover poker debts.

That was whatshisname? Calvin. Ran up the whole debt in one drunken afternoon, and seemed to think that Joseph, as his commanding officer, would be able to sort him out. As in, would have the money to hand and feel obliged to lend it to him. Possibly he was still pissed, or just so monumentally hung-over he couldn't think straight; either which way, as he left the room to tell whoever he owed that he couldn't pay, he made the mistake of calling Joseph a 'stuck-up prick'.

Joseph let it go.

He was almost out of earshot anyway.

Not so fellow Platoon Commander Lancaster.

He was on his way to see Joseph and must have heard the insult round a bend in the corridor.

Kaboom!

Right from the start, possibly because he was about as young as a newly commissioned officer could be, Lancaster rose up to own the rank. Take nothing away from Joseph: he did a pretty good job of acting the part of an officer himself, but Lancaster, well, he just *was* one. Being better than everybody else at everything didn't hurt, plus the ability to be everywhere, early, ready, and calm. Joseph never heard him raise his voice. Never, that is, apart from the day Lancaster overheard Calvin insult a fellow officer. He didn't like that. So he put a Calvin-shaped dent in the side of the drinks machine and roared at the poor bloke for a full minute. Calvin wouldn't be playing cards for a while, not given the list of shitty jobs he now faced for insulting his commanding officer. Joseph didn't find it necessary to join Calvin and Lancaster in the corridor, but possibly he should have: when Lancaster finished and entered Joseph's office his 'no bother' was half-hearted; it seemed he suspected Joseph had heard the insult and he couldn't hide his distaste at the fact he'd let the man walk away.

Ah, well.

Goes around, comes around.

As surely as night follows day.

Which it does.

Eventually.

34

Right then, Plan B.

Although the night is warmer than the one before, it's also darker. There's cloud in the way of whatever moon has risen and no ambient town-light to speak of. Suits Joseph. He wants to cut across country, unseen, swiftish. Better ditch the pack for now, then. Come back for it later, after executing said plan, which will be successful, because it has to be. The shed-or-whatnot is as good a place as any to hide his stuff for the time being. Yes, under these, bricks, stones and so forth. Joseph breaks a sweat digging a hole in the rubble-mound. He transfers what he needs – plastic bags, water bottle, plus passport (don't forget that!) – to his satchel. Then he waterproofs the backpack by sticking it inside a couple of bin liners, lowers it into the new hole, shores the thing up with bits of broken whatever, and tosses some deadish foliage over the lot. It's properly dark now, therefore hard to see the excellence of the cover-up job, but it feels pretty good to him.

The old confidence. Can't keep a good man—

Don't tempt fate.

Instead, what next?

Beat a stealthy retreat around the ruin, then head back across the field and down to the road. Which leads? Well, to the village, or hamlet, call it what you will: somewhere he can find a tap and refill his bottle, sorting out the desert storm-sized problem of wanting – no, needing – something to drink *now*. By God, thirst. We're all animals, after all.

Joseph picks up the pace when he hits the lane. Best not be seen on it if possible. Make haste! His knee hurts. Tough! Back in the day, shredded feet and all: that was him once, and this is him again now. Tabbing, it's called, army-wise. Whichever. He jogs on. Enduring!

Settles into a rhythm.

How does it go again?

What?

The chant thing.

There are lots of them.

Here's one, for example. From basic training.

'Left, left, left right left. Left, left, left right left. Left, left, I had a good job and I left. I left because the pay wasn't right so I left, right, left.'

Ha.

Sort of appropriate.

There's a light up ahead. And a sign. What does it say? 'Peaslake'. Really? Yes! Okay, so that's good, isn't it? Because he knows where Peaslake is. Of course he does. He's driven through it a thousand times. It's not so far from school. Plus he looked at a house here once, with Naomi.

He hadn't realised he was this close. It's a little embarrassing. Not to mention annoying! To have come this far and yet to have to dog-leg away.

Damn, Charlie. With your breadcrumbs.

Or just maybe it's about not quite wanting to be here, this near, yet.

If only Naomi had written a note too. Even if it had just spelled out the old I can't help you until you get some help ultimatum. Yes, even that would have been something. Still, it's a long game, this. Don't give up, not yet.

Yet? Ever.

After all, they haven't always been on the same page; they had their share of ups and downs from the beginning. The difficulty she had with Joseph's army career, right at the start of things, for example, in the bar in Kuala Lumpur, where they met. Holiday romance. It was very noisy. When he told her he was on leave from the army she cocked her head to one side and shouted, 'Farming?'

'No, army, you know, soldiering.'

Now her head drew back. 'Really?'

'Yes.'

'But . . . why?'

The fact that she was so obviously and genuinely baffled, combined with the way she was unafraid to show it, made him simply shrug his shoulders and offer to buy her another drink. He got away with it, then, the thumping music a kind of excuse. But later, after they'd met up back in England and started dating for real, he never really explained himself either, just let her work out for herself that he wasn't bloodthirsty or institutionalised. The army was something he did. Since it pre-dated their getting together she couldn't really object. And outwardly, at least, she didn't. But Naomi's own job, working in publicity for Save the Children, made the point for her.

He loved that Naomi was a good person.

Good, and secure.

The rolling way she walked, ever so slightly cowboy-legged.

So comfortable in her own skin!

Damn it, loved? He still loves—

Just stop.

Which house to scope for a tap, anyway?

This one, set back behind the laurel hedge. Joseph skulks up the grass to one side of a gravel drive. Black stripes on a pale background up ahead: this house is Tudor-style, quite possibly original. He remembers something about a visit to the vet with Lara when Gordon, the dog, broke his jaw. Tore it just about off on a sprinkler at night, running with his nose to the ground and his mouth apparently open. Stupid dog. God, it looked painful. The stoicism of animals, though: he whimpered a bit, then shut down. Did the vet live somewhere like this? Joseph can't remember. There are no lights on in the house. Everybody's in bed, or out. Is that a speedboat on a trailer, next to not one but two SUVs? Big pile of bricks they're parked in front of, that's for sure. Possibly he was mistaken about the vet: we're in oligarch territory after all. Even oligarchs need outdoor taps, though: how else do the staff keep all those tinted car windows clean? Let's just sidestep quietly down between this wing of the house and that wall. Could be a garage, or annexe. And what's that? Is it? Yes, it looks like some sort of spigot sticking out of the brickwork at knee height, up ahead.

Click!

The side of the building jumps with brightness and Joseph, frozen, has two sudden shadows.

Security lights.

Crap!

Forward or reverse?

Just . . . go the way you know!

Joseph ducks and lurches and jinks into the darkness. Mistake: night-blind, he runs straight into a low bush, falls over it even, whacks down in a flowerbed. Mercifully, it's a soft one. Still, he's winded. Lies stone still struggling to keep the gasp, when it comes, quiet. The security light clicks off again, plunging everything into a darkness way thicker than it was before. Which feels, come to think of it, sort of safe. At least the bush offers a bit of cover. Lie here. Wait it out.

There's no sound of a door, or footsteps, just black silence.

That tap.

Christ almighty, he's thirsty. Lying here on his back in the softness, his throat feels as if someone's tipped a load of sawdust down it. The longer he waits, the worse the need to drink becomes. What he'd give for a glass of water. And actually, let's face it, the longer he waits without anyone coming out of the house, the more it seems nobody noticed or cared about the security light, making it less likely anyone will care if he trips it again.

Nice thinking!

It'll take him what, thirty seconds to fill his bottle?

Joseph collects himself behind the bush. Odd phrase that: collects himself from where? Thirst-land. A sudden image comes to mind: four mugs of tea on a tray. He fishes out his water bottle and loosens the top in readiness, thinking: swoon.

Swoon?

As in not yet, just to be on the safe side . . .

Soon.

35

Remember Northern Ireland?

The regiment deployed there for Joseph's first real tour. Peacekeeping duties. Out in Rwanda, as Naomi pointed out at the time, they were killing one another by the hundreds of thousands, but in Northern Ireland, then, not so much. This was just before the peace process grew smiling teeth. Duties were schizophrenic. Joseph and his men spent half their time conducting highly visible patrols through the streets of North Belfast, more as a symbolic gesture than for any real deterrent purposes, emphatically 'we're still here, for now, with guns and boots, after your hearts and minds, for all to see!' And the rest of the time they did the exact opposite. They skulked about in the lush countryside near the border, trying in vain to keep tabs on IRA players, holing themselves up in ditches for days on end, their stomachs hollow-full of rations, focusing and refocusing their binoculars in the hope that they'd unearth an arms cache in time to get home for a proper feed. During one particularly long, humid July stint, the focus of the stakeout marched across the farmyard carrying a tray. He had trouble negotiating the rusty gate with it, tiptoed across the cattle grid, skirted a couple of puddles, and advanced straight up to the ditch. The tray had four mugs of tea on it.

'Now piss off,' he said, setting them down on the grass.

If this was modern soldiering, hanging about in Thetford and Newbury had prepared Joseph well for it. Hurry up and . . . wait. But the frustration of never once firing his weapon was nothing compared to how much he missed Naomi back then. It was a physical longing, not unlike the homesickness he'd put up with aged eight.

Ah, Naomi.

His mum loved her when they met. Of course she did: Save the Children! Mum sat rapt as Naomi explained what she did.

'I met Joseph's father on a kibbutz,' she said in reply.

'Really?'

'Yes, we sunk a well.'

(So thirsty!)

'Wow.'

'It's true. They'd mostly dug the borehole already, but we were there when the first water came up. I helped Arthur connect the pump. In the end we had to use a winch. It was more reliable.'

'You don't want to leave a problem that undoes your hard work after you've gone.'

'No. Although that was only a test well, just for the kibbutz, and they had these big storage tanks anyway, but even so, the thing is, it's all about doing something together, isn't it?'

For Naomi Save the Children was pretty much all about saving children, but she nodded anyway.

Mum wasn't about to let it lie. She fingered her turquoise necklace nervously before going on.

'I suppose it might be nice for the two of you to have something like that, you know, an activity or task, something to achieve, pulling in the same direction.'

Was she talking about grandchildren? 'Anyone want pudding?' Joseph said.

Poor Mum.

Dad's illness pretty much snuffed her out youth-wise. That peculiar sixties have-it-all mentality which yoked cause-politics to a free spirit, or tried to: gone. It's as hard to be carefree as it is waving a Solidarity flag when the plastic chair you're sitting on is bolted to the lino floor of a hospital waiting room. After his death, with the help of Sally and Fiona, two divorced friends with whom Mum had visited northern Thailand on a batik-printing course, she began to rekindle the spirit of her original self. The old ethnic throws spread themselves out all over the backs of the sofas again. Would that they could have stayed that way. But she'd also started seeing a man called Tristan who talked a lot about antique restoration but made his living developing golf courses in Spain. Tristan wore pastel-coloured shirts and called Joseph 'Sport'. Within a year she'd sold up and gone to live with him outside Alicante. Hot there. Dry. (So thirsty!) Excellent climate in which to drink sangria in the afternoon and later wear flip-flops whilst riding pillion on a scooter driven too quickly round a corner by said Tristan. The truck they hit was carrying watermelons, cherries, nectarines and so forth, and though the driver was blameless, the company he worked for insisted on sending industrial quantities of fruit for the after-party – wake, whatever – on the sweltering day of the joint funeral.

So thirsty.

Soon, as in now?

Why not.

Very slowly, Joseph stands up.

36

Whack!

The blow is as sudden and blinding as the security light, bright white pain exploding from every direction. But it's not real light, because he's instantly flailing on his side in the dark, an immense ringing in his ears and a figure looming over him, black against the deeper night.

'Got you!'

The outline grows an arm, raises it high to hit Joseph again. There's something in the man's hand. A cosh, or stick. Joseph shrinks sideways as the blow comes, so that it glances off his shoulder instead of connecting with his head. Still, the shock of the first blow has him swimming underwater. He's doubtful he can dodge another.

He hears himself groan.

'What's that?'

The man is fumbling with something attached to his belt. A gun? Jesus, no . . . Joseph heaves himself up into a sitting position. There's a sweet smell coming from something he's crushed in the flowerbed, clashing with the taste of blood in his mouth. No, not a gun. The thing jerks crazily as the man pulls it free. It's a roll of duct tape. He drops to one knee and grabs Joseph's forearm.

'Neighbourhood fucking Watch,' he says.

Joseph pulls weakly but he can't sit up: he's an anchor fallen in the mud. But he's trying!

'No you don't,' says the man.

He has one end of the tape wrapped around Joseph's wrist. Joseph feels himself yanked forward and to one side: the man is rolling him to reach for his other hand.

Joseph protests.

Sadly his kerfuffling makes the man lift his hand again, and this new unfairness swinging down to meet Joseph is definitely truncheon-shaped.

Joseph snaps to.

He catches the man's arm and pulls, hauling both of them off balance. Joseph's full weight drags them down. The man slaps into the flowerbed beside him. For a second they are nose to nose, pretty much. Then Joseph is lurching up, grabbing at the cosh, pushing the man down with his taped hand as he smashes at him with the other.

Thinking, in a life-flashing-before-eyes sort of way: Zac and the coconut.

He won it at a village fête last summer.

Joseph wasn't there.

Possibly he was in Houston, nailing down the Mobil deal.

Or maybe he was just uninvited.

Anyway, Zac brought the coconut to show him in Cleveland Square when the ordained weekend came round. How do we get into this, then? A hammer. But, of course, Joseph's toolbox was at the old house – when would he start calling it Naomi's? Never! – leaving them stumped. Momentarily!

He bought a shiny new hammer from the hardware shop round the corner and together, on a bit of central London pavement, they knocked a hole in the coconut.

The hollow thud, the pleasing sensation of something giving way.

Wow.

It's tempting to bash this chap again with his own stupid stick, but Joseph resists, partly because in their nose-to-nose state he can tell whoever it is isn't Lancaster himself, meaning he must be an underling, and anyway, that first thwack, ugh, was sickening, which is possibly why the man is so very still at his feet.

Most still indeed.

Is he dead?

Jesus.

No!

Joseph bends low over the slumped figure. Decides he should hold his wrist over the man's mouth to check he's breathing. Very sensitive, wrists. Sadly, Joseph's has a roll of tape hanging from it, and it sort of clonks the man in the face. Makes the man shiver, though, so that's something. And yes, he's still breathing. Shallowly: little sips. Come on, man, keep at it, don't stop.

Joseph peels himself free of the gaffer tape.

He smells of expensive cologne, this chap.

Is his cheek black with mud or blood?

Joseph rubs at it. Doesn't feel too wet. And he's groaning now, trying to say something in fact. What is it? A message from Lancaster.

'You trod on my . . .' the man grumbles. He tails off, losing interest.

But he's coming to, which is good, isn't it?

Yes!

Better not be here when he picks up his flowerbed and walks, though.

Just as Joseph is about to get up himself, though, a car rumbles down the lane, its headlights pouring lazily through the big hedge. The drive is nowhere near as long as Joseph recalls. He flattens himself across the prone man. There's something square in his chest pocket, hard edged, a phone. Joseph pulls it free once the car has gone.

'Give that . . .' the man says, flapping.

Joseph hits the power button and a picture of three children comes to life behind the code screen. Two of the faces are smiling at one another; the third is hidden behind one of the blank boxes. Joseph stares at the picture long enough for the screen to go black, then immediately illuminates it again, thinking damn, damn, damn, and not because he can't crack the code. He doesn't even try to do that. Just sits there slowly realising that this chap, unlike him now, is connected. Connected, but groggy. What's he saying now?

'The car needs an MOT.'

What?

Either way, he's broadcasting his whereabouts with this here phone. Meaning Joseph should get moving. He slots the mobile back in the pocket he got it from and lurches to his feet.

Then he realises: you don't need a code to call an ambulance.

Do the right thing!

Joseph does: he pulls out the phone again, dials 999, explains there's been an accident, gives the location, and rings off quickly when the operator asks his name.

There'll be a recording, of course.

So what?

He wipes the phone down carefully and drops it, suddenly thirsty again.

So, so thirsty!

But . . .

Risk it: this chap isn't operational anyway.

Joseph dashes down the side alley. Strangely, the security light stays off this time. Still, he can see well enough to find the tap and fill his water bottle. Screw the lid on tight. Actually . . . He unscrews it again and drinks the whole bottle. Good thinking! Water, from a tap: it tastes incredible. Better than Krug. Which Naomi always scoffed at: what's wrong with sparkling wine? Not the point! He fills the bottle again, shoves it into his satchel, and jogs out towards the road.

37

Lancaster.

How the hell does that man do it?

Joseph, exhausted, is taking a breather, leaning on a five-bar gate.

It's just before dawn. No colour in the sky yet, just battleship grey.

Something about having been up all night, plus the post-adrenal slump following a real scuffle, prompts him to remember the day in question, very clearly, as ever, because that was the thing about that day: it simply refused to fade.

Lancaster was sitting with his boots off inspecting a red mark on his sock. Beneath it, a burst blister. He was listening to Kenny Rogers on a tinny radio. A strong smell of Deep Heat muscle spray hung in the air. When Joseph told Lancaster where he and his men had been ordered to go he turned the radio off, put his boot back on, and asked if it was okay for him to come too. It wasn't a real question. His helmet lay turtlebacked in the dirt. He dusted it off, shouldered his stuff, and beat Joseph to the door.

This was Bosnia, late 1995. They had been led to believe, before they arrived, that as far as the real war went, they were late. Well, sort of. Back at school, when he was a prefect, Joseph wore a pale blue tie. In Bosnia he wore a pale blue peacekeeping helmet instead. Never mind that they were pimping for the hydra-headed UN–NATO force, this was more or less the same job they'd done in Northern Ireland: it mostly involved wandering around as visibly as possible wearing lots of intimidating kit. Lancaster had been at it for three months before Joseph arrived. This made him at once a reassuring presence and ever more annoyingly the expert. Joseph had no real idea why Lancaster wanted to come out on that particular patrol but he wasn't about to complain. He slammed the door of the Land Rover, slapped the dashboard, and waited for Stretton to drive. Joseph had cut a wisdom tooth the week before and his jaw started to throb when they hit the first rut.

They arrived on the outskirts of the village an hour later. Lancaster suggested they continue on foot, so Joseph told Chambers and Stretton to stay with the vehicle. Chambers loved cards, not for gambling so much as playing with them: he immediately magicked a deck from somewhere and began fanning, cutting and collapsing it with one hand. Lancaster noticed this and looked at Joseph, who climbed down from the cab into the cold without speaking.

'Put those away and keep an eye out,' Joseph heard Lancaster say.

They headed out into what was left of market day. The first stall Joseph passed displayed nothing but disposable razors. The second was heaped with slimy fish. A bunch of women talking in the middle of the square tightened together as they passed. Peacekeepers! Plus guns. There were no men around.

Up ahead, beyond the tree line, a plume of black smoke leaned lazily to the left. It made the winter-white sky look all the more anaemic.

Concentrate.

Look at Lancaster here, pulling out his map.

Joseph had already told Mehta to check the route, so Lancaster was only confirming what Joseph already knew.

Namely: they were headed towards the smoke.

Eight hundred metres down the road they arrived at what was left of a burning house. The front door had been dragged from its hinges and lay bright-painted red in the garden; everything else about the house looked black. Also deserted. Once this village had been mostly Bosnians. Then it was Serbs. Now some of the Bosnians had come back. Or was it the other way around?

Joseph really hadn't been there that long; still, he was buggered if he was going to ask you know who.

The breeze shifted and the smoke above them kinked and fanned out and straightened again. It made Joseph think of starlings. That thing they do in unison.

Mum, he thought: she loved birds.

She had them all over the house. Pictures of them, at least. Free to soar!

Or be sat on, many of them being stitched on cushions and so forth.

They moved on, Joseph trying hard to focus on the here and now. There, for example, was a tractor on its side overgrown with weeds.

And in the distance, people.

Plus a strange noise coming from up ahead.

What was Lancaster doing giving the orders, telling Reid to hang back while they crossed the icy stream, heading now towards the moaning sound. By the side of the road, as if unsure which way to go, stood an old man. He had the top button of his shirt done up but it was too big, the collar a hoop around his scrawny neck. He said something to them as they passed in a language Joseph didn't understand. When nobody answered, he spread out his hands and arms. What was that supposed to mean? Now he was taking off his woolly hat, holding it to his chest. Look at his head, steaming!

Up ahead, the noise, louder, definitely sounded like moaning and, as they got closer, it broke down into many voices.

Lancaster lifted up his hand, bringing Joseph and his men to a halt.

'Something's gone down here,' said Joseph, obviously.

Lancaster looked at him. 'Still going by the sound of things,' he said. 'This place, two years ago, was right in the heart of the clusterfuck.'

'So we just do our thing, yes. Loop through, let the people see we're here, go home.'

'Either that or we backtrack,' said Lancaster. 'Whatever we do doesn't want to involve getting caught in the—'

'Let's keep an extra eye out, then,' Joseph said, nodding at Reid, as if the statement was meant for him. This was Joseph's patrol, after all. In three weeks nobody had thrown so much as an insult at them, much less a rock or grenade.

Lancaster hadn't shaved. His stubble was copper. He rubbed a palm over his chin, and Joseph wanted to unsay what he'd said but couldn't. Lancaster shrugged, making the difficult impossible. 'If you say so,' he said.

38

The difficult, the impossible . . . Joseph pushes that day away
. . . right now it's more important to sort out: what next?

Well, Southampton hasn't moved, has it?

No.

So let's get going.

It's doable!

He is beneath a flyover rubbing the top of his forehead.
Lucky the man hit him there, where the skull is thickest.
Still, ouch. Hopefully any bruising is above his hairline. He
must be presentable now. To that end he cleans himself up as
best as he can, using a shirt tail dipped in a little of his water.
First, he wipes his face and hands. Next he brushes down
his coat and trousers. And he even has a go at his boots.
Nobody is going to pick up a ___, are they?

No, no, no.

A what?

The word won't come.

He isn't one anyway. He's a Big Beast!

Ha.

How the mighty have . . .

By now it's what, nearly 5 a.m. He sits down to wait as
dawn breaks. Stupid word for it: dawn bleeds in. When he
judges it's a sane enough time to be seeking a lift, he tracks

his way up onto the curve of the southbound slipway. Standing in full view is a horrible feeling, but that's what he has to do. The traffic is already up and running. Early-morning commuters first, then white vans, the occasional heavier truck. He keeps an eye out for police cars. Doesn't see any. Seven thirty turns to eight o'clock, nine, nine fifteen. Jesus: he started out feeling horrendously exposed and already it's as if he's invisible. Another half hour passes before anyone even slows down, but as soon as Joseph takes his first step towards it the car accelerates away, leaving him feeling oddly idiotic.

More time passes.

Clean morning has given way to fumes, despite the breeze.

Just before ten o'clock, a UPS van swerves towards him as it comes up the ramp, but it's only because the driver is checking his phone.

Joseph thinks: perhaps, give up?

And later: five more minutes.

And after another half an hour has gone by: sixty seconds.

Just as he's about to turn back down the slip road an old Mercedes Estate, approaching slowly, pulls onto the hard shoulder and drifts to a stately stop. It's an immaculate car, all chrome, unblemished paintwork, blue-clear glass. The driver is an older woman. She holds the wheel with one leather-gloved hand and searches for the electric window button with the other, finds it finally, and watches the window slide all the way down before asking Joseph if she can help. Her voice has a wartime BBC correctness undiluted by age. A sort of cucumber-sandwiches voice.

'Yes please, I need a lift.'

'I can see. But where to?'

'Southampton. Anywhere in that direction will do.'

She nods kindly. An older – let's face it, elderly – lady in a valuable – classic, even – car, stopping to pick up a lone, male, mud-stained hitchhiker. A shot of concern passes through Joseph.

She's still nodding.

Is she all there, up top?

Ha! Is he?

'Well, let me think,' she says. 'I'm on my way to Alderbury. If I take the southerly route I'll be going along the M27, better still than the M3 for Southampton. I don't want to have to go into the town if that's okay?'

She's asking him?

'Any service station en route would be great.'

'Yes, yes. Jump in. Rownhams. Between junctions three and four. Here.' She pulls a hardback road atlas from the door pocket and hands it to Joseph. 'Have a little look, see what you can see.'

Joseph occupies himself with the atlas. The car smells of oranges. Always reminds him of school. They put them out as a snack. He used to bite a hole in one side and pulp the juice out of it straight into his mouth. It made his lips tingle, aware of themselves, like his left wrist is now, where the tape was stuck to it! He knows where he is, but still, where's Alderbury? It takes a moment or two to find the spot on the map and realise that this lady is in fact offering to go out of her way. Perhaps he should tell her; he doesn't want to take advantage. Still, it's tempting not to.

Apropos of nothing she says, 'In 1955 I canoed the Danube bend, right into the heart of Budapest.'

Joseph looks up at her.

'I was seventeen. I went with my sister, Flora.'

'Wow.'

'She died fifteen years ago, right after Eddie. That was the worst year of my life.'

'I'm sorry,' Joseph says.

She's concentrating hard on the road, peering over the steering wheel. His mum would have been about this woman's age now, Tristan's moped notwithstanding. Her white hair is carefully done. Against the brightness of the driver's side window it has a haloed look, candyfloss held up against the sun.

Remember that time Lara made herself sick on the stuff?

Some sleepover or other. They had a swimming pool, he knew that much.

Poor kid: he had to hold her hair out of her face as she leaned over the toilet.

'Eddie was my husband,' the woman explains. 'This is – was – his car.'

'It's a lovely car.'

'Isn't it.'

They sit quietly for a moment and the fact of the car asserts itself. It's a bit like when the credits for a film show the name of the sound guy, Joseph thinks: you suddenly become super aware of whatever song the title sequence is playing. Well done, sound guy: good job.

'I'd never driven it before he died. Because I'd never learned to drive! He wanted to teach me but I couldn't see the point. The trip to Hungary, with Flora, we hitchhiked the whole way from Putney to Esztergom, which was where we hired the canoes. And once we'd arrived in Budapest we caught lifts all the way home. Three weeks there, two and a half back. And later, even if I could have driven, well, Eddie would have wanted to drive me. He was hopeless around the house, never lifted a finger to help, but gallant as far as driving was concerned.' She pauses as a lorry pulls past: they really are driving quite slowly. 'The point is that you seldom see hitchhikers nowadays. A couple of rotten apples and those ridiculous films, they spoiled the whole box. As a matter of fact, you must be the first person I've picked up in a year, two maybe. Nobody else has asked! Anyway, as I say, I don't much like driving in towns, but the least I can do is take the southerly route and drop you off as near as possible to where you want to go.'

Joseph nods, mutters his thanks, and looks down at his muddy boots on the spotless footwell mat.

He shuts his eyes and listens to the tyres on the tarmac, a low hum.

39

It's started again, up ahead, the wailing, coming from a group of women and children. The patrol found them in front of what was left of the village mosque. A woman dressed in a plaid shirt and long black skirt was the centre of wailing-attention, her hair matted with blood. The group parted as Joseph and his men approached. Lots of crying, full volume. Had some sort of catfight gone on between this lot? Jesus, another step closer and the woman calmly raised her hand, then struck herself hard above the right temple with a rock! The sound of it. That coconut. Now she was raising the rock again, and Joseph was lurching forward to stop her.

'No,' said Lancaster.

But it was already too late anyway.

Clunk.

She'd kill herself like that.

'Leave it,' said Lancaster. He was looking from eye to eye to eye, his rifle in both hands.

Joseph turned back to the woman, crouched down beside her, took the rock from her hand, saying, 'What's the matter?'

'Come on,' said Lancaster. 'We're here to have been here, that's it.'

40

The old lady is talking again, telling Joseph her name, Emily, and something about how she's returning from a visit to her son. He's a dentist called Geoffrey, recently divorced. It wasn't amicable. Twice a month she travels up to do her bit, as she puts it, looking after her grandchildren, making sure there's proper food in the fridge. The divorce, it turns out, was Geoffrey's fault. He cheated on his wife, Caroline, with an old schoolfriend he met on Facebook. But his mother understands: she'd seen how cold Caroline could be. The way she walked out on him and the kids confirmed it, did it not? A mother, leaving her school-aged children, never mind that her dentist husband wanted to patch things up. Cold.

'It does sound that way,' Joseph concedes.

'And now Geoffrey has to work all the hours God sends just to meet the payments.'

Geoffrey, Joseph thinks. Does he feel his regret in his guts, or do his fingers shake inside his patients' mouths?

'Clare's twelve already but she's started wetting the bed.'

Of course, the kids.

41

'What's she crying about?' Joseph asked the group around the woman with the rock. He saw the burnt hem of a shawl, red-rimmed eyes, a birthmark low on her jawline. Saw? Still sees! This girl here with the bad teeth was the only person to hold his gaze. 'What's happened?' he asked her.

She replied unintelligibly, grabbed the nearest child by both shoulders, pulled him to her, and said something else.

'English,' Joseph said.

Another young woman stepped forward, the one with the singed headscarf. 'Her brother. Her little sister,' she said.

'What about them?'

'Come on,' said Lancaster. 'Let's go.'

(Why didn't he listen to Lancaster? He should have, but he didn't, and the not-listening grew teeth and bit him and still won't let go!)

'They took them.'

'Who?'

She said a word Joseph didn't understand and added, 'Bosniak family.'

'Another family? Not hers?'

The girl's look said he was an idiot. 'Yes. Not hers!'

'Okay, another family took her kids. Why? When?'

'Three hours.'

The bloodied woman raised her fist again. Joseph reached out, saying, 'No, no, no.' And he was surprised when she placed the rock in his palm.

Very good.

She didn't let it go immediately, though. He had to sort of work it free with accompanying reassurances.

She'd stopped wailing now, he noticed. They all had. Her face was wet with snot as well as blood. She had a white mark running from the corner of her mouth up across her cheek, at odds with the homeliness of her youthful, beautiful even, skin.

Despite the icy breeze Joseph could feel his ears burning.

42

Now Radio 4 fill the car. 'I like to catch up on the news when I can,' Emily says.

'Sure,' he says.

And it's a relief, at first, to hear of a fresh uprising in Syria, lower than expected unemployment figures, broken manifesto promises, and an unexpected win on the cricket field.

But hold on.

A stab of what's really happening prods Joseph to concentrate.

He's left a man for dead in a flowerbed!

No, no, no, not dead.

And he's right. Even as the more detailed news starts up after the headlines, there's no mention of anything that could be that.

Nor is there any reference to a missing banker, Airdeen Clore, or any late snippets about a financial angel hitting random strangers' bank accounts with Hail Mary gifts. Joseph feels the seatbelt tight across his chest and realises he's leaning forward to listen. He'd like to hear, say, that a dairy farmer in Normandy or a childminder in Prague has reported a suspect payment of, for example, $41,345 into their bank account, but . . . he doesn't. The news just fizzles out into the weather.

Meaning everyone's keeping quiet.

Well, you would, wouldn't you!

The bank is pulling the mother of all cover-ups: that much is clear.

And nobody is keen to give away what they're so grateful to have received.

Possibly.

Joseph is wringing his hands.

No, no, no, he thinks: even if said dairy farmer, child-minder, car-wash owner, priest, whoever, did query a deposit, the whole point is that he, Joseph, with the help of his man in Milton Keynes, has successfully short-circuited the electronic money trail.

Hence no story to report.

Makes sense.

The seatbelt goes slack again but his mouth still feels dry.

Think the thing through again.

First, Milton Keynes man, with his ingenious binary witchcraft. Expensive chap, bastard clever. Though he drove a Lexus coupé he wore trainers and below-the-knee shorts to the meeting at McDonald's in Luton. Isn't it amusing that Joseph only met him as the digital watermarking expert on that Uzbek oil and gas arbitration? Because he was suggested by Lancaster, no less!

Ha.

Ha, ha.

The legal team replaced him before the hearing for some reason or other, but Joseph kept his card. Instinct. Set a thief to catch a robber, et cetera.

So far the fraud team at the Financial Services Authority, working with the bank's enforcers, will have traced the missing funds into accounts held by a Russian doll sequence off offshore shell companies. Joseph sees them stretching into the foggy distance. And where the dolls blur out, there's a sort of cliff wall, invisible but there, he can sense it, beyond which: Switzerland.

Costly peaks!

Tranche after tranche of inaccessible, veiled, Swiss bank accounts.

Even if those banks could be penetrated, which, given the amount Joseph coughed up, they cannot, the money only stayed there for a heartbeat, before being dealt blind through a further kaleidoscope of offshore accounts, each one held in the name of a dead World War One soldier, as it happens.

Joseph's idea: thank you Commonwealth War Graves Commission, handily online.

From the trenches the money passed to the beneficiaries, who, though they might try to find out where it came from, will discover zip re its true origins, because said origins are through a trench and up an Alp and down a cliff and across an endless plain shrouded in mist. Gone. Beyond gone, in fact. Expensively! It cost Joseph three-quarters of a million dollars to ensure they *never existed*.

What didn't?

Ha.

'I always take a few provisions when I visit,' Emily is saying now. When Joseph is slow to respond she says, 'Just to stock up. Geoffrey isn't the best shopper.'

'Right.'

'Porridge oats, for example.'

'I see.'

'He feeds the children all sorts of sugary cereals, but a bowl of hot porridge is better for them. Particularly if you put some banana and golden syrup on it. I took two boxes.'

'I'm sure they appreciated that.'

Hedgerows slide past in the pause that follows. Eventually she risks a quick glance at Joseph beside her and smiles. 'Possibly,' she says. 'Either way, it's a nice feeling, trying to help.'

She's right, of course.

Ha.

43

That's all he wanted to do himself, help the woman with the
bloodied head.

'The other family took your kids three hours ago,' he
said, still squatting beside her. 'Where did they go?'

'Home,' said the other one, with the singed shawl.

'Where's that, then?'

'Next village.'

Lancaster's gun had dropped to his side. He said, 'So it's
a domestic. Come on, Joe.'

'I don't think so. It's not her family that took them, is it?'

'No,' said the woman with the shawl.

Joseph's boots creaked beneath him in the mud. Somebody sniffed. The woman whose kids were missing had the
same dark hair as Naomi. 'Tell her it'll be okay,' Joseph said.

The shawl's voice: 'It is not okay.'

'She's probably right,' said Lancaster.

Joseph looked up. 'Are we here just to stroll about or
what?'

'That's right, stroll about following orders. That's our
thing.'

Joseph patted the woman's shoulder. 'Tell her we'll help,'
he said. 'Show us which way they went.'

'Christ,' said Lancaster, and, 'Fucking hell.' But he

didn't object further when they started out to walk three miles down a slab road whose verges were, for the most part, greyscaled out. Something with caterpillar tracks had torn the concrete edge to bits, so that what grass there was either side of them was covered with cement-coloured dust. Joseph took charge. Lancaster therefore held back. Literally: he brought up the rear. The longer they walked, the more Joseph could feel eyes on the back of his neck, though every time Joseph looked over his shoulder Lancaster's gaze slipped off over the hedge, the fields of weeds, that fir copse. Lancaster's rifle butt was jammed up against his right bicep, showboating alertness. He didn't want to do this, but if that's what they were doing, he'd do it properly.

A mangy horse stood tethered in a gateway. The woman with the burnt shawl led the patrol past it alongside a broken-faced house. Out of the corner of his eye, Joseph thought he saw a shape lurch through the blackness inside, but nothing came of the movement, nothing other than a swoop of fear so similar to the feeling he'd had in the moment of finding his father dead in his armchair that Joseph stopped. Something horrible lay ahead. He knew it. What's more, he understood himself completely: given the chance, he'd turn back.

But, he just couldn't.

Not then.

Because . . . Lancaster!

Couldn't admit it to him. 'It' being . . . his mistake.

The patrol concertinaed to a stop, Lancaster last.

Joseph pretended he'd halted to ask the woman how far they had to go.

As it happened, not far. The houses here stood spread out along the road in their own plots of land. Two or three more plots later, and they were there, next to a stone wall, set back from which stood a neat, whitewashed cottage. Very Disney. A leafless vine of some sort hugged the lintel, and smoke curled from somewhere behind the pitched roof.

'This is here,' said the woman with the shawl.

Everyone stopped. It was quiet.

'Her kids,' Lancaster started. 'The family she says took them. They live here?'

The woman with the bloodied head pushed past him to the garden gate, which was painted dark green. Joseph stepped aside to let her through. As he did so there was a quick cracking noise, then another, and another.

The air was unzipping.

With bullets!

Spitting dirt there, there and there, behind them in the road.

44

Apropos of nothing, the car slows down.

'What's this?' says Emily. 'Something's not right!'

She pulls herself forward on the wooden steering wheel.

Joseph tenses up. What does she mean?

She's not looking at him.

Sort of shuddering, though: is she ill?

No. It's a problem with the car. The engine slurs and gives out and Emily panics and lets go of the wheel entirely, the car coasting across the gentle curve of the dual carriageway.

Jesus!

He quickly leans across to steady them into the slow lane. A truck ploughs past. Their speed drops from forty miles an hour to thirty, to fifteen. Ah. Below the speedometer the petrol gauge is orange, the needle levered down beyond empty. Joseph drifts the Mercedes onto the hard shoulder where it rolls to a sedate stop. For good measure, still hanging onto the steering wheel, he pulls up the handbrake. Emily's breathing, quick and shallow and panicky, is audible in the traffic gap. She's shaking. Joseph pats her arm.

'It's all right,' he says.

'Oh goodness.'

'We ran out of petrol,' he says.

They sit in silence until another car whips past close by, the Mercedes rocking in its slipstream.

Emily says: 'I could have sworn I filled it up last Tuesday, but I must have . . . forgotten to.'

He looks sideways at her.

'My cousin Ralph lives in Glasgow,' she says. 'They have a terrible problem there: he's had the petrol sucked out of his tank twice. But this is my fault.'

'Do you have breakdown cover?'

'The AA, you mean?'

'That kind of thing.'

'No. My husband always said insurance was for pessimists.'

Joseph has a policy, and he's pretty sure it attaches to the person, meaning him, not the car he happens to be in, so he could call somebody out to help himself, except that he can't, of course.

'It's one view,' he says.

Emily is checking the road map. 'We're about here, I think, and if I remember right there's a garage at the next junction. Not too far. But if we're only . . .'

Joseph is still looking at Emily. She made an effort for her visit, with eyeliner and a dusting of something on the wrinkled plane of her cheek. Damnit! How has this old lady managed to beach herself on a dual carriageway with a mud-stained fugitive?

'I'll go,' he says.

'Really?'

He can't tell if she doubts he'll return, doesn't know for sure if he will or not himself.

'Yes, I'll go. Just sit tight. I'll be back with petrol.'

'So stupid of me, forgetting to fill up,' she says.

'We've all done it.' He pops his seatbelt.

'I'm sorry,' she says.

'You're helping me out. It's the least I can do.'

He climbs out of the car. A pylon is humming to itself nearby. He should tell her to get out of the car and wait on the verge. That's what you're supposed to do, for safety's sake, isn't it?

'I won't be long,' he says.

45

Joseph walks the gritty hard shoulder trying not to remember what came next, but it's no use: this is one of *those* days.

He didn't see anything in slow motion.

He exhibited no catlike super alertness.

He felt no muscle-memory training kicking in.

He didn't even see Reid get hit, but there he was, rolling around on the verge of grey grass, clutching at himself.

Look at him!

Joseph just stood there.

And after a pause, and another clipping noise, something struck the side of Joseph's neck.

Ouch.

Something else, much louder, had started next to him, a shuddery whip-cracking.

Look at Lancaster there, unleashing with his SA80.

Both the top windows of the cottage had already exploded.

And somebody inside was screaming, and the vine was quivering.

The hand that came away from Joseph's neck was wet with orangey blood. Plus there was the problem of this awkward shape of the woman in the headscarf bent sideways between the gateposts, unsure whether to duck forward or back. At least he understood that. Joseph dragged her behind the stone wall. Her jumper smelled of onions. They ended up huddling beneath Lancaster, whose gun was still trained on the house.

How infuriatingly fucking competent!

The screaming had stopped. Lancaster drilled another couple of rounds into the house for good measure and sat back. His face was white but when he glanced down at Joseph he was smiling.

'My arm,' said Reid, who had already pulled himself through the weeds to sit with his back against the wall.

Joseph kneeled up, shouldered his own rifle, flicked off the safety catch and trained the sight on the front door. It took all his effort not to pull the trigger: he only managed it because he knew a burst of fire from him, then, would be totally ridiculous.

'You've been hit,' said Lancaster, which helped. He leaned to look and said, 'Only a scratch.'

Joseph later had fourteen stitches down the left-hand side of his jaw to close up the cut, but still.

For now he was okay!

'It doesn't really hurt,' he said, to cement that fact.

'Good. That window. Top right.'

Lancaster turned to attend to Reid. Why hadn't Joseph thought of that? Because he was covering the house already! For a long time he looked at the house over the muzzle of his rifle, the empty window socket, the shredded curtain hanging still inside, the render beneath the window split with bullets. The front door was ajar, he noticed. After a few minutes a tortoiseshell cat walked through the gap. It sat down on the front step and looked away. The two women had started talking, a whisper at first, then more loudly. Now they were arguing. The one whose children were missing was loudest. By the time Lancaster had finished strapping up Reid's arm she was standing beside him, pulling at his shoulder with one hand and jabbing at the house with the other. She evidently assumed he was in charge, too.

'She says what are you waiting for?' the other woman said.

Blood had leaked into Joseph's collar. He was doing a lot of blinking. Beside him the mother had stopped muttering and now moved forward.

'She says she's going to get them,' her friend said.

46

What's that ahead? Something else to think about, thank God. The garage. Emily was right: he's come upon it at a junction a little way down the road. Once this place would have been two pumps and an attendant in overalls. Now it has sprouted a minimart, a kind of garden centre, and a coffee concession. There's also a toilet, though they call it a rest room. What he would do for an actual lie-down. Joseph runs a basin full of warm water and carefully washes his face and hands, which look bloodless no matter how hard he scrubs.

He chooses a plastic jerrycan, pays for it, fills it up, and returns to pay for the contents, because that's what the checkout guy insists he must do. As he's waiting in the queue a second time he spots himself on CCTV above the counter, swiftly looks down, and finds himself inspecting the bumper packs of Haribo, Murray Mints and whatnot. His eyes snag on the Maynards Sours: these are Lara's favourites, and before he knows why he's put them on the counter.

She'll be grateful, he thinks.

No, no, no.

He pays for them anyway and trudges back along the hard shoulder, round the final bend, to find the car with Emily still inside it. She has a newspaper spread over the wheel. He opens the passenger door, fuel can in hand, and says, 'Success.'

She smiles gratefully, and he knows she was worried he might not come back.

'What's a breed of large penguin?' she asks.

'Sorry?'

She taps the newspaper. 'I'm struggling. Seven letters.'

'Emperor,' he says.

The word, right there: how heartening!

It's an old car. She has to climb out and unlock the petrol cap with a key. Joseph would have done it for her, but now she's beside him, solemnly listening to the glugging as he tips the fuel into the hole.

'You're in some sort of trouble, aren't you.'

The last drops drain from the spout.

He screws down the lid.

'Trouble or not,' he says, 'you needn't worry. You should have enough petrol now to get you home, and I can make my own way from—'

'No,' she says, cutting him off. 'I was going to say the opposite. You're welcome to come with me, to my house. Rest, have something to eat, see if you can't find a way to solve your . . . problem. That is, if you don't have to go to Southampton straight away. You've done me a favour.' She nods at the fuel can. 'I'd like to do the same.'

47

They found out later that the woman with the blood-matted hair, the children's mother, was called Katja, and that her friend with the singed shawl was in fact her sister, the children's auntie, Anis. When Katja walked towards the house Anis followed. That didn't surprise Joseph as much as the fact that Lancaster went with them, but he did, leaving Joseph no choice but to tell Reid, who already had his rifle trained on the house with his good arm, to cover him while he went too.

Those yards between the gate and the front step: bloody hell!

Each step was an invitation.

You got Reid in the arm and me in the neck.

Why not finish the job!

But it didn't happen. They made it to the front door un-shot-at.

Once through it, the first thing Joseph saw – because how could he miss it? – was a decorative swipe of blood stretching along the parquet floor of the hall.

Though Lancaster told her to wait, Katja followed it straight into the back yard, leaving footprints as she went. Joseph and Lancaster held back to clear the house, room by room. It was empty. Making it likely Lancaster had hit the gunman, who'd dragged himself bleeding outside. If there'd been others, they'd fled too.

The bedroom with the blown-out window smelled all wrong. It took Joseph a moment to work out why: as well as hitting the gunman one of Lancaster's bullets had struck a can of hairspray on the dressing table by the back wall. Joseph was about to pick it up when a terrible wailing started behind the house.

He followed Lancaster downstairs and outside to find Anis holding Katja in the doorway of a brick outbuilding, both women wailing because of what they could see inside. Some twenty yards beyond them lay the gunman, still alive, propped against a bale of chicken wire. He had dropped his pistol. Joseph picked up the gun and shoved it into his webbing and stood over the man for a moment. He wasn't going anywhere. Given that, Joseph had no choice but to join Lancaster and the women by the brick shed.

Dead children: he knew that's what he would see, but he hadn't expected it would be like this.

The outbuilding contained some sort of bakery. There was a calendar on the wall turned to February, the wrong month, depicting an Alpine-looking chalet in thick snow, and there were sacks of flour on the floor, and a rack of metal cooling trays stood next to one wall, opposite a row of kitchen units topped with a long stainless-steel work surface. Squat in the middle of the room, planted on the brick floor, stood a huge oven. A homely light shone from inside, illuminating four small feet, blackened and split and pressed up against the door glass.

Before he knew what was happening, Katja had broken free of her sister, who had in fact been holding her back, and she made it to the oven. Heat billowed from within as she opened the door. Joseph took a step away and Lancaster told her to stop but of course she didn't. She burned herself pulling the first child out, shrieked, couldn't hold onto the corpse, dropped it hard on the brick floor. The head was canted back, mouth prised open, stopped with something round. Katja took whatever it was out and threw it to one side. The object rolled towards Joseph. It was an apple.

'Damn,' said Lancaster. 'Unbelievable.'

Despite the burning heat Katja hauled the other body out of the oven as well.

Joseph, soldier in charge, just stood there.

Look!

An apple in this one's mouth, too.

What's happened here?

The answer's pretty obvious!

Go on, then, spit it out.

Somebody had killed these children and cooked them, or worse, put them in the oven alive.

Now here was Katja, with her bloodied head and burnt hands in her lap, her two dead children curled black on the floor in the doorway of the hut.

Joseph could feel his back teeth flexing in his jaw; the torn skin on the side of his neck was smarting now, a richly deserved sharpness!

One of the children was twisted backwards, a balletic little shape, while the other's fists were tight black balls.

Joseph, man of action, shut the oven door.

Well done, very good.

Next, he picked up two empty hessian bags from a storage bin under the window and laid them over the children's bodies, careful, though he didn't know why, to arrange them writing-side down.

'Unbelievable,' Lancaster said again.

'Can you stop saying that.'

'But, Jesus. What do you think makes a person decide this is the thing to do?'

Later, they found out: Katja and Anis's younger brother had killed the Bosnian baker's wife and three children eighteen months beforehand. He shot out the windscreen of the wife's car as she was approaching a pontoon bridge. All four of them drowned upside down in the frozen river, and though Katja's brother had since died himself, his roasted nephew and niece were somebody's idea of revenge.

48

He accepts Emily's offer of help, since . . . he just does.

She drives them to her house, a square-set child's drawing with roses wired to the brickwork, a spider plant on a window sill in the kitchen, and photographs – of Geoffrey and his children, presumably – all over the walls.

There's a collection of wind-up toys in the fireplace next door, some of the toys without keys, and a pleasant smell of cedar logs when he bends to look more closely at: what's this?

A tin monkey frozen mid-drumbeat.

The manic expression on its face!

Emily explains her husband made these toys in his retirement, and because he seems interested, she shows Joseph his workroom with all the tools still laid out, screwdrivers and Allen keys and miniature spanners, pliers, a tiny hammer, all as he left them.

They return to the kitchen to sit at the dark wood table, on which Emily places a cold ham with a rind of yellow breadcrumbs, Stilton, pickles, and . . . a pair of Pot Noodles, at odds in their midst.

They eat in silence, Joseph seriously considering explaining his missing status, what he's done to the bank, Lara, Zac, the goddamn unopened letter in his satchel, all of it, and so on. But he can't quite begin, and opts for: 'This is very kind of you,' instead.

'There was a time, after the divorce, when I thought Geoffrey might do something stupid. He was that low.'

'Right.'

'It's a mother's worst nightmare.'

Joseph thinks of his own mother. The Green Party flyers on her sideboard, ready for her to push through letterboxes, whatever the weather; her bookshelves piled higgledy-piggledy with gardening manuals, self-help books and detective fiction. That murdering idiot, Tristan.

'What turned him around?'

'A British Gas engineer. I know, it sounds stupid, but his boiler broke down and the engineer who came to mend it fixed him, too. The gas man was retraining to be a counsellor, saw something strange in Geoffrey's demeanour, asked him if he wanted to talk about it. And he did. And it worked.'

'I see.'

'I couldn't help him myself. I was part of the problem just because I was me. He couldn't admit how low he was to his own mother. It's just the worst, that your child might do that to themselves, isn't it?'

Joseph nods.

'Anyway.' She pauses, clears the plates, says finally: 'He's all right now.'

'Good.'

She's sweet: she's trying to tell him that it will all be all right in the end. Geoffrey the dentist pulled through.

He will, too. Possibly Geoffrey's low point didn't involve a $1.34 billion crime, a hammerhead called Lancaster, and a memory that *just won't go away*.

49

Somebody's idea of revenge.

Wasn't it obvious whose?

Joseph walked away from the two women, the two corpses, Lancaster, and the pervasive horrible burning smell, knelt down and dry-retched over a flowerbed with no flowers in it. He shut his eyes and tried to imagine he was somewhere else but that was never going to work; the next time he opened them a string of saliva connected him to the turned earth. He stood up.

'It is, though, isn't it,' said Lancaster behind him. 'Unbelievable.'

Over Lancaster's shoulder the man he had shot sat slumped against the chicken wire, going nowhere slowly.

'I'll sort this,' Joseph said.

'What?'

Joseph, moral crusader, could hear himself breathing fast. He looked out across the scrubby hedge at the unplanted field and trees beyond it. There were knots of birds in the upper branches. Roosting crows perhaps. No, they weren't big enough. Starlings.

'Save the children,' Joseph said. 'Peacekeeping.'

'Sit down, Joe. Put your head between your knees. You look like crap.'

'Somebody did this.'

'No shit.'

'Him.' Joseph pointed to the man sitting by the chicken wire.

'Possibly.'

'It was him.'

'Maybe. Come on, Joe.'

Joseph pointed to the women. 'Best get them inside.'

'Take it easy,' said Lancaster. 'I'll radio this in.'

'No.'

Lancaster took off his helmet and passed his hand over his head, his cheek, his chin. His face was pink. Never mind the dusting of stubble, he suddenly looked young for his age, which was pleasing. All that competence was just an act: he was as clueless as the next man when push came to shove. Joseph was the next man. No, no, no. He pointed at the women again. 'Just get them out of here,' he said.

'Calm down.'

'I am calm,' said Joseph evenly, walking towards the man.

'Okay, but slow down. Wait.'

Joseph paused and pointed at the women again. 'I am waiting.'

'Okay. Good.'

Lancaster squatted next to Katja and Anis and took his time encouraging them inside. He pointed at the sacks on the floor and said, 'We'll bring these to you.' The word 'these' was obscenely unspecific. By the time Lancaster had ushered the women inside, Joseph's breathing was steady again.

50

Joseph excuses himself to use the bathroom; when he returns to the kitchen Emily is nowhere to be seen.

He waits.

Where the hell is she?

He should leave.

But he doesn't want to, and doesn't quite know why.

He pulls on his boots, opens the back door, and finds Emily at the bottom of the garden. She's wearing a headscarf, an old Barbour, and she has tucked her slacks into wellies. She's also holding a crowbar in one hand. If the clothes fitted her once, she's shrunk within them over time.

'Something's up with the drain,' she explains. 'We're not on the mains. The septic tank is ancient but I had it emptied not long ago. Sometimes the sump bit leading to it gets blocked.'

Joseph looks around and sees a row of neatly pruned fruit trees, a compost heap, a squirrel running along a distant fence top.

'The sink wouldn't empty,' Emily goes on. 'My husband was a practical man. He used to sort of jab at the hole under here to get it going again.'

Joseph holds out his hand for the crowbar.

'First the petrol, now this: I couldn't possibly let you,' she says, but allows him to take it from her anyway.

'This thing?' He sticks the point of the iron into the soddenness surrounding the slab and works it upwards, not particularly wanting to see what's beneath it. Scummy liquid full of peelings and worse swimming in a hole which, when he prods it, has some sort of fibrous mass stuck deep inside. He jabs harder at the obstruction. Here's a good deed. Costs nothing! If he can just gouge and thump and break apart the crap in the bottom of the hole all will be well. Sure, some of it is spattering back up at him, and Emily is telling him to stop, but he's started and he's bloody well going to finish.

Thump, spatter, thrust, fleck, twist.

He's not done anything like this for years!

A good old physical problem.

Solved!

With a sucking sound the watery sludge in the drain suddenly drops away.

'There!' he says.

'Your clothes.'

He looks down at the mess.

'You'll have to let me wash them.'

'I've really got to get going.'

'But look at you! You have to clean yourself up.'

She's almost scolding him.

It's sweet.

She's also right: his clothes are properly filthy now, and he stinks.

So he complies. He allows her to lead him indoors, loan him her dead husband's dressing gown, and use the plastic, avocado-coloured bathtub, while she runs his clothes through the washing machine.

He lowers himself into the foam, slides beneath it and resurfaces, thinking: baptised. After he's scrubbed himself, the bubbles are grey and there's a scum line round the sides of the bath. He lies there thinking would he, Joseph Ashcroft, ever let a stranger use his bathroom, or feed them a Pot Noodle, or indeed offer them a lift?

No. He would not.

But an elderly woman has done all this for him, partly, at least, because she wants to help him sort himself out again.

In fact, she's prepared to do more.

She's made him a cup of tea to drink, in her husband's dressing gown, at the kitchen table, and says, 'Your clothes will take time drying. I made the bed up in the spare room. You're exhausted. I'll show you where it is. Have a lie-down. If Southampton can wait, that is.'

Joseph lets her lead the way, thinking: it's a funny old ___.

No, no, no.

Funny old ___.

World.

The bed is cool, its sheets thin. He slides in delicately: a misplaced heel might tear this old clean sheet. She's put a glass of water on the bedside table. That's what he's talking about: kindness.

He holds the glass up, watches bubbles rise within. Then he puts it down again, leans back, shuts his eyes, and sleeps soundly.

51

More or less.

There's just the memory of the dying seagull to deal with first. He found it in the back garden when he was nine, hanging at head height in a bush. His football had rolled into the flowerbed and he didn't notice the bird as he stretched beneath the bush to retrieve it, but as he stood up it was just there, its blank eye an inch from his face. He jumped back. Yuck! The seagull didn't flap or screech. So was it dead? No. He stared at its downy blue-white breast feathers, slate stripe along one wing, the edge almost green, and saw the beak open and close slowly. Then the wing scissored forward. The bird looked mechanical almost, but wasn't. It was alive, dying. How long would that take? And how had it got there in the first place? Couldn't just have fallen out of the sky, could it? Impossible to say. Joseph wanted to take the bird out of the bush and end its misery but he didn't know how. He was frightened. He took his football inside and spent the afternoon trying not to think about the seagull, and the next time he went into the garden, it was gone.

But the injured man slumped against the bale of chicken wire, well, he was still there when Lancaster returned, and Joseph was still staring down at him, remembering that seagull for no good reason at all, except the obvious one.

'What were you thinking?' Joseph asked.

The man took a breath but didn't answer. Probably couldn't. The entire left side of his body – coat, jeans, even his one muddy trainer (how had the other one come off?) – was stained with blood so dark it looked black, yet both the hand pressed against his chest and the exposed side of his neck below his beard were bright red with it. Now the man twisted his head up a little, trying to see Joseph perhaps, but he couldn't turn his neck far enough to pull the manoeuvre off.

Poor guy: very shot!

Joseph crouched over the man. 'Can't answer?' he said.

A bluebottle landed on the shot man's collar. Joseph waved it away for him, stood up, had a little walk around, stopped to look at him again. He was a chunky man, barrel-chested, broader across the shoulders than Joseph, powerfully built. But who was he? A baker. With an oven. Perhaps he'd grown so strong lifting bags of flour? Or maybe he wrestled, wearing tights? Or lifted weights. Or swam a lot. Yes, he was on the local water polo team. Not just on it, he coached it, and coached young children to swim as well, taught them how to swivel their hands when doing backstroke, dip their little fingers into the water first, keep their hips up, their arms straight. A community-minded sportsman. What's more, the curve of that nose looked intelligent, which meant he had also been to university, to study economics perhaps, or political theory. No, that didn't fit with the being a baker bit. Or did it? Probably he was offered a place but couldn't go, what with the war and so forth.

The fly had landed again, on the man's bloodied ear now. It crawled inside. He was offered a university place but couldn't go because he had to stay behind and run the family business, man the oven, bake the bread, because his father couldn't, because he'd died, died sitting upright, in a dark brown armchair . . .

No, no, no.

'Joe?' Lancaster was using an annoying snap-out-of-it voice.

'Yeah?'

The man let out a long sigh. Was he tired? Bored? Did he wish he hadn't done it, hadn't joined the army to prove something to his father, who was dead already, and therefore not even able to take offence?

No, no, no.

The fly had done his time inside the ear and was taking a walk up that excellent sideburn and across the man's forehead.

'They're waiting for us,' said Lancaster. 'Come on.'

'Check out his beard.'

'What?'

'It's great, isn't it.'

'Fuck his beard. Come on.'

'Sure,' Joseph said. 'Just give me a minute.'

He didn't really want to do it.

So he didn't have to.

He could stop himself!

Here's how: by folding his arms, burying his hands under his armpits, holding himself in place.

It wasn't that hard.

But then the tip of the man's tongue sort of poked out between his black lips and everything was obvious. Katja's children were dead, but this chap here wasn't, not yet.

'I never did find out what happened to that bloody seagull,' Joseph explained.

'What seagull?'

'There could have been some sort of miracle. I mean, I don't actually know.'

'What are you talking about?'

'If we go inside now and come back out later he may be gone.'

'Whatever, come on.'

Joseph reached into his webbing. Lancaster saw what he was doing and said something, but Joseph was already pointing the man's pistol at the fly on his head. Lancaster lunged at him, shouting something Joseph never heard, because he shouted it too late.

52

Listen to the heating pipes, and the wind through the tall trees in Emily's garden. Feel the thin soft sheets.

There's the seagull at head height in the bush, with its floppy wing.

And here is a shadow spreading out from under the fully slumped dead man Joseph shot.

There's a voice, too, tiny, objecting.

It's Lancaster: he's a million miles away, and coming to get you!

'What the fuck did you do that for?'

Joseph shrugs beneath the covers, pulling them up to his chin.

'Why? Oh Christ! Why!'

'It's pretty straightforward.'

'No. No. No. I can't believe you just did that. No.'

'You shot him first.'

'What?'

'He was dying anyway, I think,' Joseph says eventually.

'You moron! That's not the point!'

'What is the point, then?'

'You killed him on the ground, right in front of me. What are we supposed to do now? You're expecting me to just

. . . I don't have a choice now, do I?! What am I supposed to do?'

There's no answer, not in the treetops, not beneath the covers.

53

What happened next? For at least a minute, nothing at all. Joseph and Lancaster just stood over the dead man taking him in. Joseph had shot him in the head and now he had a big triangular blackness above his right eyebrow, a cross between a hole and a split.

Baker of bread and children.

Wrestler, aspiring student, swimmer, coach, whatever.

All irrelevant now, what with the missing part of his head.

Now that he was no longer breathing, Joseph marvelled at the new stillness. It had less to do with the quiet and more with a sense of calm.

The fly had gone, he noticed.

'Give me the gun, Joe.'

'Eh?'

Lancaster's face was grey. Joseph felt suddenly sorry for him. But then Lancaster shook his head and, woah! Joseph's pity soured to defiance.

'Oh come on. A fucking oven.'

'We don't know for sure who—'

'Apples.'

'We don't know.'

'Of course we do.'

Lancaster drew himself an inch taller. 'We have to radio this in.'

Joseph looked at him carefully and saw Lancaster's Adam's apple move in his throat, giving him away.

'Radio what in exactly?'

'Don't be a dick.'

Joseph turned from Lancaster to the dead man to the brick outbuilding, with its door still ajar, and the two sacks in front it, each covering a dead burned child, and he looked at the blank-faced back of the house through which the children's mother and aunt had obediently retreated, and said, 'Of course. Let's call it in.'

Lancaster nodded in relief.

'It being the patrol, the women by the church, the trail here, the contact, clearing the house and finding the dead kids in the oven.'

Lancaster tipped his helmet back and ran his hand over his face.

Joseph knelt beside the dead man and used a clean bit of his trouser leg to wipe down the pistol's handle and the trigger. Fiddly work! He persevered.

'Seriously?' said Lancaster.

'I'm just giving him his gun back,' Joseph said, laying the pistol in the man's hand. There was a ring on one of his fingers. They wouldn't stay clenched, but no matter; Joseph managed to wedge a forefinger in behind the trigger guard. 'Apart from this one, yours is the only gun anyone fired,' he said. 'And you unloaded in self-defence, because this fucker ambushed us. Nobody has to know anything other than

187

that, do they? We found three dead bodies when the shooting stopped, one of whom belonged to the guy who'd been firing at us, trying to stop us discovering the other two, who were kids. Go find the radio. Call it in.'

Lancaster's face looked like it was made out of crumpled paper.

Meanwhile, Joseph, well, he was brick-built, certain!

And yet . . .

Joseph put an arm around Lancaster. He caught the acrid smell of sweaty fear, but couldn't tell who it was coming from.

'It's the bigger picture that counts, Ben. Why did you come out today? We're not just tourists. No need to make a drama out of this. We've sorted something here.' Why did his throat feel so tight?

A wood pigeon cooed in the distance, the exact same sound the wood pigeons made in the trees outside the dormitory window at school.

'You watched me do it.'

'I tried—'

'Tried what?'

'I don't believe this.'

'You saw the whole thing.'

'I—'

'Oversaw it, almost.'

Lancaster shook his head but said, 'Okay, all right, all right.'

'What we have to do now is carry on carrying on.'

Lancaster nodded without conviction.

'Let's make a start, then.'

54

Joseph wakes late to see a bar of sunlight falling through the gap between the curtains. He swings his legs out of the bed. They look pale and white and old, unfit for purpose. He's lost weight: he can see his hip bones. Once he has dressed he heads downstairs, following the pleasing smell of stew. Emily insists he eats a bowlful, and even offers him the use of her laptop. She's probably hoping that he'll make contact with someone, but once online he taps straight through to Reuters to check for news about the bank.

There's nothing.

Still nothing!

Damn Lancaster: it's an incredible cover-up he's orchestrating. Incredible and . . . disheartening. The only explanation Joseph can think of is that they're waiting until they've got him in hand to parade as the guilty man, before they reveal the full extent of what he's done.

But he knows that makes no sense.

It's just that the only other explanation is too depressing to articulate.

Yes, they'll be redoubling their efforts to find him before the story breaks itself.

But he'll frustrate them.

He'll show them by pulling off Plan B.

Which means, yes, he'll actually disappear.

To Southampton!

At least that makes scent.

Sense.

Actually, both!

He needs to throw them off the scent, doesn't he? And the best way of doing that? By laying a false trail. To a dead end. Literal death would be great, but there's the problem of a corpse, and it's good that he still thinks it a problem, isn't it, because it means he doesn't want to provide one.

So either he has to be presumed dead, or just gone, as in abroad, far away.

In Southampton he can feign both happenings: slip the net or die trying, appearance-wise, at least.

Joseph mops up the last of the stew with a piece of granary bread. Emily is giving him a bit more Geoffrey detail, probably to make him feel he too can pull through, but he's not really listening, because he's thinking instead, reaching the conclusion that for his plan to work he needs to lay down a big marker in Southampton, making it very clear that he, Joseph Ashcroft, was there. How best to do that? He comes up with an idea and discounts it because, listen to her, she's offering him as much time as he needs to recuperate, and damnit, her kindness tastes of Worcester sauce, so wholesome, making super gratitude the right response, not theft.

Theft? No, no, no: he's only going to borrow it.

She'll report it missing. It'll be found. They'll work out that it was him, Joseph Ashcroft, who took it. Job done.

There's the key on its hook by the door.

Coffee? He doesn't mind if he does.

And sooner or later, yes, he hears her apologise for rabbiting on so, and saying she'll leave him be while she does a few chores.

Chores. Great word: Joseph hasn't heard it in ages. Bankers don't really think about chores, other than to outsource them.

Off she goes, wearing her little slippers.

And wow, he feels bad in advance.

But it's only a car!

A nice red classic and therefore an obvious one.

Plus her dead husband's pride and joy.

He should leave her a note. But there's not really time and what would he say other than sorry. In the utility room he puts on his clean coat and laces his boots and shoulders his satchel and there are the keys to the Merc, right there on the hook with the brass chicken's head, or at least they were, because they're already in his ungrateful thieving hand now, which is entirely justified given the wider scheme of things.

Ah, the wider scheme. It's like a park, or a playground, for outfits like Airdeen Clore to do their stuff in.

This is different.

He skulks out of the back door, careful to walk on the flagstones instead of the white gravel. Quickly he reaches the car, crosses to the driver's door, unlocks it, climbs in, shoots his bag into the footwell and bends forward to feel for the little lever that will let the seat slide back on its runners, and it's as he's fumbling for it, head to one side, that he sees Emily in an upstairs window. She's looking right at him. His fingers find the knob. He eases the seat away from the pedals, eyes still locked on the old lady.

Is she smiling?

Damnit: there's a hot sensation in his neck and face.

He should just climb out and apologise: I'm sorry, I don't know what I was thinking.

But he doesn't. Can't. He's done it now. He's slotted the key into the ignition and turned it to hear the engine purr, and he's let off the handbrake and looked up again – he couldn't help it – as the car eases forward.

Framed in the window, Emily waves.

What an ocean-going schmuck he is!

Ha.

If he wasn't so hot with guilt, he'd be able to enjoy the ocean-going thought as funny, given that he's actually going to the ocean, or the sea, at least, Channel, whatever.

Just shut up!

She'll get the car back.

Just – after he's gunned it down this lane, out onto the open road – later.

55

They crunched back through the house over so much broken glass it seemed they'd shot up a glaziers, with water from a holed tank or pipe dripping through the hall ceiling, diluting the blood on the floor, each of them carrying a child's corpse in a sack, Joseph's stupidly light in his arms, so light in fact that it couldn't be a real body, could it, except that it was, and they found the women with Reid and the others, and perhaps because of the morphine they'd given him, or perhaps not, when Reid worked out what was in the bags he flipped out in all the wrong directions, accusing everyone – the little crowd that had gathered at a respectful distance, poor Katja and Anis, even Lancaster and Joseph – of it being their fault.

'Who are you people?' he shouted. 'You're monsters, that's who!'

Joseph didn't disagree, just stood marvelling at the scene, leaving it to Lancaster to calm the man down, which he did by digging a roll of wine gums out of his webbing and offering it to him. A wine gum. When Joseph saw the packet, steady in Lancaster's hand, he knew, as in knew absolutely, that Lancaster would keep the secret, tell no one, come what may.

And he was right: neither man mentioned it ever again.

56

The old car drives like a powerboat on a glassy lake. It takes Joseph a while to get used to the steering. Feels like he has to turn in before each corner, set the course for the bend ahead. Soon he finds himself on a straighter dual carriageway. The hedge alongside it is newly buzz-cut: raw white wood flashes among the dark stems. He heads south.

He turns on the radio for the news, but it's dominated by a story about another ancient DJ added to the list of 1970s perverts. For years those guys must've thought they were home free. Now they're paying.

Stuff catches up with you in the end.

Except when it doesn't.

When Joseph reaches Southampton, he follows signs for a multistorey car park and runs the old Mercedes up the concrete ramp to the top floor, the tyres squealing even at this low speed as he uncoils the car round the tight bends. They need a top-up of air. If he'd noticed earlier, he could have sorted that for her. He rolls to a stop in an empty bay. No rush now. He has bags of time before the last ferry, which sets off after dark. He uses the time to write Emily that note, combining an apology with thanks (she waved him off, after all!), and adds a postscript suggesting she has the tyres looked at. He puts the seat back and whiles away the rest of the day in the old army lying-in-wait mode, plus, admit it, a fair bit of napping.

Excellent.

He even dreams.

Of Naomi, plus Lara.

He has to make her a costume for a school event, World Book Day or possibly Comic Relief. She and her little friend Harriet, the one with the glasses, have decided to go as Laurel and Hardy, so he makes a fat suit by putting Lara in one of his old Jermyn Street shirts and stuffing it full of balled-up pages from the *Financial Times*. He and Naomi aren't speaking, and the whole hands-on-father costume initiative is supposed to encourage her to break her silence, and it does, but not in the way he expects: she stops en route through the kitchen, laughs at Lara, and congratulates him on dressing her up as a fat cat.

Joseph wakes up.

Naomi.

When she realises what he's done.

She'll be so cowed.

No, no, no!

So *proud*.

It's dark enough now, so he sets off to case the port. And yes, it's pretty much as he remembered, because yes, he did his due diligence. Not just for this trip, no. Beforehand, back in the day, when he *bought* this port, lock, stock and funnels. Not for himself – what would he want with a port? – but for a port-keen client. Bought two others as well that summer, in fact, but this was the only one they persuaded him to visit in person, suffer the guided tour, dot the portholes and cross the anchors, so to speak. The bloke who showed the team around had a large nose and took his job incredibly seriously. Joseph had to pinch his inner thigh to stay awake through the grindingly slow tour of the loading bays, cargo containers, ships' berths and so on.

Now he has to find the right ferry. That one, the smaller of the two, parked nearest the eastern end of the horseshoe. He hangs back from the relevant ticket office until there's no queue, waits a moment longer, then advances. The woman in the booth has taken advantage of the customer gap to open a packet of mini sausage rolls. She bites into one as he arrives and turns away to chew.

Because some people are just good, polite people!

Above her and to the right, a security camera.

Politely now: smile.

Joseph books a one-way ticket and holds his breath as he pays with his credit card, half expecting Lancaster to have cancelled it, but no, of course he hasn't, sale accepted, because this is exactly what the crafty bastard will have been hoping, that he, Joseph, will run out of cash and slip up. In fact, he only has a few notes left, so the credit card is actually quite necessary. To buy the ticket he has to give the woman his name, address, inside leg measurement, everything.

In for a penny!

Details in the system: electronic breadcrumbs. Meaning he doesn't have much time. Lancaster will already be pecking them up. Right now there will be people en route to the port, the ship, Joseph, and even if they don't manage to board before the ship sails, which in all likelihood they will, Lancaster will waste no time in organising a reception party in Dieppe.

So, let's get on with it!

57

Joseph walks briskly up the gangplank, past a skinny boy in a ridiculous steward's uniform, and heads towards the ship's stern, keeping to the lower level. There's a map screwed to the bulkhead at the foot of these stairs. Joseph looks it over. A ship's toilets are supposed to be called heads, but here the stick-man-with-his-legs-spread sign will have to do. He finds the gents behind a heavy sprung door and, wow, that's an aggressive lemony smell indeed. This cubicle here is empty. Joseph locks himself inside. Then he takes off everything but his trousers and shirt. That's right, jacket, jumper, even his boxers, socks and boots. These, plus everything else, he stows inside not one, not two, but three heavy-duty rubbish bags, each of which he seals with a triple-looped elastic band.

Back out in the main bit of the bathroom he catches sight of his face in the mirror. Bristly. Plus the colour of porridge. Woah. Can he really go through with this?

Has to.

In a minute.

No, now.

Otherwise, the ship will sail.

Yes, but for now, just spend sixty seconds hanging on to this here sink.

At school they kept the porridge warm in big baking

trays, then cut it out with cheese-wire to serve. It's true: each serving was a little slab with straight edges. Square porridge!

Get a grip, man.

But he already has: an iron grip on the metal sink.

And his feet are buzzing on the equally metal floor.

Because? Is that deeper shuddering the engines kicking in?

Go, go, go.

Joseph slips out into the corridor and works his way swiftly to the ship's stern, or as far back as he can get on this lowest level, right to where the last lifeboat is slung. Dockside lights bob and sway, and that's a proper thick rich diesel smell, and there, he spots one, and another, and a third – the third being closest. Ladders, all bolted to the jetty wall, thirty or forty metres away, ladders he noticed while listening to the guy with the enormous nose drone on and on and . . .

Hold on.

He's squinting hard at the nearest ladder and yes, no, yes, he sees that he's right, the bottom rungs don't quite reach down to the shifting blackness of the water. He doesn't remember that detail. Due fucking diligence! Oh, Jesus. Possibly a tidal problem. Doesn't matter: if he can't reach the bottom ladder he'll be shafted, meaning he'll drown.

Think.

What he needs is a bit of rope.

He could have bought one. But he didn't. What a complete fucking . . .

And yet, hang on, this is a ferry, with lifeboats, and in all probability, yes, back there, a lifebelt on the metal wall. For pulling-in rather than simply-bobbing-about purposes, it is fixed to a length of rope. Just wait for that couple, clearly having some sort of domestic, to reach the door and go back inside, before quickly liberating the lifebelt, which is more easily said than done, a right drown-while-you-wait-shaped fiddle in fact.

He gets it free just as the engine pitch shifts again.

Now, before anyone comes!

Really?

He's actually going to do this?

Just get on with it!

Meaning: yes he is.

Ha! Soldier! Big Beast! Now!

Joseph ties one end of the rope to the neck of the bin bags. And quickly! That'll do. Now he lowers it over the railing. Remember that thing on Dartmoor? With the cold lake. Hands like lobster claws. Well, keep a goddamn firm hold of the other end of the rope, now. And shimmy over the railings. Wow, the metal is cold. Hang on tight. Lean back. Can he see the bin bags on the rope end, bobbing below? Check! With the free end also reaching the water? Also check. Good! Now, hold both bits of looped rope super tight and lean back and step down, hanging on, not slipping, and Christ, this is hard, lowering himself evenly, one step and rope-hold at a time, but yes, that's right, and again, and—

Woah!

One half of the rope gets away.

Meaning: Joseph falls.

58

Five months after *it*, it being what he did to the deserving baker, Joseph's tour was over and nothing beyond the roasted children – everyone heard about the apples – had come to light. Joseph carried the day in his face, though. Needed fourteen stitches. The medic who put them in did a terrible job and the scar, a candy-pink swoosh below Joseph's jawline, never entirely faded. They sent Reid and his shot-up shoulder home to recuperate. Joseph never saw him or the two women, Katja and Anis, again. He never found out if they knew what he had done, and anyway, even if they had, were they about to complain? As for Lancaster, well, he and Joseph didn't speak about it again themselves because it hadn't happened.

Except that, well, *it* had.

And because it had, not four days after returning home, Joseph found himself making an appointment to see his commanding officer, Major Terry Riceman, or Very Nice Man as he was known. Riceman had decorated his office with his own photographs, most of which, Joseph noticed, as the Major made a good stab of welcoming him home, were black-and-white landscapes with fences prominent in the foreground and something small on the horizon. A barn in that one. Some horses there. A pylon. He was a small man with a paunch but he carried himself stiffly, like a Stafford-shire terrier.

'You as well?' he said after Joseph had explained his plan.

'Sir?'

'I appreciate that it was a trying tour, but these things recede. You'll see.'

'It's not Bosnia, sir. I enjoyed it. In fact, I'm not sure the army will give me another opportunity like that. Which is partly why it's time for me to move on.'

'Did you two rehearse this?'

'Excuse me?'

'Those were more or less Lancaster's words. Good gig, he called it, rewarding, but . . . blah blah blah . . . time for a fresh start.'

'No, I didn't know he . . .'

Major Riceman was inspecting his fingers. He picked up a letter opener and used it to scour the edge of a cuticle. Joseph watched. Why justify himself to this man? Behind the Major's desk, through the window, a yellow rope was swishing lazily among the leafless branches of one of the base's big beech trees. A chainsaw buzzed briefly, followed by the dull crack of a branch hitting tarmac.

'And are you heading off in the same direction?' Riceman asked at length.

'What direction is that?'

'When I pressed him, Lancaster revealed he intends to bat for the money men.'

His clipped diction was as phoney as his photographs. Joseph said nothing, waited for him to explain.

'Mr Lancaster is selling his skills to something called a corporate security firm. Not quite mercenary work, but not much better. He probably thinks he's going to be some sort of commercial spy, but I imagine it will mostly involve him drinking tea in prefab huts, patrolling light-industrial estates with a torch, that sort of thing.'

'We haven't discussed it.'

''Course you haven't, but you must have a plan of your own, no?'

The rope flapped loosely among the branches again. Remember leaping from the lower branches of the big pine into those rhododendron bushes at school? Great fun, that. Joseph nodded and said, 'Arboreal work, sir.'

'Come again?' Riceman narrowed his eyes.

'I'm going to retrain as a tree surgeon.'

'You're joking?'

'Sir?'

'You're an officer. To swap that for monkeying around with a saw, pruning things?'

Joseph thought of saying something about liking the outdoors and wanting to be his own boss, but, 'Will that be all, sir?' came out instead.

Riceman sat back, his shirt buttons tight across his stomach. The chainsaw revved once, twice, a third time, but he still didn't cotton on. Joseph stood before him. Riceman puffed out his cheeks and shook his head and said, 'I suppose so, yes.'

59

Splash.

The cold blackness hits Joseph from all sides at once. It swells within his clothes, which cling and balloon as he hauls himself upwards.

Jesus, that hurt.

Remember the time with the toaster, the stuck bagel, plus fork?

Well, this is like that: after the first, obliterating belt of electricity, every nerve shrieking.

He breaks the surface.

Breathe!

And tread water, lying back: work out which way's which.

Something brushes his face. It's the rope, which followed him over the rail.

He grabs hold of it and, keeping himself afloat with one hand and his egg-beater feet, reefs the rope in. The bags are still attached to it. Every time his ears dip below the surface, he hears the thin buzz of the ship's engine.

Quick, get clear.

He sculls away on his back. There's nobody leaning over the railing above him, no faces looking down. It doesn't take long to reach the deeper darkness beneath the looming dock wall. There, to the left, the ladder. He drags himself along the slimy brickwork until he's beneath it. And it's a bloody good job the rope followed him because yes, the bottom rung is tantalisingly out of reach. He treads water in the shadow, feeling for the free end of the rope. Tying a knot in it is absurdly hard: he has to dip beneath the surface and bob up to breathe. And when he's done, it's no mean feat throwing it the measly few feet through the ladder. He tries, fails, takes in a lungful of water and drops beneath the surface to cough into the deep. Tries again, also fails. With each throw the leaden cold takes a firmer hold. When, finally, the knot drops back down to him through the bars, he's just about spent. But he still has to tie the rope to itself and haul himself clear of the water, before the cold saps the last of his strength.

Lara.

Zac.

Naomi.

He's hanging onto the rope now, but he's still in the water, letting it take his weight, gathering himself.

Gather quickly!

His fingers are frozen hooks.

Back and shoulders? Also locking stiff.

Possibly: give up?

Wow, that's a delicious, lemon meringue pie prospect.

No, no, no.

Lar-ac-omi.

His head dips beneath the surface again and as it does he hears a fierce shift in the engine whine. Jesus! Get on with it! He regains the surface just in time to hear a mighty horn blast, and the – wòw – blind panic is quite something: up he goes, all in a surge, onto the bottom rung.

60

The bottom rung: that's where you'll start.

Very Nice Man. He said that. Sent for Joseph a few days before he was due to leave the army for good, sat him down, cupped his little paunch, leaned back in his chair and revealed, trying not to sound like it had kept him up at night, that he'd been thinking about Joseph's 'idea about the trees'. Wasn't it a young man's game? Not that Joseph, at twenty-four, was old, but still: such a job as tree surgery had a shelf life, didn't it, and well, had Joseph considered any other avenues? Because unless he built himself a lopping and pruning empire in which younger men did the actual monkeying, he'd possibly regret the decision come what, forty-three or forty-four?

When Joseph conceded that he wasn't in fact dead set on arboreal work, Riceman sat forward in his chair.

'Have you given the City any thought?' he asked.

Joseph hadn't.

'Specifically, banking.'

'I know nothing about money.'

'Apparently, you don't have to. It's a well-trodden path on leaving the regiment. To tell you the truth, I thought about it myself back in the day. Still . . . you're open to the idea?'

Joseph shrugged.

There and then Riceman picked up the phone and put in a call to Airdeen's head of recruitment. They'd been at school together. Joseph was thinking how banking at least ticked the something-his-dad-would-not-have-approved-of box. Meanwhile Riceman was spouting phrases so banal – 'leg up', 'show him the ropes', 'safe pair of hands' – Joseph almost wondered whether the whole thing was a wind-up. But it wasn't. And a month later there he was, walking into the bank's foyer, five minutes early for his induction day, tailored suit trousers breaking over polished toecaps, with a brand new Aspinal briefcase at his side, because if you're going to do business, look like you mean it, yes?

He'd fought in two wars but his mouth was very dry.

Also, his briefcase was empty.

There he was anyway, a brogue on the . . .

61

Bottom rung.

As at Airdeen Clore, once on the ladder Joseph wastes no time in climbing up it. Despite his bin-bag luggage, he reaches the top without difficulty, but there he pauses, dripping, just below the level of the dock, face pressed to the wall in the dark as the ferry sounds its horn again, performs a nautical three-point turn, and slews away into the night. There's a saltwater smell in the rotten concrete close up. Remember that harbour wall in Pembrokeshire? Jumping in and climbing out. Yes, but that was a summer's afternoon; now he's shaking with the cold, which is called ___.

Damn gap is understandable, given the headache, but ___?

That's it: *shivering*.

When the right word comes, he peers over the top. There, to his left, is the Portakabin in which, some eight months ago, he was offered a plate of Jammy Dodgers and custard creams to go with the coffee in a plastic cup while the bloke with the big nose talked about the steps his team had taken to reduce costs. Who was that guy? Why was he, Joseph Ashcroft, Big Beast, even required to talk to him? Well, he was. By bigger beasts. Such things exist? Admit that? Yes, and now he's required to make a dash for it, and work his way into that gap between the makeshift build-ings.

Wow, his heartbeat is ridiculous. Ah, that time the wash-ing machine skipped off its bearings or axle or whatever. Well, much the same spin-cycle whoosh-clatter fills Joseph's ears now.

And his fingers are at best semi-functional: he has a ter-rible time getting his wet T-shirt off, doesn't even bother to undo the bin bags, just claws his way through to the dry clothes inside. These he yanks on damply, everything: hoodie, jacket, boots. Trousers-wise, he'll have to make do wet. At least he's out of the wind here. He pulls his hood up. And gradually, by holding hard to himself and bouncing on his toes, he starts to feel himself again, not as in 'feel like his old self', but more 'feel the bits that have gone numb, like trunk, arms, and head'.

What's he doing?

Waiting, that's what.

The ship will be well out into the Channel now. Noth-ing else is sailing or docking until the morning: he checked. The car-hire concessions will have shut for the night. Porters gone home, plus whoever else there is, or was. Yes, by now there'll be practically nobody about. What's the phrase? Something to do with something in a cupboard? He nails it: *skeleton* staff.

And look at that cat sauntering past, its shadow swelling on the chain-links. Joseph isn't sure how long he would have waited for just the right moment to throw his bag over the fence and hup himself over it, had it not been for that cat turning up. It was a sign. Saying: I, a cat, am relaxed enough to stroll on by, because the coast, quite literally, is clear.

So get on with it.

He does.

He climbs the fence and drops down on the other side in a car park full of white vans, one of which he immediately ducks beside, thinking: ice floes. He's like a polar bear, swimming between them, making his way towards the continental shelf or whatever it is. Actually, it's the exit. There's a kiosk, but he can't spot anyone in it, and a barrier, but that's to stop vehicles entering, not people getting out. He can just walk round it. Even so, best do that unobserved. So let's wait here between this refrigerated truck and that transit van until the lone car drifting by has gone and then, as in now, walk as nonchalantly as possible out of the car park, bag over shoulder, pretending to look at a something in his hand, a mobile phone, perhaps.

And keep walking.

Along this service road. Over the junction. Past these raised flowerbeds, which appear overrun with weeds. And on and on, all the way into town. Where it's well, well past closing time. There's vomit on the pavement there, watch out. What day is it, anyway? Joseph has no idea. Does it matter? No. All that matters is that he has pulled it off! Probably. A minicab slows beside him but he turns his face to the shop window. An estate agent. Wow, the houses, they're practically giving them away down here. With his next bonus he could no doubt buy that one with the sea view. Probably. Still, he's done a far better thing.

Hasn't he?

Only if it was successful.

Look: they'll bite on the ticket transaction and see that he boarded the ship and the search will skip sideways to France. There'll be no record of a passport check at the French border, which will suggest either that he gave the border police the slip, which is possible, what with his skill set, or that he jumped overboard, opting for a burial at sea, which is also possible, given his predicament. They're not about to imagine he swam home, are they? Because that would be like swimming back towards the shark, Lancaster, which would be, purple, porous . . .

Huh.

Preposterous.

62

Most people at the bank seemed to think that a bit of sleep deprivation was macho, but if you've spent a week on rations in a ditch, staying up for a couple of nights in a warm office, eating takeaways and doing things to spreadsheets, things Joseph soon discovered he was actually pretty good at, is hardly a terrifying prospect. The only thing that Joseph had to muscle through was Naomi's disappointment when he cancelled things they'd arranged to do: dinners, trips to the cinema, weekend breaks (he could afford them!), et cetera. Fact was, she hadn't been as delighted to have him leave the army as he'd hoped she would be.

'A banker now?' was what she said when he told her.

The 'now' was annoying.

'Why not?' he said.

'No, totally. Why not.'

And months later, when they were lying side by side in bed one Sunday morning, she said something else that got to him: 'I met your friend Lancaster the other day.'

Joseph rolled over to face her.

'He was in town.'

'What did he want?'

'Nothing. Just to know how you were, how you'd been since you got back.'

'Odd that he wanted to ask you, not me.'

'I suppose so.'

'What did you tell him?'

'Not much. That you'd moved on with the new . . . career. But, to be honest, compared to him you've hardly changed.'

'How's that then?'

'He was just a boy last time I saw him; now he's all grown up.'

'We're all older.'

'If I didn't know him, I don't know, I wouldn't want to run into him on a dark night.'

'Lancaster?'

'The shaved head, muscles on muscles. I barely recognised him.' She turned her face to the ceiling. 'I think he was more interested in what you may have told me, to be honest. About what went on out there. He kept asking if you'd been in touch with any of the guys, that sort of thing.'

Joseph didn't fill the pause.

'But you've told me nothing, so I just put him at ease.'

A burning sensation built in Joseph's chest. He shut his eyes. Blackened feet, a triangular split, apples.

'It's a while ago now,' he said.

'A year. Nearly.'

'Yeah well, there's no sense dwelling on it.'

'Dwelling on what?'

'Stuff,' Joseph said.

Naomi sighed.

'What is it?' he asked.

'Stuff,' she repeated.

63

Joseph does not return to the multi-storey car park. They'll find the Mercedes there eventually and it'll work its way back to Emily, who'll put two and two together. Scrunched note notwithstanding, she'll understand.

Hopefully.

Either way he has a new mission to complete.

The job now, with the false trail laid, is to go to ground properly. He knows where and he knows how. Just has to pick up his kit en route. Doubly important now that he's not seen or recognised along the way. So that rules out catching any more lifts or taking public transport. Instead, he's got to tab it out. But 'it' is actually quite far. What, seventy-odd miles along the road?

Doable, and yet . . .

Fewer as the crow flies, but pushing on over stiles and through hedges is a lot more time-consuming.

For now he's walking purposefully out to the edge of town into a bit of suburban estate, complete with traffic-calming measures and cul-de-sac signs. He checks his watch: three thirty-nine. Not a soul about. Everyone here tucked up in their beds. Lucky them, but strangely he doesn't feel tired himself now. He's too busy scouting the driveways. There are some decent cars parked in front of these little boxy houses. Mostly newish. Strange, splashing that much cash on a shiny car to stick outside your Barratt home. Still, in his time Joseph has spent good money like an idiot, so who's he to judge?

He's not about to pinch another car, because actually he has no idea how to start one without a key, but he is checking them out, looking for . . . Yes, here's one, a Volvo estate with a set of roof rails. And on top of the rails, a pair of those bike-stand things. Which will mean, possibly . . .

Joseph tries the garage door, which doesn't budge.

No joy there, then, but round the corner in the next close he spots another bike rack on a people carrier and this time it's easy to force open the door of the little shed to the rear of the two-up-two-down house. Inside there's not much starlight but, using his hands, he finds not one but three adult bikes to choose from. This one here is a racer. But the next one has panniers and, bonus, lights. He lifts it carefully onto the garden path. This is what insurance is for. Still, he feels a bit bad, so he pulls some notes from what's left of his cash – which doesn't, it seems, leave him very much at all! – and puts them under a flowerpot just inside the shed door.

The bike has a clicky back wheel, so best carry it a little way up the road. Skirt that pool of streetlight. And swing a leg over the saddle here. Wow, it's somewhat large, this bike. He's nicked it off a giant. Joseph either has to shimmy forward on the saddle or pedal standing up, which does the job for a mile or so, before it's actually quite uncomfortable, damnit. He's not been on a bike in ages. You never forget, blah blah, but your thigh muscles do. And the bag is a bit

awkward, slung across his back like that. Still, he's making good progress, and he can endure. He goes on another
couple of miles, gets into a sort of stride, works with the
pain, does his best not to hate the bike and the long-legged
freak it belonged to. He can't take the most direct – motorway – route, for obvious reasons, has to cut up through East
Meon, Liss and Liphook instead, names he recognises dimly,
though what's this just short of Haslemere: a seam of grey
sky in the east, dawn breaking, colour creeping in.

He's done thirtyish miles. That's more than he's cycled
in the last decade. And on a bike so big he can barely reach
the pedals.

Hold on.

Dismount.

Didn't Lara's bicycle have a sort of . . .

He checks the seat post.

Aha.

Calmly he opens the quick-release clamp and drops the
saddle a couple of inches, refusing to think about the pointlessly hard time, raw inner thighs and whatnot, he's given
himself over the last three hours, out of sheer . . .

Look: traffic is starting to build. There's a car or two
waiting at this junction. That chap has his shirts hung up in
his rear window. He's off somewhere for the week, possibly
staying in a Travelodge. Ah, the luxury of a cheap hotel. Not
for Joseph now, though! No: he needs to be closer by, somewhere he knows he can hide out completely, unobservable
yet observing.

What?

He's got to keep an eye on them.

Who?

Don't be daft, one quick-release stupidity is enough.

Lara.

Zac.

Naomi.

Christ, this hill. Why does one in every five cars cut so close to him? Maybe he's not vacupacked in luminous spandex like that bloke who just shot past him, but still, he's here, struggling through these pine woods, trogging on. He's forgotten how hilly this part of the world is. You just don't notice them in an Alfa Spider. The Alfa, ha. Black with red leather seats. The smell of them! He bought it brand new with his first real bonus. Sounded great ripping through these tree tunnels, despite Naomi's 'really?' when he parked it out the front.

Oh, Naomi.

It was just a car.

Maybe it cost a bit more than he should have spent on himself, the bonus actually being a little less than he'd been expecting, or hoping for, at least, but not to have bought it would have been to admit that fact, wouldn't it?

Yes!

Got to keep up appearances.

Anyway, if he had the Alfa now, he'd chase down that white-van man and give him a talking to at the next junction, for whipping by so close to a cyclist, him, former Big Beast Joseph Ashcroft, who isn't even wearing a bike helmet, for God's sake!

At least it's easier going with the saddle at the right height. Keep turning the pedals. Just a few miles now, miles in which to answer the question: where to ditch this bike? How about a pub car park? A sort of pay-it-forward gesture, helpful to the next person who needs a ride home. He could even pop in for a plate of egg and chips before leaving it outside, couldn't he. Tempting, but no. This village pub doesn't open for another four hours anyway. In the end Joseph props the bike next to an ancient red phone box on the village green. And from here he sets off on foot, feeling oddly buoyant.

Well, he hasn't sunk yet, has he?

64

Joseph kicked off his brogues and sat down on the leather sofa. It was 11.15 p.m. on a Friday. He'd just got home after a punishing week in which he'd mostly been selling a budget airline. Naomi handed him a glass of champagne. Actually, fizzy white: their compromise.

So far, so normal.

Then she said, 'I'm pregnant.'

The bubbles were suddenly sharp on Joseph's tongue. He stood up, sat down, stood again and walked over to some pot plants. Arrayed like that, in a semi-circle before the bay window, they looked congratulatory. Rightly so! Why, then, was Joseph swaying in front of them, fear dropping through him, making it important to grip the back of the couch?

Naomi knew he'd lost his father young, but not how.

What with his mother dead in Alicante, he'd sort of left out the specifics of Huntington's chorea.

Of course, he'd meant to tell her at some point, but never quite got around to it, because let's face it, whole weeks, months, seasons went by without him thinking about it himself. Not much, at least. Certainly not with a name, plus implications. The disease was a bit like that homeless guy who'd set up camp in the alcove to the left of the bank's service entrance: Joseph had got good at looking the other way.

There was never a right time to tell Naomi about it, because it wasn't necessarily relevant!

Now, however, it was.

Joseph was thirty-one. He'd never had a symptom, and he'd never taken the test. He was a rational man, yet that 'and' had somehow developed shades of 'because'.

That's right, the causal links had jiggled themselves about; not confronting the disease by seeing definitively whether he had the disease was what he did to ensure he didn't have the disease.

But if he *did* have it, there was a chance the child might have it, too.

Which meant he had a *duty* to tell Naomi about it now, didn't he?

She'd stopped taking the pill without warning him?

Oh Christ.

'That's fantastic news,' he said.

Naomi put down her glass and they held each other. Wow, did she feel good in his arms. Differently good: better. Now was the moment.

'Fantastic,' he said again.

'I know.' Her hair was soft under his chin. 'Nine weeks.'

'Wow.'

'You're okay with it?'

'Of course I am! I mean, did you . . . was it . . . ?'

'Accidentally on purpose, yes. I was going to tell you, but I didn't think it would happen this quickly.'

Now was the moment, now!

'You're not angry about that?'

Now!

But no, he heard himself saying, 'No, no. I get it. I mean, we were always going to have kids at some point.' He rubbed her back. 'Some point is now!' – NOW . . . no! – 'It's . . . decisive of you. I like that.'

They stood holding onto one another, Joseph looking over the top of Naomi's head at the piles of correspondence, newspapers and CDs – Jarvis Cocker staring back knowingly at him – and the moment stretched out, meaning he could still bring it up, still, still yet, yet still . . .

But no.

All he eventually said was, 'We're going to need a bigger place.'

65

Right now, en route to pick up his luggage, not so much from an airport carousel or five-star bellhop, more from underneath some rubble, he's headed for somewhere more bijou. Yes, forget neoclassical column frontages, abstract topiary (surely a contradiction in terms?), integrated salmon pools, underfloor heating, blah blah: think bum hole instead.

Bum?

For God's sake.

Bomb.

But that's what they called them! Back in the day. Bum holes. Yes, well: they were eleven, not forty-four. Still, that means it's not a *mistake* as such. Bum hole is the correct memory, so it's not a slip caused by . . .

Stop thinking about it.

Instead: might as well take the footpath here, with all the flint bits poking through that ground alongside. It looks like the reddish earth has a million grey-white teeth. Trudge on. Do the dog-leg around this big L-shaped field. He knows roughly where he's going because he used to walk Gordon, the actual dog . . .

That was afterwards. A long time afterwards!

No, the bomb hole was a thing from boarding school. It, meaning the school, stood on a ridge. Still does! Beneath the turreted red-brick building and across the flat valley floor there were sports pitches, but the sides of the ridge were flanked with woods. And in the woods: long culverts overspilling with ferns and stunted, scrubby hawthorns and rhododendron bushes interspersed with beech and ash and fir trees (every year the groundsman would cut one down to use as a Christmas tree in the hall) and even the occasional oak.

That looks like an oak tree there, in the middle of the field, as a matter of fact.

Ah, back in the day. The teachers turfed them all out into the woods for whole afternoons at a time. Thousands of good trees to climb. Joseph remembers the races. Up that tree with the smooth bark and across the long bough to drop into the canopy of the other one and half fall half slide back to earth. They timed each other with digital watches that were new, as in not long invented. Back in the day. Poor old Ben Doherty: he fell out halfway down and broke his arm, but he swore he'd done it slipping off the retaining wall behind the pool and even if they didn't believe him, the teachers didn't try to stop them going into the woods. They were out of sight there and that was all that mattered.

Joseph is puffing a bit. Not far now, though. Through the trees at the top of the rise and down the other side. That little copse with the ruin in it should be off to the right. Do the thing properly: scope the site to check nothing has been disturbed. Yes, and keep to the hedgerow now for the final approach.

All looks fine.

All is!

Ah, familiar rubble.

Mess of brambly branches to one side, under which, safe and sound: kit.

Excellent.

In fact: that's a relief.

Tiredness sweeps it.

It's been quite a time, after all, what with pounding that drain in Emily's garden, the drive to Southampton, making it through to the ship wired on adrenalin, jumping off said ship, that freezing water, climbing the rope and ladder, skulking about still so cold, forging on to liberate the bike, riding the bike a cool sixty miles, plus a final push on foot to here: no wonder he's exhausted. Let's just settle down in the corner to rest a while, before . . .

Because although this is a good spot to hide in for a while, it's not actually good enough, is it?

Location, location, location.

Bomb holes.

In the woods, at school.

Paul Holmes said somebody in his brother's year had actually found an unexploded bomb in one once, but that made no sense: if it hadn't exploded there'd be no hole, and anyway Paul Holmes also said he'd seen a wolf.

Ha.

The bomb holes were real enough, though, craters six or eight or ten feet wide and most of them so deep you could stand up in the middle. They were caused by stray bombs dropped from German planes in World War Two. If only one had hit the school building, Paul Holmes said, then they wouldn't have to do French. Good point, but stupid: there wasn't a major city nearby so the Germans were terrible aimers; if they'd tried to hit the school they wouldn't even have hit the woods.

But they weren't trying to hit anything sensible, were they? Their planes were just full of anti-aircraft holes and jettisoning their payloads wherever, which meant the woods. Not only the woods in the school grounds, either: they'd pockmarked the whole area. Joseph knew this because one Sunday afternoon he had hopped the iron fence to explore the Forestry Commission land that ran east towards the village. There were more bomb craters in those woods, too, all grown over with brambles and ferns. He liked going there, so went back, alone, privacy being in short supply at boarding school. As in non-existent. To find it, you had to escape. Leaving the school grounds was a risk, yes, but by telling nobody about it he managed never to get caught.

They didn't build dens out-of-bounds. No, they used the best school-woods-holes for that, clearing out the brambles and laying branches over the top, thick sticks first, then thinner ones interwoven with ferns, and on top of that they scattered leaves and kicked up earth. Camouflage! Necessary because as soon as they started building their den, other kids did too, and since they were other kids that meant they were on the other side. Gangs formed along year-group and friendship fault-lines. Over the next few weeks each gang built its own den, or battled to take over someone else's, or tried to destroy what it couldn't win.

A bit like at Airdeen Clore.

Ha.

And then on another Sunday afternoon, Mark Fenyard stole some matches from Mr Stead's jacket. Mr Stead taught woodwork. He only had seven fingers and he smoked a pipe. Everyone pocketed a slice of bread at breakfast and later went to the woods to toast it over a fire of leaves, cardboard, pine cones and toilet roll. For some reason they decided to make the fire in the den. There was no chimney. The smoke didn't smell as nice as Mr Stead's. It was soon so chokingly thick in the den that everyone else climbed out, but Joseph was still crouched over the fire with streaming eyes holding the bread on a sharp stick in the flames when the Myers gang launched their raid.

Hostile takeover.

They'd seen the smoke and crept up. The first Joseph heard of it, everyone was yelling and a branch came jabbing through the ceiling. He tried to grab the end of it but couldn't and then more light spilled into the den as one edge of the roof came up. There was a lot of earth and wood in that roof. Myers and his gang shook it and kicked at it and the whole thing collapsed in on top of Joseph and the fire. Falling earth blotted out the flames. He managed to drag himself out backwards covered in dirt and twigs and from the outside the den now looked like a nest, gently smoking. He wasn't hurt. And the funny thing is that it was funny! The Myers lot ran away. Everyone saw Joseph wriggling himself free and laughed at him, saying he was an idiot, but meaning he was brave, and he liked the idea of being a brave idiot very much.

Still does.

When awake, that is.

66

Just as he realises he's nodded off, Joseph snaps to in a confused panic, with the same Christ-where-am-I? feeling he's
had a few times on the motorway, driving when tired. That
can kill you: read the signs! Best wind the window down
and sing at the top of your voice or possibly bite the inside
of your cheek. No need for that here. He's pretty safe sitting
against this wall at zero miles an hour. But he's thirsty again,
and hungry, admit it. Well, there'll be a shop in the village,
and he's going to have to risk swinging by for a few provisions en route.

En route to where?

He knows. It'll be perfect! Of course it will. They think
he's in France, or at the bottom of the Channel, so the last
place they'll look will be . . .

Anyway, he should get started if he's going to make it to
the shop, shouldn't he?

Yes.

Right, then, repack this kit properly, and scuff up the
brambles again to give the ruin back its rural ruinousness.
And let's head out, making like a rambler, yes, a heavily
equipped rambler taking an early summer break through
the beautiful Surrey hills: rambling!

Ha.

Because he is rambling on, thought-wise, isn't he?

Rambling among the brambles, a right shambles.

Stop it.

Since when did he, Joseph Ashcroft, Big Beast of linear decision-making in matters of war and wealth, get so . . . sideways, off-kilter, diagonal, in terms of head space? Is it a sign? Like the missing words.

Just open the letter: find out for sure.

No!

Why?

Because not opening it is his only defence.

That gummed-down St Thomas' envelope flap is holding back the tide.

And anyway, he's misremembering things. The inside of his head has always been a scrambled sort of place. Sure, it made decisions, choices which he acted on by doing things, things which, looking back, seem pretty authoritative and organised, but who is he kidding, the actual thinking bit behind the decisions was always a mess of noise and light.

Because all heads are full of that!

We get on despite it, don't we?

Yes we do, and right now Joseph must get on, as in make his way along this here yellow-green hedgerow, pick up the footpath and head down into the village, in search of the shop. The first houses he passes, a pair of Edwardian stacks-of-bricks, are set back behind nine-foot evergreen hedges. Very reassuring. And what's that up ahead? It is indeed a shop, but sadly not the right sort: all it sells are four-by-fours. Joseph actually bought one a while back, because he just did. No, not to spite Naomi. They make hybrid versions now anyway. 'Treacherous school-run driving conditions, here in Surrey,' she'd said. He backed off, then backed back on and bought one. And in a way that was lucky, because if he remembers rightly he'd made the suggestion at the end of quite a frosty month.

Further on into the village proper is a pub festooned with hanging baskets, behind which there's a lovely garden. He remembers drinking cold white wine in it with Naomi one sunny July afternoon when the kids were small, Zac strapped asleep in his stroller, Lara off ferreting in the flowerbed, and the wine going down a treat, neither he nor Naomi saying much, but both – he was sure of it – feeling the same warm perfect shiver when he reached out and covered the back of her hand with his own.

Ah, lovely moment!

Lucky man!

Cut short, sadly.

No, not by that. He didn't do that until much later.

By the wasp. Remember? Of course he does. Poor Lara suddenly started screaming among the hollyhocks, catapulting Naomi – and Joseph, just a second or two later – up off the wooden bench to help her get the damn thing out of her hair. It had stung her three times: shoulder, neck, ear. He dug some ice out of the cooler bucket but Naomi waved it away and off they went back home to find the antihistamine cream.

There's the shop, look.

'Shoppe', actually.

Ha.

He's never been in it, has he? Never stopped here while driving through? No, because there was one closer, run by that chap from Poland with the glass eye, and between him and Ocado they, meaning Naomi really, had the household bases covered.

Look at all these little advertisements in the window. Here's one for a 'dog companion'.

As in, a companionable dog?

No, someone to look after yours.

Possibly that's who Naomi leaves Gordon with during the day.

Because of course, as well as keeping the kids, she also managed to hang on to the Labrador–lurcher cross, even though it was Joseph who bought the dog in the first place, for Christmas, for Lara and Zac, and yes, Naomi, he was fully aware of the 'for life, not just for Christmas' slogan, meaning this was not some impulse purchase prompted by his having missed both their carol concerts.

Joseph's eye snags on another advertisement.

'For sale: trampoline.'

Surely Naomi hasn't?

No, it's a different number entirely.

What's this other notice here, then? Neighbourhood Watch: keep alert. It seems some poor pensioner disturbed an intruder and won himself a right hook. Well, he was lucky it wasn't worse.

Joseph takes his hat out of his pocket and pulls it on. His face hangs before him in the glass front door. Properly bristled!

Just be swift in here, fetch the necessities, a rambler rambling subtly through.

He opens the door softly but a bell tinkles anyway, announcing his arrival, and suddenly the backpack is very large in the confines of the shoppe, as if he'd ridden inside on a horse. Should have dismounted. Tries to do so now, but clatters a stand of postcards with the backpack in the process.

'Pop that down there if you like,' says a voice very close by.

Joseph flinches, turns, sees a pleasant-looking woman, albeit with wonky teeth. She is leaning forward on her countertop, smiling at him and indicating a spot just to the left of the door where she's suggesting he rests the damn—

'Thank you.'

And damn again! Straightening, Joseph sees that they were serious about the Ye Olde bit of the Shoppe: beyond the rack of vintage postcards the place appears to sell mostly retro sweets in big jars ranged behind the woman's counter and down that far wall. Black Jacks, Sherbet Lemons, Liquorice Allsorts, Kola Cubes, et cetera. At least there's a drinks fridge, although that too is full of ginger beer and cloudy lemonade. Not quite: there are bottles of sparkling water on that bottom shelf, and yes, as he tracks down the far side of the central aisle he's relieved to find a small selection of actual food, chosen mostly it seems for the famous labels. Heinz baked beans, Fray Bentos pies, Colman's mustard, Del Monte pineapple slices. Christ, his mouth is watering. He starts gathering up a few tins, then realises he'll need a basket, and has to retrieve one from beside the counter. Actual wicker!

'Shout if I can help with anything,' the woman says. It's not just her teeth that are wonky, her smile is as well. In fact her whole face is a genial Picasso, off kilter and . . . amused.

Joseph's eyes slide to one side.

'I'll take a pound of sugared almonds,' he says, spotting the jar.

(Lots of calories in nuts, see.)

'A whole pound?'

'Make it two,' he says, and while the woman is sorting that he heads off to fill his basket with Gentleman's Relish and Piccadilly Piccalilli, as well as the Heinz beans and so forth he already spotted. Oh, for a few packets of just-add-water rations to keep the weight down: the little basket, solid with jars and tins, is ridiculously heavy given their combined nutritional value. In fact, it's ridiculous all round: looks like he's about to go native with some sort of knock-off Fortnum & Mason hamper.

Ha.

Look, the empty jars may come in handy, at least.

He adds a couple of bottles of Malvern mineral water to his hamper and waits patiently while the wonky woman rings them through her vintage till. No barcode scanner here. Joseph eyes his rucksack, resting against the wall. There's not much room in it. And anyway, he doesn't fancy opening the top up here, so he accepts the offer of a bag. Inevitably, it's a paper one with the Shoppe's logo on the side, and he needs two of them, and it seems he's spent some ninety-six pounds on these bits and pieces, which is notable mostly because of what he realises as he receives his change, namely: that's it money-wise. As in, those five twenties were his last notes. And that's as it should be. He's timed it well. From here on in he'll have to make do without the green stuff.

Exiting the shop with both paper bags and his rucksack necessitates a bit of a kerfuffle, because, Christ, this thing here is done up too tight, and the postcard rack . . .

The woman, keen to assist, comes out from behind the till to help him heft himself in, strap-speaking.

She's still smiling.

Short of actually holding up the place with a gun, could he have made himself any more obvious?

'Wow,' she says, when he's finally sorted.

'We're off on holiday,' he replies, as he picks up the paper bags.

She opens the tinkling door wide. 'Well, enjoy!'

And out he goes, blinking into the sun, which is in his face, coming as it is through the tops of those trees.

That's not why his cheeks are burning, though.

Ignore it!

Concentrate instead on that beautiful hillside, the low sunlight turning up an extra dimension of purple shadows among the bursting leaves. Look at that red kite or possibly buzzard soaring above the hilltop. Tremendous.

That's the way he's headed now, quickly over this patch of village green and out along the lane towards the footpath, trying not to worry about the children on the slide over there, with their mother or nanny or au pair glancing up at him, freighted rambler, trudging on.

67

Remember nanny-gate?

Ha.

He was only trying to help.

Naomi started it, sort of, by sitting beneath that cruel light. She was reading an Amnesty update at the kitchen table one February evening and the standard lamp made her look suddenly older, more careworn.

'Tough day?' he asked.

She looked up and frowned. Wow, creases.

'Well,' she said, 'it started with Zac throwing his porridge at the wall and Lara refused to go to school again, but it's only a stage.'

'We could get some help.'

'Meaning?'

'Someone to mind the kids. An au pair or whatever. So you can . . .'

Because the fact was, everyone at work had at least one nanny, some of them two, a spare for when the main one had to sleep and so forth. Bankers' wives expected it. The few who had their own careers to go back to did, and the many more – younger, often Russian ones, it seemed, for whom work meant choosing a marble floor or fundraising with a champagne glass in one hand – spent their time doing that and keeping up appearances. Joseph could afford a nanny. He said so. Why was Naomi, crumply, looking at him like that?

'It's not the money,' she said. 'Though why waste it?'

'Would it be a waste?'

'They're our children. I don't see the point in someone else looking after them when we can. Kids can be hard to take even when you love them. I mean today . . . without the love . . . an au pair or nanny wouldn't do as good a job.'

'Yes but, you know,' he nodded at the magazine. 'You could do a bit more of what you want.'

She'd always planned to go back to work part-time. She'd said as much, and eventually did! Other wives were happy enough giving to local charities; Joseph's would help run a global one. He was proud of that. He poured her a glass of wine and told her so. She thanked him, agreed that yes, she still wanted to go back when both kids were properly settled in school, and went on, 'But for now nobody else can look after them as well as I can.'

I? We!

It was all the fault of that damn light, which was too bright.

Unforgivably unforgiving.

It made him factual. 'Yes, but they're wearing you out.'

'Why do you say that?'

He looked at her evenly. 'It's obvious.'

She stood up and went to the sink. It was the same ropey kitchen that had been there when they bought the house. Why she didn't want to improve it with solid wood cabinets, granite work surfaces, plus possibly add an Aga and one of those special pure-water taps, he didn't know. When he hosted the poker evening James Lassiter had mentioned the name of an Italian design firm. And, technically, he was Lassiter's boss. Sort of.

'I'm going to bed,' said Naomi.

'But your wine.'

'You finish it. I need my beauty sleep. Evidently.'

'Naomi,' he said, but couldn't quite bring himself to deny it. Why? Not because he didn't love her, but possibly because he didn't in that moment love her enough.

68

Damn au pair. She's not even watching the kids on the slide, although what could she do, realistically, if one of them fell?

Catch him!

From that height, it'd hurt.

Yes, but exactly: for Lara and Zac, Naomi would throw herself under a bus.

So would he!

Damn lamp.

All he had to do was swap in a gentler bulb.

A little job.

Right now, though, the job is lumping himself and his kit into the woods. The school is still there, he knows it is. Down through this sweep of mostly pine trees, which by the way smell terrific this evening, he can even see an edge of the far games pitches. But he's not going anywhere near the grounds. He's skirting them, going beyond, heading for the stretch of Forestry Commission land on the other side.

It's quite steep here.

He's puffing hard.

Why not stop for a rest and crack open one of the water bottles? Good idea. Joseph wipes his brow and takes a long swig. As soon as the coldness hits his stomach he feels cavernously empty, so he digs out the sugared almonds and eats a handful. Lord, they're tasty: the crunch of the coating, the fibrous goodness within! Joseph tips a few into his pocket and savours them as he works his way deeper into the woods.

It's around here somewhere.

Handy if he found it before sundown.

But wow, these rhododendrons, even thicker than he remembered, or imagined, make searching tricky. A system would help. Instate one! Track down the slope towards where the fence hits the field. That takes a good quarter of an hour. Walk twenty paces along the field-facing edge of the woods. And search back in up the wooded hill. Harder work still. Push on, keeping a keen eye in and around and beneath the trees and bloody rhododendrons. Look, they'll be helpful when he's settled: put up with them for now. Just keep going! What's it called when gun dogs search a thicket for birds? Quartering? Searching methodically from side to side, into the wind. Something like that. He just has to quarter this here woodland in search of a bomb-hole crater he last saw thirty-three years ago, because . . . because it will be ideal.

But damn, the light is failing.

Darker in the woods than by the field, obviously.

It is, particularly in the purple dusk, pretty tangly.

He thinks of alveoli. Those tiny end-of-the-line sub-branches of lung. This here is proper oxygen-producing green belt. Untouched for . . .

It's amazing the way the eyes adapt to the encroaching darkness. He's been going for what seems like an age when he reaches – and remembers – the drop-off ledge. Of course.

A spine in the landscape, raised three or four feet, with a gully running down one side which, if he's right, leads up to . . . yes . . . just up there, where the backbone gives out onto a little rise, within that deeper darkness, the tree tunnel folding in all around, bushes beneath, ram on through them, find the hole within.

Joseph pushes through the thicket to the rim of the crater. It's hard to make out where the slope starts, and the weight of the pack puts him off balance. He lurches, slips, drops to one knee, and sort of topples into the bramble-filled hole.

Ow.

At least it's here!

Of course it is: holes don't move.

Just get yourself out of these straps, man.

Lord, there's enough undergrowth down here. He can't really see through it, or pull himself free. As soon as he moves, a cord of something thorny scratches his neck. But once the pack is off he's able to squirrel himself sideways more or less, reversing up the angled side of the crater, dragging the bag with him.

Really, it's dark.

No point starting now: he'd just have to redo the whole thing in the morning.

At least it's not a cold night.

Although, having stopped moving, and with the sun down, it's hardly warm.

He's lying on his back, looking up through brambles and branches to the sky, and seeing more or less none of it, just charcoal abstractions.

Kip here.

It's not ideal, but.

Just . . . start in the morning.

Moving slowly, a man underwater, Joseph finds his bed-roll, the sleeping bag, and one of the tarps in his pack. He sweeps from side to side to test for big lumps in the ground. When he finds a flat enough spot he spreads out the tarp and bedroll, shimmies into his sleeping bag, and pulls the flap of tarp he's not lying on over the top of him.

There, a draughty Joseph sandwich.

It'll do until first light.

Which will come eventually.

Much faster if he actually falls asleep.

There are still a few sugared almonds in his trouser pocket: he can feel them pressing into his thigh. Dig them out. Do a bit of nibbling.

This is much worse than the ruin, despite its holed roof. Yes, but imagine how fine the shelter he'll build tomorrow will be by comparison. At least he's safe here, tonight, for now.

That's right, ___ half full.

Glass.

If you're going to stay awake, at least do a bit of planning.

Planning? He's already done it! Nothing more to add.

Remind himself why he's here, then. Think of all those lucky people he's helped with the bank's money.

$1.34 billion!

Ha.

As in: really?

Stop it.

But actually? That's still realistic, is it?

Yes. Of course it is. Think of the Caymans; think of Milton Keynes.

In fact, let's not.

Go over the entrance again instead. How is that supposed to work?

Well . . .

69

Joseph dreams of portcullises, pinging elevators, draw-bridges and oven doors.

Which, as ever, wakes him up in a sweat. He's way too hot. Of course he is: never mind the oven, he's fully dressed, he's in a heavy-duty sleeping bag, and he's wrapped in a plastic tarpaulin. Result: he's horribly thirsty again. He drinks half his remaining water in one go, noting that the greys above him are a clearer mesh now, three-dimensional, dawn coming through.

Time to set to work.

First, make sure this is the right spot.

Yes, it's high up on the slope, deep within the closed canopy of mature trees, with plenty of smaller rhododen-drons and other assorted brambly bushes crowding in, cover within cover. The crater itself has a couple of clumpy things growing in it, and a sapling, possibly a birch? Doesn't matter: just cut the lot down. Joseph unsheathes his hand axe and takes the tree and bushes out at ground level, the purplish blade soon dull with earth. He drags the bushes up out of the pit and looks around. With the shape of the spine, the gully, and the hill, most of the surface water should run down there to the east, where, look, the sky is pinking up.

Okay, so this hole. Dig out the leaves, take the thing right back to the soil. As he remembered, it's sandy, loamy: also good for drainage. If he builds a little lip on the upper side of the slope, he can keep the den drier still. Because that's what this is, right, a den?

Or lair.

Big Beast.

Ha.

Joseph spends a good hour clearing the bomb hole of mulch. He uses his short-handled spade. Once he's stripped out the debris, he stands in the lowest point of the depression. The ceiling won't quite be above his head height, but he can always dig down and, in any event, there will be enough room above to sit comfortably on the cot-bench he'll build . . . there, across the up-slope end of the hole. He stretches out his arms. There's a metre or so between his fingertips and the pit sides. Which means he's going to need longish boughs for the frame.

Smells good in here, quite garden centre.

He pulls the felled bushes over his kit and heads out to find the right wood.

It needs to be green, not dead.

A hundred or so metres to the southwest, he comes upon something suitable, a coppiced ash, birch, whatever-tree that has grown back with lots of true boughs, thicker than his thumb, spearing straight up.

He chops a bundle.

Rubs mud into the exposed white stump-flesh.

Carries the lot back up the hill and trims them down next to the camp.

The offcuts will come in handy.

Two trips later he has more than enough lengths of sturdy stick for the frame. Back in the day they just plonked branches across the bomb hole, but he's not eleven now, he's a grown-up ex-soldier, skilled! He lashes the poles together with snips of cord, making a square big enough to cover the entire hole, quartered with two boughs, then cut into eighths with four more. He has a few poles left over so he weaves a couple of them into the frame too, making sure to leave one of the edge squares unobstructed. That one, there. Using the cord, he measures its sides. Roughly two and a half feet by two and a half feet. Big enough for a door.

Right, let's make that next, then.

He sits back on his heels. Pops another sugared almond. They're addictive. Mid-morning sunlight is filtering down through the canopy, dappling everything. Wow. It's actually quite good fun doing this, making the door, a frame within the frame, just a few inches bigger all round, subdivided with thinner little offcuts, tied together snugly, there, satis-fying: something you can see.

Because you won't see it later, with any luck.

Next, cut a couple more lengths of cord to make a hinge, tying the little square over the frame edge, like that, a trap door, the wrap-around knots good and snug.

Now pick up one end of the whole big lattice-structure and give it a shake, double-checking all the poles are secure, which they are, because he's not an idiot, and drag-lever-lift it into place to check that, yes, he measured correctly, and the roof covers the hole. Or will, at least, when he's . . .

Joseph stands back, hands on hips. His trousers definitely feel loose. As he's running his finger around the inside of his waistband, a bird caws somewhere in the trees above. He looks but can't see it, even when the noise comes a second time. Sandpapery, a saw cut. Possibly the voice of a crow. They do that to warn each other about predators, don't they? Which could mean that someone is coming.

Joseph crouches down, checking this way and that, through the undergrowth uphill to the north, over the spine to the east, down the southerly slope and through the densest stretch of brambles to the west.

He stays very still.

Minutes tick by.

But the crow doesn't caw again and he can see nothing moving in any direction, not even a leaf.

Probably the crow saw a bird of prey en route to somewhere else.

Still, crack on: the sooner he's completed this roof and camouflaged it the sooner he'll be able to relax.

Remember that God-awful away day, early on at Airdeen Clore? The instructor with the shapely hips. 'Once you've built your raft and rowed it across the lake, then you can relax.' It wasn't even a real lake, more of a big pond, ducks included: it would only have taken a minute to stroll round to the other side. Lancaster was there. He'd just joined the bank's security team. Within eighteen months he was head of it! Anyway, standing before the pond, the womanly instructor pointing out the logs and twine, Joseph said to Lancaster: 'You'd think an army stint on the CV might exempt us from this . . .'

Lancaster didn't reply, just walked straight off to join his team, who of course won a jeroboam of Veuve Clicquot each at the end of the day.

70

Anyway.

Time to stretch the tarpaulin over the frame. Joseph takes the big plastic sheet he covered himself with during the night, unfolds it completely, pulls it out flat on the ground, as best he can, given the brambles. Then he lifts the frame up again and manhandles it to one edge of the tarp. Carefully, he lays it down. Good: the tarp is more than big enough to wrap over the outer edges of the frame. He fetches his roll of duct tape from – sod's law – the bottom of his pack. Wonderful stuff, duct tape: in the army he learned you can fix pretty much everything with it, even a bullet wound. Working methodically, he folds each edge of the tarpaulin back over the side pole and tapes it securely to itself. He even runs two great long strips of tape right the way across the middle of what will be the underside of the roof, for good measure.

There, a giant square-drum-skin-billboard-artist's-canvas!

But it's not finished yet. Because he still has to cut out the small square section of tarpaulin around the door, and tape that to the little frame. Hurts to think the roof will be less watertight because of it, but how else is he to climb in and out? No way else, that's how. The fact that the door panel overlaps the frame hole helps things, and he'll position it so that the door opens facing down the slope.

Considering how best to manhandle the roof into place, he pauses.

Think ahead.

Once the roof is on, some things will be harder to do inside the den. The most important? Well, that's what these leftover poles are for, foresight-wise.

Which is?

Some sort of raised thing.

Yes, to stand a chance of being comfortable, he must make a shelf on which to lie, something suspended a foot or so off the ground, in the hole, down at the end furthest from the door.

What's the best way to do that?

Use what the hole has: edges.

Take this first pole, dig-jab one end of it into the bank edge, and push the sharpened, cut-to-size other end into the opposing wall. Make sure this first beam is properly secure. And repeat with a second, third, sixth, ninth, thirteenth length, each one a little longer than the last and lashed to the next, and the next, and the next. This takes some time, but it would take a whole lot longer if he were trying to do it under the lid. Joseph saves the thickest, strongest pole until last, and really digs that one in extra deep, tying it off super tight.

There!

Where's the bedroll?

Joseph ferrets it out of his stuff, allows it to inflate, and tapes it tight to the top of the shelf. Faithful duct tape! That'll hold the whole thing more firmly to itself, won't it?

Yes.

Still, he sits down very gingerly.

The bed sags a little, clicks and creaks, the sticks working themselves deeper into the walls. Look at that earthworm, wriggling for cover. Never having liked worms much, Joseph leans the other way. Is this end of the cot higher than that end? A little, but the shelf, which is, yes, just about as wide and long as he is himself, holds firm!

For now.

If he needs to he can always make some legs to buttress the thing in the middle later on, can't he?

Yes, he can.

Joseph puts the rest of his kit in the hole, leaning tidily against the foot of the cot bed.

He feels absurdly proud of what he's made!

But he's not finished yet.

He has to manhandle this roof into place next, doesn't he.

Right, then: let's do that now.

Carefully.

Don't jab a hole in it.

You'd have to try: the tarp is made of pretty strong stuff, a sort of woven plastic.

Joseph lifts up one corner of his roof, walks it gingerly into place, lays it down tenderly, as if it were a work of art.

Which it is!

Because it represents the first of the four challenges for any survivalist, which are, in order: shelter, fire, water, food.

He checks that the entrance works.

It does, sort of.

He can slide in feet first through the hole and down the internal earth bank at a comedy angle, dropping the trap door satisfyingly shut behind him. Won't be a problem to cut a steeper chute later, and that hollow within the hollow just there will double as a fire pit, which should work well with the raised door above it, which, excellent, is also a chimney.

Inside, with the roof shut, the crater is now dark, save for a few cracks of light where the edges of the roof don't sit flush with the ground. He'll soon sort that. Out he climbs again and digs and cuts and scrapes and settles the roof panel more firmly in place. Has to go deepest on the southwest corner, where an unhelpful root is forcing the thing proud, but the axe takes care of that in the end, and by 4 p.m. he has the roof properly embedded over the hole.

The fall of the land, the fact that the bomb hit a gentle slope, is helpful, because it means the roof slopes, so water won't pool on it. Joseph isn't too worried about collecting rainfall that way as he has point three on the list – something to drink – covered: he knows there's a stream not far to the east, where these old woods meet the Scots pine plantation.

He wipes the sweat from his forehead with a hand he subsequently sees is streaked with mud. Camouflage!

That's the next job. He uses the leaf mulch already cleared from the crater first, scattering that all over the dark green plastic. When it's exhausted, he takes a bin bag and pushes through the brambles, gathering up more leaves and twigs, and strews that on top of the roof too. If, as *he* did after all, someone was to push through the woods to this point, they'd still see a bit of a clearing, an unnatural flatness over and next to the ex-hole. He sorts that by carefully laying the undergrowth he cut from the crater on the roof edge, bushiest bits facing outwards, and he cuts down more of the thorniest bushes he can find and drags them to cover the roof, the gap between these two beech trees, and there, next to the spine, too. In time these bushes will wilt, the brambles shrivel, but he can add more. He stands back, skirts the outer edge of his camp, ducking under branches here and pushing through this clutch of holly. Ow, or rather – man up! – ticklishly unpleasant. He unhitches a leaf from the branch, marvels at its defensive waxy stiffness, goes on, dragging leaves over a footprint here, kicking up some dirt mulch there, checking that he's not left obvious signs of himself round and about in constructing the hide.

Which, as far as he can see, he hasn't.

Not that he's some Navajo tracker.

He pauses, Big Chief Joseph, and does the patting-your-open-mouth-while-exhaling-a-whispered-but-sustained-'ah' thing.

He's done a pretty good job.

So now he picks his way carefully back to the bomb hole, lowers himself inside and pulls the door-hatch nearly shut. This offcut will act as a kind of prop, for ventilation, a little light, et cetera.

Not that there's much day left. He's been working more or less flat out since dawn. Bar that false crow alarm, he's not been disturbed. Which is good, isn't it? Yes. And now . . . he's exhausted.

71

And hungry, and thirsty.

Very!

These two urges have a different shape here in the half-dark, under the pole roof, the tarp, the dirt and leaves and camouflaging undergrowth. Yes, down here with the worms, the aching emptiness in his stomach and the taut dryness of his lips take on a sort of holy significance. He is in exile. Earthly possessions (his, plus a chunk of the bank's) offloaded. A husk of himself and atoning, he is supposed to feel this way . . .

Pah!

Joseph digs out his water bottle and finishes what's left. He'll strike out for the stream after dark. He still has at least half of his sugared almonds, but best ration them. Instead, he twists off the lid of a tin of what looks like – yes, he holds it to the stripe of grey light to check – Gentleman's Relish, and with his spoon-fork, which takes a while to find, he tucks in.

Here he is: Joseph Ashcroft, top-level Airdeen Clore executive, eating gourmet relish off a spork, straight from the tin, in a hole in the ground.

Top level.

Well, almost.

Stop it.

He was bound for the top, wasn't he? Steinmann-Jones said as much on that clay-pigeon day with the guy from B&Q back in February 2015. Steinmann-Jones was wearing actual plus fours and appreciated Joseph's commitment to the team, because that's what he said, in his little nasal voice.

'You're a safe pair of hands, Joseph.'

'Thank you.'

'With a little more zing . . .'

Pah.

Forget that.

Smell the salty dirt, the cut stick-stems, the empty plastic water bottle, the goddamn relish tin.

Listen to the hush of treetops, the distant birdcall, the earth-sigh (which, possibly, is far-off traffic).

Feel the weight of his body spread out on this stick-and-bedroll contraption. If his hair was longer it would brush the sandy wormholes, while his boots press in at the other end.

He has never felt safer.

Or more trapped.

Both halves of this one feeling are yoked, precedent-wise. Think of bed. That's right, the one he and Naomi shared for twenty-two years. For twenty-one and two-thirds of those years he had the exact same safe feeling last thing at night, no matter what had gone on during the day. Even when the kids were tiny and sure to wake up within an hour: that moment of closing out the day in their bed, curtains shut and lights off and darkness pressing in, was a safety so secure it felt like abandonment.

The last third of a year, until she found out, not so much: that was the trapped bit.

And after she did, boom.

All – his – fault!

What a moron.

Yes, well. He's doing his best now, isn't he.

He can be proud of the den, at least.

Plus this cat.

Cat? *Cot*.

Surprisingly comfortable, all things considered, though admittedly not what he's used to: seven bedrooms nestled in the Surrey Hills, or two thousand square feet of round-the-clock portered mezzanine in Cleveland Square. Which, admittedly, might have been an ill-advised extravagance.

Why?

You have to look the part!

Within reason.

Well, he got what he deserved. Look around!

What goes around, comes around, and . . .

Goes to ground.

Round and round and . . .

72

When he awakes it's properly dark and he's forgotten where he is; confused, he sits up quickly and hits his head on a roof strut. It doesn't hurt. In fact, he smiles with pleasure, thinking: *still safe!* He checks his watch. It's 3.15 a.m. He's slept a solid six hours, which isn't bad for a first night in the shelter. The thirst is back, though, a cardboard ache behind his tongue.

He has what, an hour and a half before dawn?

Get a move on, then!

With the hatch fully opened, there's a little starlight to see by. As his night vision strengthens, half-tones creep in, silvery-grey bracken here, charcoal tree trunk there. And all around the crosshatched rhododendron stems. It is very quiet in the wood, a fact he only realises when an owl hoots, making the silence loud. He finds his empty bottle and the deflated water carrier. Thank you, Charlie. Stuffing both into his satchel he climbs out, shuts the hatch, drags the cover bush back into place and sets off, through the tangled wood towards the stream.

Which, sadly, has moved.

Or rather, isn't where he remembers it to be.

On the plus side: neither is the Scots pine plantation.

Has he gone the wrong way?

He retraces his steps.

Wow: here's the spine already.

What with all the sidestepping and soft footing, he'd actually gone no distance at all.

He's lost a good half an hour. Nothing for it but to strike out again, this time pushing straight up to the sandy track bordering the top of the wood, so he can follow it west along the ridge top, making much quicker progress unobstructed, these hoof prints little lunar craters in the half-light, and there, where the mottled charcoal treetops hit a line of deeper blackness, that must be where the old woods end and the plantation begins, meaning if he follows this iron fence line downhill, crosses this little lane, and takes the footpath opposite, it will – finally – lead him down to the stream.

Which surely he should be able to hear about now?

But he can't.

He's just beginning to worry that he's wrong again when he makes out the spikiness of reeds up ahead. And yes, there beyond them, a movement of light that is the water's surface. But it's not flowing at a noise-making pace. It's just a silent, mirrored blackness, narrow enough to step over in places, and not more than a foot or two deep. Joseph has to kneel in the wet edge to submerge the water carrier, which burbles as he fills it. He fills his bottle for good measure, and is tempted to drink from it straight away, but he's not about to make that mistake. This stream flows alongside hedge fund managers' hedges, past private equity investors' 'Private!' signs, and through bankers' back yards. It could be full of anything! He must boil this water before risking drinking it.

Let's get back to camp and do that, then.

But Jesus, this now-full water carrier is palm-cuttingly heavy.

Should have brought it in the pack.

Rather than lug the thing all the way back up the hill and around the top of the wood, Joseph opts to follow the fence line the other way. Just along here it borders an open field. He approaches slowly, aware that the darkness is losing its clout, not yet dawn but not far off it. As the field opens up before him, there's a sudden movement ahead that makes him flinch. But it's just rabbits. A lot of them, bouncing for cover. Dropped marbles, Joseph thinks, the hedgerow a sofa they always end up under. No, snooker balls.

Takes him back.

Rabbits, in clusters, on the edge of the school field, visible through the classroom window in the early evening, nosing the hardbitten grass while he, Joseph, was supposed to be working, but couldn't, because of the rabbits.

He was what, ten?

He liked rabbits!

He wanted to get close to them.

But when the class burst outside, the rabbits scattered like, yes, a pack of snooker balls broken hard. One minute they were there, the next they'd ricocheted into the bracken.

So one morning, almost as early as this, he'd crept out of bed and gone down through the boot room at the back of the dormitory building. Smelled of wet cement, the boot room. The door wasn't locked. He circled wide into the school woods, found the boundary fence, picked his way along with wet pyjama legs from the bracken. Worked forward slowly. Got to the edge of the grassy bank, on which: more rabbits than he'd ever seen. Fifty, at least, nibbling about in ones and twos and threes.

He was close enough to see the pale pinkness inside the nearest rabbit's ear. For a long time he just stood there staring at it. The pinkness made him want to do two things at once. First, take aim with a catapult. And second, stop anyone (including himself) from doing anything like that at all. If he'd seen himself about to do it, he'd have stamped his foot in warning, because that's what rabbits did.

A spider's web strung with dew beside him was just as confusing: absolutely beautiful, but he still wanted to tear it apart.

He didn't break the web or stamp his foot, just went to take another soft step forward. How close could he get before the rabbits fled?

No closer. Either he'd been standing still too long or he was trying to move forward too slowly; he lost his balance and pitched forward onto one knee. His steadying hand landed in a clump of nettles. Damn! When he looked up the rabbits were gone.

He still likes rabbits.

Possibly, though, he'll have to come back and set trips.

Traps.

Because: needs must.

Right now, he needs to drink.

He makes it back to the woods as the sky beyond them lightens. There's a spreading mat of quilted cloud in the east, the edge of which is now pink. It makes him think of setting fire to the torn edge of a newspaper.

Ah, news.

What he'd give for some.

But it's not his priority now. Today's all about bedding in, staying hidden, doing a professional job. He approaches the den site cautiously, double-checks nobody has disturbed his camp, which of course they haven't, because he's picked an excellently surreptitious spot, right in the middle of the tangliest, most awkward bit of the scrubby wood.

He moves slowly, tuned in. Look, for instance, at that incredible flame of orange lichen up the side of that big beech tree, and the mini flower-shaped moss on the fallen log beneath it. There are mushrooms of some sort growing along the rotting bark, inky spokes on their undersides. He has no idea whether they are poisonous or edible and isn't about to find out. Pushes on further up the bank instead, noticing that there are more pines mixed into the tree-scape higher up, which makes the ground prickly with needles and cones. Round to the west, beyond the spine, it's all beech nuts and bracken, and yes, now he's closer in to the camp he sees where the rhododendrons really take over, providing marvellous tight cover, within which, softly softly, he comes upon the hide.

Yes, the wood is all just as he remembered it.

Home sweet home.

73

Down in the bomb hole he unpacks his Primus stove and the little aluminium kettle, fills the latter with water and sets it on to boil. While he's waiting, he dig-smooths an area to the left of the entrance within the crater on which to set out his cooking utensils and provisions, remembering that they did pretty much the same thing when they were kids, creating little shelves in the bomb holes' sides, places to hide the stolen matches, loaves of Sunblest white bread, pocket knives. The kettle takes a while. In fact, he's too thirsty to wait, so he pops one of his water purification tablets in the water bottle and gives it a shake, waits sixty seconds.

Christ, that burnt metal taste.

Odd, but so good!

Takes him right back to time in the field.

Time with Lancaster.

Strange.

That was what Joseph felt when Lancaster approached him asking for his backing with the Airdeen Clore job, after a gap of some three and a half years. He'd half expected, or even hoped, he would never hear from him again, and it was at once reassuring and discombobulating to take the call and agree to meet up. By which he meant: here was Lancaster giving Joseph back the upper hand.

Or was he?

'You owe me for my silence. You help me get this job. And . . . we're all square.'

That was what he meant, really, but of course that wasn't what he said.

What he said was more like:

'I wouldn't want to tread on your toes.'

They were three pints in already, standing at a tall table – no stools or chairs – in an All Bar One somewhere in the City, at 10 p.m., Joseph having agreed to meet up after work. Around them: a gallery of bloated pink faces, cufflinks, et cetera.

'Another?'

'Sure.'

Lancaster somehow cut straight to the front of the bar queue. What was this about? Christ, the noise in this place, people not so much talking as bellowing. Joseph had had to reschedule a conference call with Dallas to be here. Not great, boss-wise. Here was Lancaster again, parting the crowd. Same certainty around the eyes, but a lot else had changed. The size of his neck, for starters. And, as he turned sideways, the slab-like chest. You would get out of the way for him. Still favoured the squaddie haircut but now it looked more . . . freighted with intent.

They raised their glasses.

'It's just that the Kroll job has limitations,' Lancaster explained. 'I've been wanting to move in-house for a while. This Airdeen Clore role looks bang on, and the headhunter reckons I'll stand a good chance.'

'Sure, why not?'

'Yeah, a very good chance, she said, particularly if some-one in your position could put in a word.'

Joseph took a gulp of cold fizzy lager and nodded, while actually thinking: me? In the scheme of things he was still more or less plankton in the Airdeen Clore sea. Still, no sense undoing the misconception.

'I'll see what I can do.'

'But only, you know, if having me around wouldn't com-plicate things for you.'

"Course not. Just think hard before you jump. They're a pretty aggressive employer: all up-or-out, that sort of thing.'

'I think I can handle that.'

The lager was so cold it made the backs of Joseph's eyes ache, while simultaneously helping him not give a damn about that or much else. A man in his position. Ha. It hadn't been a particularly stellar month. Quarter, even. What with the dressing down Sara Blumenthal gave him after the pulp plant refinancing debacle, shaking her head at him in the lift like that, almost hard enough to dislodge her stupid Alice band. But maybe he was past that now, ladder-wise. Up or out! He was still there! Joseph shrugged and said, 'I'm sure you can, Ben. Anyway, what are you talking about: it'll be great to have you around.'

Lancaster's smile looked genuine enough, relieved, almost.

'It's good to see you again,' Joseph heard himself say.

'You too, mate. You too.'

74

Joseph's kettle is agitated, shivering on the little stove. Happily, it doesn't whistle. A brew, that's what he wants. He lets the kettle boil a good long bug-killing while, then puts a teabag in his lightweight aluminium cup and pours the steaming water on top. It'll have to be powdered milk torn out of one of these sachets and stirred in with the clean end of the spork, but never mind. The mug is instantly hot in his hands, a sort of anti-thermos. He holds it reverently, trying to remember the name of the corporate catering firm the bank uses. Purdles & Co.? Pendles? The number of their monogrammed napkins he's used over the years; how can he have forgotten? He thinks of the platters of assorted sandwiches set out on big walnut boardroom tables during deals made in meeting rooms on the ninth floor. The crab ones are the best, washed down with Darjeeling tea. Would you like a cup? Food plays a part in even the keenest negotiations. I'll just think of my next point while I pour this out for you. Biscuit? And so forth. Generally, as a Big Beast, someone else would do all this, but, you know, never underestimate the personal touch.

Also, tea in bed.

The first time Lara brought some up at the weekend for him and Naomi, teabags still floating murkily within.

That was a negotiating tool, too: what she really wanted was to be allowed to watch Saturday-morning cartoons.

Sure! Go ahead.

But to be honest, this first sip now, here in the hide, with the mineral earth smell rising and the birdsong outside, the trap door raised a couple of inches to let the morning light, filtered by the trees above, stream in, well, this brew tastes pretty much as good as any other cup of tea he's ever drunk, full stop.

Simple pleasures.

Sadly, he knows they'll end.

Meaning: he knows there's only so long he can put it off.

'It' being?

Stop!

Best off staying practical.

Consider the weather, for example. He's been lucky to have had the chance to get set up in the dry, but knows it won't last. Soon he'll have to deal with a bit of pain.

Rain.

Yes, yes. But what was it that chap with the ponytail said during the induction week, outlining the bank's ethos and so forth? He had a German accent and wore brown suede loafers and paced about as he shouted, 'What are we best at here? Making hay while the sun shines, at all costs, right?'

Joseph had nodded along with the others.

'Wrong! Wrong, wrong, wrong! I mean, of course what we do here is make money when the market is good, but . . .' the ponytail shook excitedly as he slapped the lectern and went on, '. . . but any idiot can do that! The hard part, and this is what we do best, is to make even more money when the shit is hitting the wall!'

'Fan,' Joseph thought, or thought he thought, because it turned out he said it aloud.

'What's that?'

Startled, Joseph realised the man was asking him to repeat himself.

'The shit hits the fan,' he said. That's the expression. 'Or possibly you mean, "We make even more money when our backs are up against the wall."'

'What's your name again?'

'Ashcroft. Joseph.'

'Ashcroft.' Joseph recognised the 'you're dead' look in the man's eye, because he'd seen it in Drill Sergeant Atkinson's, back in the day, and the memory of being bollocked in the army made the man's ponytail laughable. 'Right,' the man went on. 'Wall, fan, whichever, both! When the shit hits the fan and our backs are to the wall, that's when we make most money of all!'

Well, that was a nice idea, wasn't it? From time to time it sort of worked. Got them through 2008 better off than most. But 2008 was ancient history: Big Beasts stalked a different landscape now, with different obstacles.

But enough of that.

This is the landscape that matters now.

Take a deep breath; enjoy it!

He has his cot to lie on, these lovely reasonably dry earth walls, treetop-filtered sunlight, et cetera. Look at that root he exposed when digging the little shelf. It has a knobbly bend in it, making it a sort of J-for-Joseph shape, possibly; either way it's useful as a handhold when climbing out of the den.

Let's call it what it is: home!

For now.

That's normal. A home is only ever temporary. Doesn't stop you caring about it, though, does it? Christ no. That shitty little flat he and Naomi first bought, well, he felt as fond of that when he first put the key in the lock as he did closing the deal for Nine Pines.

He puts his hands behind his head and shuts his eyes. Ah, that first flat. Nineteen ninety-five, April, the scabby cherry tree in improbable bloom, up the Vauxhall Bridge end of the Wandsworth Road. It was an admirably central location but also a complete hole. The corner shop sold fried chicken, VHS cassettes and four-packs of Stella through a metal grille. Back then a junior army officer and charity worker's combined income got you one floor of a rundown Victorian terrace. One room really, divided by double doors that didn't shut properly. To find the toilet you had to go through the galley kitchen.

He remembers the smell of the place: damper than this bomb hole, that's for sure. With that wonky wall out the front, beyond which: buses. Interminable buses! What numbers were they again? How can he have forgotten? Either way, the people on the top deck of the double-deckers were at exactly head height if you were sitting on the sofa in the front half of the living room. Head height and no more than twelve feet away through double glazing that didn't work, because the soundtrack to that period was buses, eight of them an hour, grinding by day and night. He and Naomi used to sit on the old second-hand sofa she covered with a throw, watching *ER* on the television as the passengers rolled noisily along outside.

Did they care?

No!

Because they were together, and this was their place, or the mortgage provider's. To think that when he came out of the army, stopped defending the realm and so forth, and joined Airdeen's instead, he paid off that loan with one bonus.

Good times ahead, property-wise.

They were. Think of Nine Pines! He cased the joint properly before asking Naomi's opinion. Knew where the sun hit the columns in the morning, and which terrace caught the last light. Distance to the station and thence the City: acceptably close. Distance to neighbours: acceptably far away. The hedge height more or less edited out the other fund managers, CEOs, accountancy partners and so forth anyway. The place had a pool! And big mature trees, set well back from the sort of sweeping lawn you imagined when you imagined big sweeping lawns, the horse chestnut, the beech, the two big maples, and of course the big Scots pines, all of them encasing the grounds in a display of here we are, grown-up goddamn trees at last.

Naomi, when he took her to see it. She was having trouble persuading Zac to drink formula from a bottle at the time, all twisted round in the car, wrestling with him in his seat.

Joseph had to cut the engine and say, 'Look!' before she would take it in.

'At what?'

'The gates. And the drive. The house at the end of it.'

'Why?'

'This is the one.'

She craned forward in her seat, her lovely neck taut before it bobbed back incredulously.

'I've seen smaller conference centres.'

'We'll fill it. Mostly with plastic baby toys to begin with.'

'Is that a roundabout at the end of the drive?'

'Pretty gauche, eh, but we can get rid of the statue. The place needs completely redoing. That's why it's on at only two point nine. But the size of the plot, and the location.'

'Two million nine hundred thousand pounds?'

'Yeah, renovating will be a stretch, but.'

Naomi's mouth – lovely but compressed now – said she disapproved of the idea as a matter of principle, but the way she leaned forward in her seat again to take a better look gave her away, and five months later he offered her a piggy-back across the threshold (corny, but what the hell) as the estate agent stood coyly to one side.

A stretch.

That's the thing, bonus-wise. You never can tell.

The statue, a stag with its head lowered, was metal, some sort of alloy, not bronze. They put a Santa hat on it at Christmas when the kids were young – Naomi's idea – and the stag is still there now.

He'd love to see it again.

269

Here in the woods, though: real deer. Beat that!

The way you had to mow up to its feet, hooves, whatever, with the little mower. They had a contractor sort the big lawn out back. He also did the pool. Quite expensively.

Joseph opens his eyes and sees the tarp suspended across the lattice of roof-sticks, super focused for a second there, like a falcon, if a falcon's eyes worked really well close up, which possibly they don't, given that they're mostly for looking at tiny things miles away. Like something that lives in a hole, then. A hedgehog, or a rabbit, or a rat.

Yes, well: those creatures do all right, despite falcons, eagles, et cetera . . . Lancasters.

Ha.

And how do they do all right?

Mostly by sitting tight.

75

Which is what Joseph does, for six days.

Bar a couple of trips to the stream in the middle of nights two and four, he stays put, not always in the hide but very close to it.

And it's not as hard as all that, seriously!

Sure, he's quite grubby, and that makes him a bit itchy down below, but he has a go at washing in the brook and, fact is, he does know how to put up with a bit of physical discomfort, because he's done it before, on exercise and in the field. It's not so much the tricks of the trade he learned in the army that stand him in good stead as the deep sense that because they're all part of his experience, the rich Joseph-ness of Joseph, he'll cope.

Even the rain, which arrives on day three, is doable. The den holds up well. After an hour or so he notices water seeping in where the roof meets the ground just above the foot of the cot, but he takes the spade outside and banks up some fresh earth to blot, block and divert the leak.

Admittedly, the bomb hole feels pretty damp as the afternoon wears on, and therefore colder than it did, but hey, he's out of the wind and wrapped up in proper clothes and, in any case, he has the option of lighting a fire.

He's already wasted no time in gathering up dead bracken

for tinder, sticks for kindling, plus some good fallen branches, snapped or sawn up, for fuel. He's also dug a fire pit to one side of the door entrance, and lined it with rocks: they'll retain some heat after the flames die away.

This will have to be a small fire, of course, given that it's in the den, but he's confident propping the hatch up will give the smoke an escape route. On the plus side, a small fire is all he needs to heat the space up. Also, it'll produce less smoke, reducing the risk of attracting attention, though to be honest he's starting to feel pretty secure here, the only other warm-blooded wood-visitors he's seen being two badgers and that young deer.

Actually, the first fire is quite a choky experience.

As in, within a couple of minutes the den is an eye-watering smoke hole: Joseph has to fling the hatch completely open to air the place.

And although it's gone nine at night, almost as soon as he does that a dog starts up barking, quite nearby it seems, making him seriously consider blotting the fire out entirely.

But the barking stops as quickly as it began, and with the door-hatch properly open, the little fire sort of works: certainly it heats the space up, and the rocks were well remembered, because they're still gently warm when, smoke and fire experiment finished, he battens down for the night.

76

Day seven brings a question: what next?

In truth that's not the right question. Really, it's 'when's next?'

Because he knows what he wants to do, doesn't he?

'Wants' meaning 'has'.

Sort of.

As in, he knows but can't bear knowing.

And that's okay, because hey, decisiveness can be over-rated.

Take, for example, Joseph's decisive stand on the Padstow holiday house, which he bought as a gift for Naomi. It had a jetty, planning permission to extend up a floor, plus a small orchard. And he'd just bought it! Wow, he had to pull some strings to manage that. But was it the right decision in the end? Maybe not. She was super kind about it, smiled and said thank you, et cetera, but the sort of 'no, really' smile that means 'really: no'. And even when he got her to admit it, later, in bed, she held him as she pointed out that she'd repeatedly said she didn't want a second home, ever, and that surely he knew she'd meant it.

'Yes, but I thought that had more to do with unnecessary pressure on our finances.'

'It didn't.'

'Which I've sorted.'

'You're not listening.'

'I am.'

'What do I want, then?'

'We can rent it out.'

'That's not the point!'

'I'm lost.'

'Please sell it.'

'Really?'

'Yes.'

Her hair smelt so good. He wasn't angry. Not even when he thought of the pointless extortionate stamp duty. Probably he'd make money flipping the house despite it, though sadly he didn't.

But that was later.

For now he just said, 'Okay, I will. I'm sorry.'

Decision, decidedly undone.

77

In the end this new decision sort of makes itself, as in Joseph finds himself thinking, hey, they – meaning Lancaster – clearly bought the Southampton stunt, because if they hadn't they'd definitely have winkled him out of this here hole by now, and since they haven't, they won't be expecting him any time soon, will they?

No.

Expecting him where?

At the house, of course.

Really, he's going there?

Yes! Under cover of darkness, obviously.

But why?

Because it's just over that ridge and needs must.

Needs?

As in, he's run out of tinned delicacies, sugared almonds, et cetera, and for some reason none of the many rabbits who live at the edge of the field bordering the southern tip of the woods have been fooled by the three snares he set there on the way to fetch water from the stream at the end of day four. Excellent snares they are, too: it only took him a couple of goes to remember how to run a length of cord from a sturdy stick to a wire noose positioned on the ground between funnelling twigs and whatnot, though possibly the wire is a bit thick, it being more garden centre than garrotte, but thank you anyway, Charlie, for trying.

Rabbit number one: what have we here, then?

Rabbit number two: bless!

Rabbit number forty-six: there are more than enough of us; it's almost tempting to help him out, no?

Rabbit number ninety: no.

He's thought about fishing instead, but the best he could expect is to refill a relish jar with sticklebacks plus possibly a frog, and sadly he didn't think to ask Charlie for a net. Quite probably there are things to eat in the woods, fungi, speciality fruits and so forth, and he has had a good look around for anything resembling a berry or button mushroom, but he's no expert, and the only bush he found with anything fruit-like growing on it – hard, bright red pellets – looked a bit unviable.

Bush: good choice, now back off.

Okay, okay.

But he's hungry!

So hungry.

Having no belt, he's had to cinch in his waistband with twine, and there's a sharpness to the bones beneath his beard.

He's got four pounds sixty pence in his pocket. That wouldn't go far in Ye Olde Shoppe. Possibly he should not have given quite so much away. But actually, no, it wouldn't have made a difference, because face it, he's not really shoppe-presentable now. In fact, despite his best efforts, he's a mess, outdoors being a fairly muddy place, and mud being persistent stuff. Still, that makes for good camouflage and, while we're looking on the bright side, the hunger has a generally clarifying effect: he's alert and quick-thinking and hyper-aware and . . .

Hungry.

That too.

But there's a solution what, two and a half miles away, in the shape of his own house. Or ex-house. Or . . . ex's house.

Bollocks to that.

He bought it, more or less.

Certainly he notched up more mowings of the front roundabout, frequently tangling the Flymo cord in the alloy stag's hoof-feet.

And although Naomi changed the locks last December he doubts very much she'll have messed with the combination on the side door to the double garage, behind which, unless something strange has happened, sits a Capital Titan chest freezer full of food.

So that's the plan, then, to rob Naomi and the kids?

No, no, no.

He hasn't missed a payment, or not until very recently, at least, so it's his food too, and you can't rob yourself, can you?

No!

The bank wasn't Joseph Ashcroft, and the share of the money that was his he gave away knowingly.

He's not eaten anything since that last can of baked beans the day before yesterday. So he has no choice. Waiting until well beyond nightfall and setting off for Nine Pines with an empty rucksack is not so much a decision as a fact. Look, he's already done it.

There is less moonlight tonight, fewer stars, more dark cloud. This makes walking through the woods more of a stumbling-tangly job. He goes slowly, yet takes a fall near the boundary fence, something thorny whipping him across the face as he trips. Ouch. He's cut the soft skin beneath his left eye. Quite deeply, by the wet feel of his cheek. Not to worry: it's no shrapnel neck slice. He's nearly at the fence and the going will be easier when he picks up the footpath.

Which it is.

He knows where this path leads.

Up here, to the junction, which turns onto the bridleway that used to be part of the cross-country course at school.

Still is, probably. He can remember running along this sandy track thirty-five years ago in shorts and a pair of Dunlop Green Flash. Of course he can, just as he remembers walking here with Naomi, Lara, and Zac, on many a Sunday morning. There are blackberry bushes here. If it was a sunny September afternoon . . . but it's not, it's a pitch-black May night, and he's not been here in the dark before. No, but this little path here, behind the Days' house, this is part of Gordon's home-circuit: he's walked the dog here a million times on winter evenings. Possibly not a million. Some, though. Generally, he was late home and Naomi had already done it.

Gordon, ha.

The name was a compromise. Zac had wanted to call him Flash. Possibly they should have let him.

Joseph pauses.

Will Gordon be a problem?

Pretty good nose on a Labrador–lurcher cross. Remember Lara's game with that stuffed badger? She could hide it anywhere around the house and Gordon would sniff it out in minutes. But at this time of night he will be curled up chasing imaginary rabbits in the kitchen, right over on the other side of the house.

Which is . . . just there.

Behind that beech hedge.

Nine Pines!

78

He skulks forward until he can make out the chimney stacks silhouetted against the night sky. They make him suddenly light-headed. The feeling is like love, but undercut. Not by hate exactly, more like resentment.

What's he talking about? He adores this place.

Take those chimneys, for example. There are twenty-two of them. Ten down the main end of the house and two clumps of six on the far side. One year a pair of rooks decided to build their nest in amongst the main stacks. Big bastards, rooks, plus bold: they used to strut around down the bottom of the lawn as if they owned it, and when you got up close they'd just give you the eyeball, as if to say: I'm a rook, what of it?

Get off my lawn!

They did in the end. Possibly because, although rooks are famously clever birds, rook chicks: not so much. One of them chose to end its first flight by picking a landing spot in the pool. Joseph hooked out its limp body with a net and burned it on the bonfire, the big parent rooks watching him the whole time from not quite far enough away. They decided Nine Pines wasn't for them after that.

Nine Pines!

Actually there are ten.

Either an Edwardian idea of a joke, or a self-seeding thing.

Joseph creeps along the hedge to where he knows it's thinnest, on account of the horse chestnut shade problem, and works himself through a gap, much like the deer that ate all the clematis that year. He's at the bottom of the garden now and from here he can see that the house, a hundred or so metres away, is not entirely dark. There's a light in a window upstairs. That's Lara's room! Joseph checks his watch. It's a quarter to midnight. She must have fallen asleep with it on, unless she didn't, meaning she's still up.

He's mesmerised by that light.

Lara.

Christ, what he'd give to see her now, to talk to her, or at least give her a hug.

She's just there. A short stroll away. As is Zac, whose window is at least dark, and Naomi, who also appears to have turned in for the night, either there, or . . .

Might she have moved back into their bedroom?

Don't think about that.

But might she?

Stop it.

She might, but probably not, though, because of . . .

Naomi: 'You . . .'

No.

'You fucked . . .'

Not now, please.

'You fucked her . . .'

Do you have to? Now? Yes, apparently.

'You fucked her in our head?'

Bed, bed, bed.

And there it is, laid out like a dead dog in the sun, which might as well have come straight out in the middle of the night, illuminating the length and breadth of the striped lawn bisected by the path up to the pool and the tennis court and the hedge cut to look like the top of a castle, crenellated, yes, that's the word, and he got it first time, because he's still got *it*, he's still rapier-sharp, perfectly capable of running multimillion-pound deals, and of building a hide in a bomb hole, and of reading a screen full of figures faster and more insightfully than any of the younger guys coming up, Rafiq included, especially Rafiq in fact, despite his Harvard maths whatsit, and he's also capable of evading goddamn Lancaster, because he's Joseph Ashcroft, damnit, and he's not ill, because in fact he's in the prime of his life, and therefore still perfectly able to pull abstruse words like abstruse and crenellated straight out his *head*.

He did fuck Heidi in their bedroom, though.

Yes, but hold on: he's not denying now and never has denied that he did make love to Heidi Sparks, his twenty-four-year-old PA, in his and Naomi's room, once, on a Tuesday afternoon.

Why?

Well, there's a question.

And he'd love to sit here and debate the answer, but strangely he's not going to.

Naomi: 'Heidi Sparks? What kind of a name is that?'

He didn't answer that question, either. Naomi, leaning back against the kitchen island (which had recently acquired a big dead-central pan-burn, courtesy of Zac, and yet she still refused to get a proper kitchen put in!) let her eyes fall to his feet and work their way slowly back up to his face, as if seeing him for the first time, looking him over with genuine curiosity.

Then she laughed.

Not a long laugh, just a sort of 'huh'.

Meaning: wow.

Also meaning: that's it, we are now dead.

Don't exaggerate.

But that's what it felt like, truly: her 'huh' was the final bullet, wasn't it?

Maybe, though other stuff came beforehand. Namely the time she found him sitting on the laundry box with his head in his hands, possibly weeping, definitely lost for words when she said, 'Do you want to talk about it?'

'What?'

'I know what's eating you up, Joe.'

It took Joseph a minute to manage: 'Know what?'

'Really?'

'I'm lost here.' (True!)

'You don't have to talk to me about it. But you should see someone. I know—'

Joseph, hopefully: 'The bonus was a bit disappointing, yes, but everyone's was down. Next year—'

'It's not that, Joe.'

'Then what?'

'You need some help.'

'For what!'

'Look at you.'

Joseph stood up and looked out of the big window instead, at a hard blue sky cut by a contrail that, though he stared at it for a while, didn't want to fade.

Naomi sighed, then said, 'Ben Lancaster told me all about what happened.'

'Lancaster?'

'Yes, ages ago.'

'About what?'

'What happened on your tour. The real reason you left the army.'

Joseph couldn't help it: he let out a snort of relief.

Which may have been, well, unwise, since it led to the ultimatum re the counselling, which Naomi seemed to think would actually help! With what? Post-traumatic stress disorder. She'd read up on it. Bless her. Allow a thing like *that* to fester and it might make a person somewhat erratic. Which explained things.

Joseph tunes in to the actual aching gnawing feeling in his belly that's making his head light and his hands shake now. Yes, let's think about that instead. It's something annoying he can do something simple to solve, isn't it, because that's right, it's straightforward: he must eat!

Immediately he remembers he's hungry, Joseph is absolutely ravenous again.

The big chest freezer, then. He skirts the lawn until he reaches the wrought-iron gate, behind which is a path of flagstones which leads round the side of the house to the double garage.

This flat bit here is where Zac fell off his skateboard and cracked his head open, or cut it, at least, concussing himself in the process, while Naomi was out, meaning Joseph was in charge and hadn't made his five-year-old son wear his tiger-striped helmet, a fact she didn't bring up either when she joined them in the A&E queue, or when the doctor was putting in the stitches, or at any point afterwards actually, because she knew he was beating himself up about it anyway and, back in the day, that, meaning kind, was what she was like.

Still is, deep down.

He knows it.

And he also knows the code to the side door of the garage, because he set it himself, and C2244Z pressed quietly into the keypad – ta da – works, so there.

He's in.

79

Best not turn on the light. No windows to speak of, but the gaps round the edge of the up-and-over double doors to the front of the garage would be clearly visible to anyone who happened to look, not that they would, it being midnight, though they still might, so let's not take the risk.

Anyway, it doesn't really matter, because as the freezer lid comes up with that little squelchy sucking sound he's always quite liked a light comes on inside.

What have we here, then?

Joseph does some rummaging, turns up a box of Calippo ice lollies, ferrets one out, rips it open immediately, shuts the freezer, sits down with his back to it and eats the whole thing in the dark. Christ, that tastes good. You'd never have thought eating an ice lolly alone in the dark in the garage in the middle of the night could be so satisfying, but it is. He bites his way through the lolly quickly, upends the nearly empty tube and feels some of that unfreezing stickiness run down his chin. It's not until he's finished that he realises he has no idea what flavour slash colour it was: orange, yellow, red?

He opens the freezer again to see – purple!

Ha, some sort of non-poisonous berry concoction, probably.

Beat that, woods.

It's tempting to eat another but something stops him. That's strange. The big Lexus isn't where they normally park it, and he didn't see it on the drive. There's just Naomi's old Golf in here, plus a huge empty space, and that wall of storage units filled with paint, weedkiller, bags of charcoal, old bits of pram, paddling pools, sprinklers, toolboxes, plus assorted forgotten crap. Also the kayaks strung up in the roof, the kids' bikes on the back wall, next to his and Naomi's, below the windsurfer, wishbone, daggerboards, sails. And the old golf clubs. That electric go-kart was a mistake; it never held its charge long enough for both kids to have a go, and Naomi refused to give her blessing to a second because they weren't that into the first one anyway. Why not? With two they could have done some racing up and down the drive, around the roundabout and so forth.

Something else besides the big car is missing as well.

That's it, not there in the space behind the big gas barbecue.

The . . . jet ski.

Where is it?

Humph.

(Naomi: 'Really. You've only used your speedboat twice in three years.')

(Joseph: 'Our speedboat. And so what?')

Has she sold it?

And the Lexus?

She's probably flogged the boat as well.

And . . . so what!

She's right.

Meaning: they must get shot of the whole lot.

It's inevitable now anyway, really, so forget about it, because what matters is the job in hand. Which is? Let's have a proper look in the freezer, open up the trusty rucksack, and fill it with those free-range sausages, that organic chicken, some line-caught Alaskan salmon fillets, that pork joint, and a pack of British minced beef. There's not much point taking the pizza. Or is there? It'll thaw and then he'll have the cheese and peppers and whatnot. A pack of frozen peas: why not? The backpack is pretty heavy now, though there's still room in it, and Joseph still hasn't really dented the freezer because it's huge and what Naomi said would happen ('we'll just keep eating what's on top while the stuff below sits in permafrost') has happened. Well, Naomi, now's your chance to see what lies beneath. Will she notice, do you think? Possibly. Strangely, this thought doesn't so much worry as excite Joseph. Who else knows the door code? Might she see the missing food as a sign?

He could pinch more and make it absolutely obvious someone has been foraging but he doesn't, and not because he's worried about the meat spoiling before he can eat it, or the weight of the pack. It's because he wants a reason to come back.

Does he need one?

Don't answer that.

Instead, let's ram a handful of these Calippos into the bag's side pocket (keeping one free for the journey home), shut the freezer lid softly, and beat a careful retreat.

This he finds very hard to do.

Because what he wants – with every fibre in his tired body – is to let himself in through the front door, take off the brogues he's not wearing, turn back the hands on the big grandfather clock, further back than that, much further, years, to a time before he even clapped eyes on this great big house, the oven door, his father dead in a chair, the album *Live Rust*, right back to the very start, and then he wants to wind time forward selectively so as to be able to climb back into Naomi's bed.

Damn, she's just up there, making this difficult!

'This' being walking across the lawn, away – from her, from them, left right left towards the little gate, this strolling away and off into the balmy night.

Balminess notwithstanding, it's hard!

That's why he's doing it so slowly, backwards, or sideways, at least, keeping one eye on the house until it's out of sight, though even then he has to fight himself free of its super gravitational pull.

Perhaps a popsicle will help.

Calippo, whatever.

No idea what colour this one is either, but yes, the little sugar rush is better than a poke in the eye. He doesn't need another one of those: the cut just beneath his left eye is actually pretty painful. Let's hold one of these frozen lollies to it as we make our way home. That makes it go sort of numb, which feels better, but with the pain now gone his stomach takes over, kicking up a hunger storm.

Right, well, that's something to do, isn't it? Take his mind

off Naomi and the kids, and the hunger, of course, by cooking a square meal.

80

Back in the den Joseph strips frozen chicken thighs from their packaging and drops them straight into his aluminium cooking pot. He adds a handful of Cumberland sausages too. This lot can all cook in its own juice. He sets the Primus flame on low and settles back to wait. How long will this chicken–sausage casserole take? Well, the gorgeous smell of the meat suggests swift progress, but he knows he must cook it all properly. After a while, he peeks beneath the lid. The chicken thighs have shrunk a fair bit. He tips a bit of the juice slash grease run-off, there being – wow – a lot of it, into the bushes beyond the mouth of the den. Help yourself, ants. He'll just keep a little of the gunk back to stop the sausages sticking. Which they don't, not really; because they're browning, not burning, as he waits some more.

Oh, just get on with it!

There being no need for ceremony in a hole in the ground, he tucks in straight from the pot, wolfing whole sausages and sporking up chicken thighs to bite bite-shaped bites from, cave-man style. No need for condiments! Just: meat. Blimey, he's hungry. Though the bottom of the pot comes into view he's still chomping on. But no, best save those few bits there for tomorrow morning. He eats one last sausage despite this good intention before putting the lid back on the pot. And then, belly swimmingly full, he takes to the cot shelf for the night.

Or half of it, at least.

Somewhere around three o'clock he wakes feeling odd.

Though he tries to go back to sleep, the sensation won't shift.

In fact it gets worse. In short order the oddness turns into discomfort which in turn becomes a yellow fact. He feels very sick.

Twenty minutes later he's on all fours, having crawled a few yards from the bomb hole, and the contents of his stomach are spread somewhere in the darkness around him, but he's still retching and retching and retching, until he's rid himself of every last drop of bile, sausage chunk and chicken shred.

Even then, he keeps on throwing up nothing for a good long while.

Somehow, between bursts of dry-heaving, he manages to crawl back to the hole, and once there he half falls through the hatch to lie flat out on the dirt floor.

It feels like he's torn his own stomach out.

The rest of him is going through some sort of hot 'n' cold spin cycle.

And his head, his head. It's full of jackhammers.

He's hugging himself, physically holding himself together, but then that starts to hurt, because everything hurts! He's squirming to rid himself of himself, by turns thrashing weakly and lying very still and squirming up against the earth wall again.

He doesn't know how long this goes on for, but it goes on, and on, and on, until at some point he sort of forgets his own existence and shuts down, overcome.

81

It's broad daylight outside; the hatch seam is glowing and he can see the pattern of branches above the roof tarp, bisecting each other greyly.

Why is he lying here, flat on the floor and not on the cot?

Doesn't much matter, forget about it!

But my God, the thirst: there's no ignoring that.

Well, at least he's ahead of the boiled water game.

He rolls over to find the container and hears himself groan thinly. Wow: infant-weak. Remember those new lambs, still umbilically connected, staggering to get up in Shropshire? Pulling the container towards him takes a huge effort. Even unscrewing the plastic lid is a trial. But eventually he manages, and slop-fills his cup, and raises it to take a few gulps, gulps that quickly become double gulps, the lovely cold feeling spreading through him as he drinks deep, such a relief at first, but a relief quickly undone by the roiling sickness which wells up again almost immediately, and he's too slow, too weak, absolutely unable to make it out of the den this time before once again he throws up.

Damn!

Actually: no worries.

Look, it's mostly just water, already sinking in.

And anyway, it's not as if he's planning to entertain visitors any time soon.

Ha.

He rests his face on the earth.

Seriously, though, he's going to have to rehydrate somehow. They taught him the importance of that in the Brecon Beacons. He sits up again and pours out another cupful of water, sets it beside the cot, and levers himself onto the little sleeping platform, moving very carefully.

Easy does it.

Meaning: small sips.

He takes one.

Some time later, he takes another.

It's dark when he refills the cup.

Then it's day again.

And then night.

82

Time passes, as it does. Two, three, days? He has no firm idea. He's able to stomach the water, which must of course run out eventually, and does, and he seems to be thinking straight now because he's checking his watch and working out there's just a couple of hours to go until the next nightfall, that being the sensible time to make the trip to the stream again.

He makes the trip.

It takes him an age.

He's so tired by the time he's hauled the water back to the den that he goes straight back to sleep, a purification tablet still fizzing in his bottle. When he next wakes it's mid-morning. He sets to boiling the water, but the aerosol of cooking gas gives out after only a couple of minutes. He digs in his pack for another, searching through all the pockets, but no, he already knew that was the last one: from here on in he'll have to rely upon the fire.

As he's reassembling his pack he comes across his satchel. He checks to see the envelope is still there and finds himself turning it over in his hands. Look at that bastard St Thomas' Hospital crest. He's sitting cross-legged on the dirt floor of the den, and the wood noise filtering in is particularly peaceful all of a sudden. Bucolic. What a word.

Why not open the thing finally? He's thinking straighter than he was.

No.

It's not about him.

It's about superstition trumping statistics.

And Lara and Zac.

And Huntington's chorea.

Damn: even thinking its full name sort of weakens him. He takes a metallic sip of the now-more-or-less-pure water to fortify himself, thinking: stare it down for once. *It* being an autosomal dominant genetic condition, not a recessive one. Correct. Which means it doesn't lie dormant and skip generations. So if a father has the gene, each of his children has a 50 per cent chance of inheriting it and developing the disease.

Well, Charlie is in the clear.

And yes, yes, yes, Joseph has always understood that doesn't alter his odds.

But still, not knowing *for sure* has been part of his defence from the outset.

How so? Not knowing doesn't affect the odds, does it? He knows that! He's a banker, for God's sake, meaning he's worked with probability for years. Yes, but it also means he knows statistics have their limitations, and that big deal-makers rely as much upon instinct as they do on spreadsheets. In fact, he's seen it – remember Sinclair and that coal-fired power plant swap?! – the higher the stakes, the more gut feelings come into play.

Are there any higher stakes than the well-being of his children?

No.

So don't open the envelope, then!

In any case, sticking to the facts for now, probability-wise, were he to find out he had the evil gene, each of his kids would then have a separate coin-toss chance. Heads you win, tails you lose. No worse than for him and Charlie.

Correct.

But that's not the whole of it, is it? Dig a little deeper and you'll see the chance of *both* of them being free of the disease is only 25 per cent, meaning *one or other of them* is more likely than not to end up taking a twitching chair-death ride.

Last time he checked, a half times a half still equalled a quarter, and he has two kids, not one.

Which is it to be, then?

Zac or Lara, Lara or Zac.

You decide!

Damn this envelope. He should use it to light the fire. But he hasn't and he won't because it wouldn't alter the fact that somebody somewhere knows the score, and he could always ask them to write it down on another bit of paper.

He should have taken the test before he got Naomi pregnant, of course, but he didn't. Because, because, because: it wasn't the way he wanted to play the game. Not getting tested was working! As in, it was holding the horror at bay. From where he's standing now he knows getting himself tested then would have been preferable to hiding in a hole in the woods with this unopened letter in his hands, but, well, just, but.

He thought he wanted to know when he finally booked himself in for the test, then the minute the needle pricked his arm – a nice male nurse with a tattoo of a kingfisher on the side of his neck took the blood – the jab of discomfort spelled m-i-s-t-a-k-e.

They don't call it blissful ignorance for no reason: he's proof positive, isn't he, that there's something to be said for actually sticking your head in a bespoke hole in the ground.

So why is he still fingering the envelope, here in the gloom?

Because: things change.

Him, for example!

As far as balances go, he's redressed some, surely? Liberating all that capital, giving it away to the deserving poor and so forth, via Monaco, et cetera, and Milton Keynes. That surely has to count for something? He knows it can't entirely make good the hurt he caused with Heidi Sparks, or undo the, er, other extravagances, the Sea-Doo jet ski and Cleveland Square mezzanine, the personal driver parked tight to the kerb, plus that Padstow holiday home with headland views, the teak-decked motor launch by Cockwells of Falmouth, et cetera, et cetera, et-bloody-cetera, all that frankly lovely stuff Naomi wanted no part of. He's given all that away, too, more or less!

83

And look at him. When he holds the envelope up to the seam of light he sees that his hands are blackened, grainy with dirt. Yes, they look like they're made of wood. His nails, grey and ragged, need cutting. That one there on his left forefinger has a proper edge to it; look how easily it slides up under the corner of the envelope flap, seeming to have a dirty mind all of its own. Get the thing over with, the finger says; you may still be too much of a pussy to look but I've got other plans. Watch me break the gummed corner of this flap as I—

Just then, the roof above Joseph comes alive.

There's a scattering, rustling sound, and a shadow works its way through the debris overhead. The sound of sniffing breaks through. It's a dog, finding its way through the broken bushes to the hatch, which, for ventilation, Joseph has propped ajar.

There! He sees a slice of black paw in the gap.

Where there's a dog, there's an owner. Nearby, probably, and headed this way.

Joseph crawls directly beneath the hatch and punches it open. Shock the nosy bastard away! He sticks his head out of the hole, sees the dog has already sprung back. It's a black Labrador, recently decanted from a four-by-four given the glossy, healthy look of the thing.

'Fuck off!' hisses Joseph.

The dog wags its tail at him.

'Get lost!'

The dog takes a step closer, but is immediately distracted: its nose drops to the ground and it barrel-wriggles through the undergrowth to the south side of the den. Joseph is up out of the hide himself, crouched low and scanning the woods as best he can for any sign of the owner, but drawing a blank: no muted Barbour approaching, no flashy Gore-Tex ramble-wear either. The dog has stopped nearby, just over there in fact. What the hell is it rooting around in the mulch for? Ah! Joseph gets it. All that chicken–sausage mess he threw up.

'Stop, dog!' he says, sidestepping through the under-growth towards it.

But of course the dog doesn't pay him any attention at all, and by the time Joseph reaches it it is finishing up, lifting its head, cocking an ear, stiff tail still wagging, giving Joseph the playful eye.

'Get lost,' Joseph repeats. He tries a growl but it sounds ridiculous. He puts his knee against the dog's shoulder and sort of nudge-bumps it away, once, twice, and third time harder. 'Just get lost!'

The dog sniffs the ground some more and wanders off. It's still hungry, because this kind of dog always is, and sooner or later its goddamn owner is definitely bound to appear, meaning Joseph has to get shot of it right now, but how? Without thinking, he picks up a half-rotten broken bit of branch, and slings it hard at the dog, hoping to drive it away, but sadly the throw isn't accurate and the stick clatters into the bush behind it, and of course the other thing this sort of dog likes to do, beyond eat everything, is retrieve sticks: immediately it squirms into the bush, tail still wagging, pushing in hard to fetch.

Joseph staggers after the Labrador, crashing through this bracken and that bush-scrub thing, his breath quick and hard in his ears, and by the time he's there the dog is in reverse, dragging the stick free, its rump exposed. He kicks it. Hardish. Sharply enough at any rate to prompt a yelp and make it squirm away, back into the bush, through it, and out the other side. Joseph sees the dark shape stop and turn and look at him through the tangles. Does he feel bad? Yes. Particularly because the blow doesn't seem to have worked. The dog has put some distance between them but still, apparently, wants to be friends. It's looking at him sort of reproachfully, the stick still clamped between its teeth, possibly still considering bringing it back?

Damn dog!

Joseph is at a complete loss.

Just then, though, the dog stiffens, all four legs rigid. It cocks its head to one side, listening. To what? Joseph strains to hear someone calling but cannot. Seems the Labrador can, though. Without warning it springs away, crashing through the bracken up to the spine. From there it dashes along the little ridge and runs off up the hill out of sight.

84

The woods are marvellously quiet again. Even the uppermost leaves are still, framed in blue, hyper-real. They look painted. A new, fuller heat has made its way into the cool heart of the woods. Whatever the date, this is a beautiful May day. Not the sort you'd want to waste inside. That always used to get to him about working in the City: sometimes he'd pause by one of the ceiling-height smoked-glass windows up on the thirteenth floor and look out across the rooftops and see, wow, that it was a nice day, and realise, just for a second or two, that an unedited version of the same day was going on in woods like these ones here, and also in fields and fells and fens, and on hilltops and up mountains and beside streams and rivers and even out at sea, and he'd wonder: what on earth am I doing standing here, air-conditioned and UV-filtered, theoretically at the top of the pile – or near it! – but somehow also wasting away?

Was it his choice?

Well, yes, but it didn't feel like one.

What it actually felt like in moments like that was a happy-enough-but-actually-possibly-a-bit-sad accident, courtesy of Major Very Nice Man, a baker with a triangular hole in his head, a dead mother in Alicante and a father, also dead, in his armchair.

None of any of this is or was or ever will be anyone's fault but his own!

Joseph takes a deep breath, coughs, doubles up, coughs weakly again. He crouches down and holds onto himself. Every bone in his body feels misaligned. When he tries to stand straight and draw his shoulders back, things don't get any better: everything aches. He feels wobbly. That's because he's wobbling! He puts his hands on his hips as if that might help him steady himself. Christ, his trousers are so loose on his thighs, hanging low despite the twine belt. It just needs retying tighter. He decides to take off his jacket, plaid shirt, and base layer, to survey the situation, so to speak, and . . . Holy crap! That's not him! He leans back from himself and his hip bones jut out sharply, obvious as fists. Above them, where the complacent swell of his belly used to sit, there's just a pallid, concave emptiness. Wow: he can pretty much count his ribs. The skin covering them is waxy and seems to be thinner than it was, making his nakedness somehow nakeder. He stands there swaying in the dappled sunlight and pinches a little grey flap of belly skin, doubtful it still has any elasticity. But of course it shrinks redly back into place when he lets go. Maybe it's the bright light, but his chest hair appears to have gone silvery. He runs his hand over the new boniness of his chest, up to his throat, now soft with beard. When he cups his jaw he can feel it hard and sharp, and his cheeks, pinched between grimy forefinger and thumb, are hollow beneath the bristles.

What has he become?

Somewhat thinner, that's what.

Well, he could afford to lose a bit.

Don't be an idiot: he's dangerously weak.

That's no bad thing, though, or at least not entirely bad.

What are you talking about *now*?

This good feeling within the achy, wobbly weakness. He's not about to give up on himself, or anyone else for that matter.

Better start by finding himself something to eat. Sadly all the stuff he fetched from the freezer thawed out and spoiled days ago. None of it is edible. But these two ice lollies, sloppy in their cardboard tubes, well, they've got to be drinkable, haven't they? Yes. So he drinks them, thinking: possibly today isn't a good day to stay in the hide anyway. The dog could lead its owner back here, for example. And so what if he's a bit dirty. He can shake these clothes out, get rid of the grubby jacket, give his face and hands a good wash in the stream, en route to . . .

85

He knows he's going back.

And in broad daylight!

Look, it probably makes no difference: the kids will be at school, Naomi at work. He'll keep himself to himself, go there the back way, case the place properly before approaching, et cetera.

That's what he does. A good wash in the brook helps him feel a little better about himself, newly spruced, sort of, presentable enough to make his way through the woods and over the stile and down the footpath with its little acorn sign to the back of Nine Pines, at any rate. Aside from the hush of car noise from the lane, plus a couple of roof-glints over the hedgerow as they take the long bend, he sees no sign of life. If he were to come upon a neighbour walking the thin path, he doubts he'd be recognised anyway: even before his transformation it would have been unlikely; the hedges work! He makes his way to the beech gap at the rear of his own – former – slice of the privacy pie, pushes through it and skirts the big lawn heading for the garage. Look at those fresh stripes. Tremendous to see the place properly looked after. Tad costly, though. Or perhaps Naomi has taught Lara to mow it, finally? She was always urging him to do that. Get the kids to pull their weight a little. Yes, maybe 'moving on with our lives' has a lawn-mowing dimension?

Nobody has changed the garage pass-code.

Or returned the Lexus to its spot, or the jet ski for that matter. There's a new gap, in fact: the go-kart is gone.

Oh well.

It's not all bad news. Joseph pops the monster-freezer lid and discovers the fortnightly food shop has happened. Thank God! Naomi – or the automatically repeating Ocado order – has laid in some more chicken thighs, sausages and whatnot, but Joseph thinks twice about borrowing those, and not just because the sight of the packets makes him sit down on the lawn tractor, catch his breath, and take a moment. No. It's just that he considers it would be more subtle to liberate something – this bit of smoked haddock, for example, and that tub of bolognese – from the permafrost.

Unlike his last visit, this time Joseph stops there, carefully replacing the newly bought items on top of all the older food before he shuts the coffin door.

No point in lugging too much stuff back to camp, is there?

That's not the point, though.

Because the point is: he can always come again.

And he does.

Two days later, at night this time, he's rummaging through the freezer again, and three days after that he's back in the middle of the day. He takes a risk that afternoon, deciding – and why not? – that it's a sensible idea to hide away in (hell, why not use the old army term: *incrementally populate*) the culvert beyond the compost, a vantage point from which he knows he'll be able to see.

See what?

It's obvious! The drive, plus the west side of the house.

Which is a good thing why?

Because that's where they'll come back to, after school.

He only has to wait a couple of hours before his patience is rewarded with the sound of a car turning onto the gravel, and there's the old Golf lurching to a stop, revealing Zac, who immediately spills out of the nearside rear door, dragging his school bag with him. He's just there! Clearly visible through this leaf-gap, not fifty yards away, leaning back into the car to retrieve some more kit, and standing up again and laughing about something, his brow clear and his smile wide and, wow, his whole self sort of stretched since Joseph last saw him, something to do with the collarless sports top he's wearing, which somehow emphasises the new elongation of his beautiful neck.

Jesus: he's grown.

The nails of Joseph's right hand are digging quite hard into his other palm.

Both Lara and Naomi climb out of the other side of the car, meaning they're mostly obscured, damnit, but Joseph sees Lara's familiar wagging ponytail as she walks towards the house, and also the length of Naomi's bare right arm as she raises the tailgate to let Gordon jump down.

Gordon.

Joseph tenses up.

Is the dog scenting the breeze? Possibly. But now he's

shaking himself loose after being cooped up in the back of the car, shaking and scratching and trotting off towards the back door, with Naomi following on behind. The sight of her further hollows out Joseph's already empty stomach. That right arm of hers is the one he lay next to (they kept to their own side of the bed, and Naomi always slept on her stomach) for twenty-odd years. Oh come off it, the sight of either arm would have had the same effect: it's the Naomi-ness of Naomi that's hitting . . .

Home.

Look! There they go.

The bang of the big side door shutting behind them reaches Joseph a half-beat out of sync, placing him emphatically over here, behind the compost enclosure, peering through this blackthorn bush at the house, in which they all are, without him.

His knees are a little damp; he's kneeling in mud.

So what?

He sinks his bum lower into the hardness of his boot heels.

Because he can't move on, not right now, not, in fact, for a bit. The sight of them just makes leaving too hard. And it's a good job he doesn't go, because half an hour later, when he's still planted there in the hedge, head bowed, the shallow in and out of his own breathing is overtaken by a faint, repetitive squelching noise, and his head snaps up as he realises, yes, it's the trampoline calling to him, from round the other side of the house. He can't see it, but that's definitely the sound of someone bounce-bounce-bouncing. Meaning one of the kids is using it!

He should see which one.

Why not? He's perfectly capable of retreating through the hedge, leopard-crawling somewhat muddily along the culvert between Nine Pines and the bottom of the Norton-Soames' orchard, and inserting himself back into the hawthorn again some seventy metres to the northwest. Don't worry about the odd scratch, plus prickles. More of a problem is the newish shiplap fence running alongside the hedge just here. Up close it still smells of wood stain. He does a very slow chin-up on the fence top, inching his eyes above the parapet, knowing that from here he should be able to see whoever is doing the bouncing.

And he can!

Partly, at least.

One half of the trampoline enclosure is in view, the other is hidden by the big oil tank. Half a view is better than none, though. And of course it's Zac doing his flips, letting off steam before Naomi calls him in for supper, because that's what he's loved to do ever since Joseph bought him pretty much the biggest and best trampoline he could find: the Sky-high Xtreme 360!

There Zac is, somersaulting into view.

Look at the way his hair catches up with his head.

And there he goes, flipping back into the bit Joseph can't see.

Here again, plus late hair.

Gone.

Joseph hangs on the fence for quite a long time, his fingers numb, his back locked, his biceps burning, all of him straining for one more glimpse, and another, and another.

Squelch-bounce-squelch-bounce-squelch.

Zac is in his own world, concentrating on landing that backflip again and again and again.

Ha.

Now you see him.

Now you . . .

Damn the oil tank. It holds 3,500 litres. Quite painful to fill up, particularly in a suboptimal bonus year.

But . . . now: look at Zac go!

Possibly, just possibly, in one of the non-flip-focused sectors of Zac's brain, there's a Dad-thought turning?

Flip, hello.

Flip, goodbye.

Flip, hello.

A non-flip thought is unlikely, face it.

What if Joseph shouted out, though? He wouldn't even have to call that loudly from here. In fact, what's he thinking, he doesn't have to call out at all. He has strength enough yet to swing his leg across the fence panel, flop down the other side and amble over to the trampoline for – 'Hey, Zac, remember to tuck your chin in' – a proper father–son chat.

But he doesn't.

Because he can't.

Instead, he just watches until his son leaves, and then he leaves too, and his hands smell of creosote for days.

86

He couldn't say hi! He knows that. But it's strange the way the brain works. For example: he also knows that he's been lowering the freezer level bit by bit with his visits, meaning at some point Naomi has to notice, but somehow that truth is more easily avoided, simply by cooking the other way.

Looking.

There is no other way to cook, just him and his little fire, lit to one side of the wide-open door-hatch, late at night, with some of whatever he's cooked – thoroughly! – left to one side for the morning. Two little meals a day do him just fine: though he's regained no weight that he can tell, he has strength enough to make the slow walk, gather a little wood, check his pointless snares.

It strikes him: it's a good job they never actually had to survive off the land whilst soldiering. The only rabbit he ever killed was handed to him out of the back of a Land Rover, next to a frozen Dartmoor stream. He was hungry! He broke its neck, skinned it, gutted it, cooked it, and ate it, as instructed. But he hadn't actually caught the bloody thing.

No doubt Lancaster's snare worked.

Joseph is out of water purification tablets now, but isn't really relying on the stream in any case: the yellow-and-green garden hose is click-locked to the tap round the back of the garage, and since he's not taking much at a time from the freezer, there's plenty of room in his backpack for a half-full water container, more than enough to last him until his next visit.

It's while he's using the tap, his midday shadow squat beneath him, one precautionary eye on the back of the house for good measure, that he spots Zac's open window. It's only ajar, but still: he knows that if that window is open a little all he'll have to do is slide the safety catch out of its groove to open it all the way.

There's a whole other fridge of immediately edible food behind that wall: he could make himself a goddamn sandwich, eggs on toast, anything!

All he has to do is climb the wisteria, itself firmly bolted to the wall, up to that porch roof, and he'll pretty much be able to step sideways onto the window ledge. It's quite a big step, now that he's taking it, and that patio down there looks further away and harder than he'd like, but he has one hand inside the window already, and the catch works exactly as he knew it would, and look, here's the window open, Zac's little desk unit thing beneath it, on which he, Joseph, Zac's very own father, is now sitting, unlacing his boots, because we don't wear shoes upstairs, do we, not at home!

Home.

Amazing.

What's Zac reading, then? Seems to be a biography of Lionel Messi? He doesn't even like football.

Doesn't: *didn't*.

At least the Percy Jacksons are still there on his shelf. Plus the catapult Naomi's father made with him when he was what, eight? Joseph remembers catching Zac standing at the end of the gravel drive, elastic taut, waiting to wang stones at passing cars. Happily he'd not yet hit one – if he had the driver would surely have stopped? – but that was testimony to the expensively secured lack of traffic in this corner of Surrey, and not Zac's poor aim. After the bollocking (possibly he was too hard on the boy; it being the weekend the Italy deal fell through could well have skewed his judgement) Joseph felt bad and set up some tin cans in front of the back beech hedge and the two of them had spent a happy half hour denting them up.

Die, Italian competition tsar, die!

What's this, though? A pot of hair gel? Last time Joseph checked, Zac paid about as much attention to his hair as he did every other aspect of his appearance, namely: zero.

Everything changes.

But not . . . Joseph steps out onto the landing and immediately hears the bip-bip-bip of the burglar alarm warning signal . . . that!

Boots in hand, he hotfoots it down the central staircase, knowing he has thirty seconds to deactivate the alarm before it goes off, deafeningly loud here, plus clinical fifteen-minute response time in the Guildford police HQ.

Marble flooring is damn slippery under sock.

(She hadn't really expected him to arrange a fitter to lay it while they were on that Florence minibreak, had she? No! And despite her 'upscale hotel' jibe, she couldn't quite hide her admiration for the underfloor heating touch.)

Never mind the heating system: Joseph's feet fly out from under him as he takes the glassy corner between the hall and the boot room, and he lands hard on his less-padded-than-it-was hip.

Ow!

But there's no time to lose: the damn bip-bip-bips wait for no man. He claws himself upright and hop-limps through to the boot room, thinking: please God don't let her have changed the code.

Fourteen Seven Ninety-Four.

The date they met.

He jabs in the numbers with a shaking hand.

And bip-hip-bip-hip . . .

Nothing.

Empty, throbbing silence, quiet as a spreading bruise.

Phew, plus: goddamn painful hip!

Joseph rubs it long and hard while hopping on the other foot, until: man, the smell in this boot room sort of overtakes him sensory-input-wise, it being just so *boot room* in here.

Meaning, thank God: not everything changes.

But look at that: there on his shelf sits a pair of his old trainers, and when he picks one up and sticks his nose in it he finds the smell of himself has long since gone.

Which reinforces the fact that many things, including some a lot more important than this formerly smelly shoe, *do* in fact, whether we like it or not, *change*.

Oh God, what else has time, with Naomi's help, edited out?

Joseph hobbles round himself in a small circle. It's a fair-sized boot room, after all.

Look, she could have thrown these shoes away, but she didn't: perhaps it's actually a good sign?

Ha.

He carefully returns the trainers to their shelf, placing his dirty boots next to them for good measure.

It's only twelve fifteen, ages to go before the family returns from school and work. Those hours, now he's back in the house – *his* house – are suddenly vertiginous with possibility.

What should he do first?

87

Well, his old shoes may no longer smell of him, but those boots certainly do, as does he, in person. He needs a good shower. That's not where he heads first, though, the pull of the fridge being just too strong. It makes him set off back across the hall, down the long wood-panelled corridor past the dining and games rooms, towards the shut door of the kitchen.

When he opens it all hell breaks loose.

Gordon, all thirty, furry, kilograms of him, leaps straight for Joseph's face, barking and wagging and licking and falling back to bounce, barking, straight up at his chest again.

Joseph staggers sideways, sinks to his knees, takes hold of the dog's ears, pulls its head under his chin, all the while saying, 'Shhh, shhh, shhh.'

He wants the dog to shut up, of course he does, but man, this all-forgiving love is overwhelming.

What's the dog doing home alone anyway?

Who cares?

Joseph has missed him.

He holds the dog side-on, feels its quick heartbeat against his own ribcage, sits like that, waits until they are both calm.

'Good boy, good boy,' he says.

There's a chorizo sausage in the fridge. Joseph hacks off

some big slices, tosses half of them in the air for Gordon to catch, and slots the rest into a cream cheese bagel. This he eats with two handfuls of cherry tomatoes, washed down with many big pulpy swigs of orange juice direct from the carton. He doesn't bother to sit down to eat and drink, just leans on one of the eighties, Shaker-style units which Naomi simply refused point-blank always and for ever to change, thinking that he actually quite likes the shabby chic look today.

Real wood, at least, if a bit dated.

He eats two apples, a satsuma and a punnet of strawberries next.

Sweet Jesus, the fresh, fruit-bomb taste.

Why not stash a couple of bananas in his bag while he's at it? And a few tins from the larder shelves, these chickpeas, some kidney beans, plus pineapple chunks. He doesn't want to weigh himself down with stuff, but the top shelf is where they kept the bottles of spirits he impressively hasn't touched for what, eleven months now, and that tube there contains a twenty-year-old Oban single malt whisky, and – he's not even thought about having a drink in ages! Meaning he's surely in the clear? Whatever – he can't resist it.

What's this on the back of the kitchen chair? One of Naomi's cotton scarves. He presses his face into the softness of it, then remembers he's still unclean, so to speak, and needs a shower. With Gordon safely behind the kitchen door, he passes the piano en route upstairs and pauses to note that the music on the stand is way fuller of, well, notes, than it used to be, but at least this change is progress, go Lara, good girl!

In the third spare room, *his room* for those last few weeks after Naomi's ultimatum, he sets down his bag and hangs his dirty clothes over the back of the chair. The shower in this en suite is a long way from the twin boilers. Takes an age to warm up. As he's standing on the mat waiting he glances sideways and catches sight of himself in the full-length mirror.

88

Oh.

As in, he actually gulps, and gulps again, to see his Adam's apple – yes, it's really doing it – roll visibly beneath the bristles covering his now scrawny throat.

He stands sideways, sees the pale hook of himself in profile, turns further and is shocked again by the new fragility of his shoulder blades, the dents above them, the wrinkled back of his neck. Hmm. That hip is an angry red. But, stepping closer to the mirror, he's more worried about the yellow-purple scratch beneath that eye. It's painful when he pulls a Popeye wink, but the pain isn't stopping him seeing all this, is it? No. Stand back again then, relish the slashes of colour within the general dirty-milk hue of everything else.

The shower is filling with steam now.

He slips inside, draws the doors to behind him, bows his head, shuts his eyes tight, edges beneath the torrent, gasps.

It's a hug from every side, a great falling relief.

With the water drumming hard on his neck and shoulders and head, Joseph opens his eyes again to see the pooling water beneath his feet. It is streaked grey. So what? Soon the tray is full of suds anyway, and after that the water runs perfectly clear down the plug hole, and by now the enveloping heat and rushing wetness has pulled Joseph to the surface of himself again; that's his blood pink beneath the skin of his inner forearm, his newly lean upper chest, the fronts of thighs and shins, and it's as if the shower is cleaning him inside as well as outside, or at the very least revealing his purer self.

Purer? Pah!

Well, he's tried.

That's the point, though, isn't it?

What's the point?

It's just there, ready to say, this point, when something about his staring at the shampoos and body washes and conditioners draws him up short. That thing there, behind the loofah. What is it?

A razor.

So?

He reaches for it.

Is he about to have a shave?

No, no, no.

There's something very wrong with this razor.

What?

It's not his.

Well, Naomi shaves her legs; no doubt it's a new one she's bought.

But this isn't her bathroom. She uses the big one with two sinks off the master bedroom. And anyway, she always does her legs, armpits and whatnot with those pink disposable razors: she's used the same brand for at least a decade. Joseph knows because he's borrowed them often enough. Before he was banished from her boudoir, so to speak.

Anyway, this one is a man's razor.

Very carefully, he returns it to its spot behind the sponge. The shower is suddenly oppressively hot. He twists the dial hard left and braces himself for the cauterising cold slap; it pulls a completely different, end-of-world gasp out of him, leaves him standing there, blowing hard, a bull in the middle of the ring.

89

Joseph shuts off the tap, pulls a towel inside the shower, pats himself slowly dry. What he'd give for a set of clean clothes. But he hasn't any, and anyway these dirty clothes are, at least, part of the new him. He puts them on like pieces of armour: armoured pants, armoured trousers, armoured top and shirt and jacket, even his armoured semi-full backpack, everything but the dirty socks, which he rams into a pocket, preferring the cool feel of the bathroom floor beneath the soles of his feet.

He pulls open the mirrored door of the bathroom cabinet, checking inside to see if he can find – yes, he knew it! – a squirter of shaving gel.

Clinique For Men, no less.

He sniffs it.

Fancy.

Joseph shuts the cabinet door and fingers his beard. It feels softer now he's washed. He decides to keep it, for good. That look in his eye is unsettling: baleful almost. He feels light on his toes. Where are they taking him? Back out of the bathroom and into the bedroom, of course.

The third spare bedroom, as was.

His room after that.

Somebody else's room now?

Serves him right, thinks Joseph, regarding the bed. If he'd brought Heidi Sparks in here instead of into his and Naomi's room might Naomi not have taken it so badly? Don't be stupid. He didn't actually fuck Heidi Sparks in the marital bed, but yes, he did have her over the dressing table, the one he used to keep his cufflinks on, plus mahogany-backed clothes brush, loose foreign change, expense receipts, and so on. Fiddly stuff, coins and cufflinks; much of it ended up on the floor.

What did he do it for?

Isn't it obvious?

Well, yes. But why in their room, for God's sake? Couldn't he have taken her to a hotel or something? Even an outbuilding. The gazebo, for example, down the bottom of the . . .

Just shut up.

Fact is, nothing is *obvious* at all. He doesn't really know why he did it, and that's the truth. Blame the automatic pilot; the little bastard has a kamikaze streak. Joseph and Heidi had sunk a third of a bottle of vodka *brainstorming* at the kitchen table before he took her upstairs: perhaps that had something to do with it?

Did he take her or was it her suggestion?

He can't quite remember.

But he can remember, most clearly, that Naomi had given him her ultimatum just a week or two beforehand: 'One minute you're screaming at the kids for no reason, the next staring into space. Zac said you threw his shepherd's pie at the fridge yesterday, because he asked for ketchup? You're scaring them. You need to see someone, get help, or else you have to leave.'

324

Well, he'd seen someone! Not quite what she meant, though, was it?

No, but—

Enough excuses!

All that's ancient history; that's not why he's here now, pulling open drawers and checking the walk-in wardrobe, for, yes, a monogrammed dressing gown, thick black-and-gold stripes of softness hanging in the otherwise vacated space. No shirts, no signs of the daily humdrum, and that's something, he guesses, but not really very much, because that definitely isn't Naomi's dressing gown, is it, and the bastard thing certainly doesn't belong to him.

90

Joseph backs out of the cupboard and sits down on the foot of the bed. From here, through the big window he can see a familiar serrated horizon of pines. They are blue-green in the afternoon sun. What's that hill called again? He can't remember, possibly never knew. Doesn't matter anyway: it's not his to look at now, is it? Whoever wears that dressing gown is free to pull back the floor-length curtains on a Sunday morning, sit here on the end of bed, and take in the lovely view.

Look, it's the third spare room. If she was seeing someone, this stuff would be in the master bedroom, surely?

He almost convinces himself there's mileage in this explanation, but then remembers the kids. She'd want to protect them, for appearance's sake, wouldn't she?

Possibly.

Either way, he doesn't blame her.

It's just that things do change.

Like him!

That being the point.

Ah yes, the point again. He remembers now: the point was all about change. He'd changed, and he wanted to show it, prove it in fact, by doing something, something grand and good and unexpected and final.

Don't over-egg it.

We give according to our means.

One good thing.

That's all he's done.

Or has he, though? Yes, that's the point! Here, in the house, he can check. Check what? That he succeeded in what he set out to do. Yes, and given the state of play, meaning his current situation, or predicament, or proximity to the finishing line, so to speak, well, it would be quite something to face that with a bit of a sense that it, meaning everything, has been worthwhile, meaning goddamn worth it.

91

Joseph has made his way into the study. Lovely smell here, too. Polish-based. He takes a deep breath, noticing anew that there's a lot to polish: the double-depth teak shelves, for a start, stacked as they are with art and architecture books purchased by the yard, and the ammonite collection, bought in its entirety online, and marvellous to look at until Naomi's 'Really, you're sure they're not fake?' put him off a bit, plus of course the ceiling-to-floor oak panelling along that wall, which Joseph had installed by that little chap from Pembrokeshire, Alwyn something; he always wore a cap and actually doffed it, yes, old-school deferential in every way, he was, except perhaps for the size of his invoice.

There's the big old desk, too, which came out of an actual captain's cabin, and the iMac plonked on it, a little too twenty-first century, perhaps, given the rest of the room's aged weight, but still there, still plugged in, and still . . . yes . . . working.

What's this, though? Joseph retypes the password slowly, but no joy, meaning: she's changed it.

Damn.

Undeterred, Joseph jog-hobbles back through the house in search of another device: Lara's laptop, Zac's, an old one of Naomi's, one of the iPads, Kindles, a decommissioned phone, anything.

Two circuits of the big house later, back upstairs in Lara's room, rummaging through the pile of discarded jodhpurs and tennis skirts – tennis? When did she start that? – on her bed, he hits the jackpot; yes, here's her iPad in its familiar William Morris wallpaper cover. He bought that case for her at Tate Britain. Cue stabbing memory of taking a forty-minute call re German pension funds in the big atrium while she bored herself stupid in the gift shop. Forget that now! See instead that it's charged. And yes, the password is still *preraphaelites*.

Meaning: he's in, connected, browsing.

It's actually quite strange to be looking at a screen again. Rocket-speed broadband, pixels dancing, the whole not-a-hole-in-the-woods world available to him again. Familiar, but alien. Like revisiting school. Ha.

Airdeen Clore, he types.

And . . .

News.

And boom, the news about Airdeen Clore is just *there*.

Because that's how it works.

Joseph scans the headlines.

'*Airdeen Clore and Goldman Sachs U-turn on Chinese Tech Giant Options.*'

'*Oil Heads Higher as Airdeen Clore Turns Bullish.*'

'*Airdeen Clore Analysts Explain Why These E&P Names are Portfolio Musts.*'

'*Airdeen Clore CEO Jonas Hertford Finally Finds Buyer for Hamptons Home.*'

'Airdeen Clore and Morgan Stanley Land Year's Biggest Energy Sector Stock Offering.'

With each new page of links Joseph's heart sinks further until – from the lightheaded feeling up top – it seems his pulse is coming from somewhere too far away to sustain him, as in, yes, wow, quick, he must drop his head beneath his knees, now! or otherwise faint.

He slumps onto the bed and hears himself groan.

What does that groan mean?

Simple: there's no news, or rather no bad news, not for the bank, and no bad bank news, baldly displayed here in Lara's room on the little William Morris-encased screen, though not entirely news to him, because let's face it he's not a complete idiot, is still very bad news indeed for the idiot known as Joseph Ashcroft.

But wait.

Just because it's not public knowledge doesn't mean it didn't happen.

Not even a bank of Airdeen's heft and horsepower could sail on with that big a hole in its hull. At the very least it would require a government bailout to carry on. Yes, without help, the ship of the bank would never have made it into port for repairs. And these stories of ongoing success only make sense if someone, meaning the government – meaning the taxpayer – has shored up the bank's position.

And that, it, they, hasn't, hadn't, haven't.

Apparently slash not.

Ugh: nothing makes sense.

Joseph is crouched on all fours on Lara's sheepskin

bedspread, the screen between his hands. He rocks back on his haunches and presses his face into the softness, breathing in deeply, steadily.

Think, he thinks; think.

What if not all of the money made it out? It's possible they – Lancaster – spotted what was happening as it happened, and did their best to shut the theft down as fast as possible, meaning they didn't head it off entirely. Many many millions might still have made it through Milton Keynes, the Caymans, et cetera, and beyond, into the wide world, and the loss of a paltry many many millions would be easier to hide.

Yes, perhaps that's it.

Meaning: he's searching for news in the wrong place.

Assuming the bank has squashed the embarrassing story of the theft for now, there may still be beneficiaries out there, total strangers who he, Joseph, has helped with a handout, a Hail Mary cash pass thrown by a heaven-based playmaker straight into the end zone of their current account: boom.

Quickly he types 'random cash gift' into the search bar.

And here's a new rash of stories to sift through.

Mostly they seem to be to do with wedding list etiquette and suggested ways of rewarding employees at Christmas, but this one here is at first more relevant:

'*Crackpot jackpot: unknown man gives strangers cash!*'

Joseph clicks on the link, his heart in his mouth, but no, it's just a story about a man handing out ten-dollar bills in a shopping mall outside Clearwater, Florida. Seems he was mostly generous to pre-teen girls, hence the call to security, the foot-chase through the car park, et cetera.

The rest of the page is irrelevant.

And the next.

But hold on, what's this?

'*Anonymous Donor Reverses Fortunes of Drought-Hit Gujarati Farm Collective.*'

This page, on the *Gujarat Samachar* news website, seems to take an age to load. So it goes, with proper anticipation! Actually, the site really is very slow. And damn, when the story does finally reveal itself, it's not in English, but Gujarati. Of course it is! Joseph has to back up and click a 'Translate This Page' link, which takes another age to shimmy forward, the translation robot working hard and quixotically to produce a story that starts:

> With its rains failed again for seven months now it pushes the small group rice collective northwestern into harder times and until unexpectedly a giver emerges. But this is the case it seems today. From overseas there have come a supporting hand of a generous with nearly half a million of . . .

Hold on.

The empty whiteness of the house has shifted. The blank space inside it is colouring itself in.

That noise there is a door slamming.

And those are voices.

Naomi's, plus Lara's. Zac's, too, asking if they can have burgers for lunch.

They're downstairs.

Joseph is staring very hard at the iPad screen. Not at the

story, but at the header bar, which reads *Saturday 28 May, 1.32 p.m.*

What a complete fucking idiot.

They're not at school. Of course they're not. Because it's the weekend. Which means they're probably returning from Lara's horse riding lesson. Which in turn means that any minute – any second! – now she'll jog upstairs to change out of her riding clothes.

92

Joseph's fingers have already started tapping at the screen. He's not sure what he's doing until he's done it. He's erased the search history and shut the browser down. Now he's returning the iPad to the pile of clothes and sidestepping pretty damn light-footedly, like a dancer, almost, albeit with a limp, to the open bedroom door. From here he can peer out at the top of the stairs. But he can't very well go down them, can he? Because the bottom flight spills out into the big hall, which is visible through any open door to the kitchen, study, living room, dining room, games room, et cetera, et cetera, et cetera.

Damn open-ish-plan living!

There's a reason he wants to take the risk and jog down those stairs anyway, but he's not quite sure what it is, not until he's made a break for it across the landing, towards Zac's room. He could run straight on to the back stairs from here, but they drop down between the kitchen and utility rooms, and that's quite possibly where Naomi is, sorting out the dog and pulling lunch ingredients from the fridge; no, better exit the way he came in, namely via hupping up onto Zac's little desk and edging out onto the window ledge.

Oh crap.

His boots.

What should he do?

A good soldier always looks after his feet!

But he put his goddamn boots in the boot room, and as with everything else at the bottom of the main stairs, the boot room is pretty exposed to the open-ish-plan comings and goings of the revamped Nine Pines.

He is crouching on the window sill, one hand on the frame, unsure of what to do next.

Well, not nothing!

Try this instead.

Quickly Joseph drops back down into Zac's room, skirts the air-hockey table and what's this, he seems to be ramming his son's moccasin slippers into his jacket pockets.

But they're a size five, and Joseph is a size nine.

So he's doing this why?

He has his reasons. Possibly they also explain why he's pocketing Zac's catapult, too. Not just because it might come in handy, but because if he shuts his eyes he can see his son's fingers curled around its handle.

Maybe now isn't the best time for Joseph to shut his eyes.

No.

If they're having lunch they're most likely to be in the kitchen, and that's on the other side of the house, which makes it not the stupidest idea in the world for Joseph to climb out onto the – actually pretty high – ledge again, and lean out to grip the trellis, trust it with what's left of his weight, and hand-over-hand-plus-foot-scrabble his way to the – ouch! – gravel below.

He pauses, back pressed to the brick wall.

The nearest cover is over there, but the nearest cover he can reach without passing a lot of twice-monthly-professionally-cleaned windows is beyond the garages, namely the big beech hedge; he can get behind it next to the wheelie bins.

Turns out gravel is quite like hot coals: run across it fast enough and somehow the hurt to your feet is less hurtful, though he's always suspected fire-walkers might actually do a bit of hopping from one foot to the other off camera in an actually-that's-pretty-painful way, and he finds himself doing the same behind the recycling.

Damn driveway: he always knew they should have gone for the herringbone brickwork option anyway.

He's out of sight here, at least.

Joseph catches his breath, marvels at the throbbing of his feet, looks back at the house from between the bins. There's a magpie on the porch roof. One for sorrow. No, phew, there's its mate, up on the satellite dish. What's that in its beak? A fairly sizeable twig. Joseph watches as the first magpie joins its other half up behind the satellite receiver, since that's clearly where they're making their nest.

Nice spot.

He has a lot of admiration for stick-built homes these days.

Still, the magpies are lucky he's not currently in residence: he'd have their nest in this here bin pretty swiftly, not because he's cruel, just to stop them shitting down the terracotta roof shingles, filling up the gutters, et cetera.

Build your nest elsewhere, magpies! Leave my home alone!

Damn dressing gown.

93

He has his breath back, and nobody has come out of the house after him, making it pretty likely they didn't see him, because if they had, if they'd seen him and thought wow, there's a thin ragged version of Dad running quite painfully across the drive to the bins, they'd no doubt immediately have run after him, all three of them, arms outstretched, shouting, 'Come back, Dad slash Joseph, we love you!', but they didn't, meaning he made it undetected, which is good, right? – but still, narrow escape notwithstanding, he's shaking all over, as in from actual head to painful feet, a physical shuddering stutter, unable, unable, unable . . .

Unable to do what?

Go back?

As in: walk back up the drive, knock on the door, wait for it to open, possibly kneel down on the front step, explain everything.

Pah!

He didn't come this far just to—

To just what?

Just pull yourself together, man. As in: chin up, shoulders back and make a move, head back to camp.

Joseph takes his own advice. It's fairly slow going, barefoot, but the shakes subside as he presses on, his horror at having nearly been caught offset by a mini surge of euphoria resulting from, well, not having been caught.

Ex-Big(ish) Beast: still at large!

If a bit compromised.

Because, let's face it, he's going to have to lie low – lower than that, lower still, as low as possible in fact – for a while now.

Well, sitting tight will certainly be less painful vis-à-vis his feet, which, crap, really don't like these stones, prickles, roots, rocks, bits of twig and so on, which pepper the route back to the den.

He makes slow, painful progress home.

Ah, the den.

He eases his way through the rhododendrons, relieved to see that the camouflaged den entrance has not been disturbed. Here we are. Just move this brush-section aside, lift the trap door slash chimney, drop the bag down the hole and follow it in.

He'll be dug in here a while now, since he can't very well risk being spotted near Nine Pines again, can he?

No.

That's the spirit.

Again, the uprush of unexpected good cheer. Because although he cannot be sure, what with the translation-in-need-of-translation, et cetera, what he read seemed to be pointing in the right direction, didn't it? Yes. Hence this mini underground air-punch!

Still, it's possibly a shame he didn't borrow a little more food, because there really isn't that much of it now he's setting the packets and tins out on the little den-wall earth-shelf, but this is all there is, for now, so he'll just have to make goddamn do.

94

Make do is what he does, more or less.

He lies up on the little cot through the rest of the day, all the next, and all the one after that, only leaving the den to use the toilet spot on the far side of the spine, and rationing what food he has – a few mouthfuls of tinned pineapple for breakfast, a biscuit at lunchtime, a third of a tin of chickpeas for dinner – to make it last. With his knife he splits open the heels of Zac's moccasins, and yes, they're still pretty tight at the toe end but, on the bright side, that helps them stay on his feet. When his water runs out, he waits until dark and hobbles to the stream – wow, that hip has really seized up – builds a fire on his return, and boils what he'll eventually drink for a thorough ten minutes before setting it aside.

On his back, beneath the den roof, he watches the patterns of light and dark change shape through the day and night, and he listens to the occasionally pattering rain, the birdsong, the wind, the squirrel-chatter and the underlying earth-hum.

This, now, is where he belongs.

And this shutting down is what he deserves.

He feels strangely focused. Yes, beyond the ache of hunger and the stiffness of his bashed hip, beyond the now-swollen cut under his eye and the headache behind it, beyond the word-gaps and the razor and dressing gown and squelch of the trampoline, beyond the bank and the debt and the bastard envelope, there's a new stillness he can half glimpse, half hear, half feel, a measured emptiness like that left behind in a house after the front door slams.

What was that quotation his dad used to like?

'And calm of mind, all passion spent.'

No idea where it came from, but that.

Yes, that.

95

Until his food actually runs out. Then the hunger changes shape. It's not that he can't bear it: his appetite has shrunk to a dot, albeit a dot radiating an ache, but the ache is so persistent he's grown used to it. Thing is, he knows he can't actually eat nothing without growing weak, and within a day of zero rations, fear of losing what strength he has left propels him to head out – quite slowly, more like a deep-sea diver than a hunter-gatherer – at dusk, Zac's catapult in hand, bound for the field beyond the edge of the wood, which he knows will be hopping with rabbits.

It's worth a try.

And look, there they are, nibbling about.

Joseph has a pocket full of decent-sized stones he's dug out of his very own ammo dump slash den. Remember the tin cans in the garden, with Zac? They got pretty good at hitting those from twenty yards, possibly nearer ten, every now and then. You don't have to creep up on empty cans of Pepsi Max, though. Moccasin-footed, he's treading super softly anyway, but look at that nearest little bastard, it's definitely clocked him already and he's still way out of range and, damn, with his next step the rabbit bounces off, not particularly quickly, casually in fact, as if to say: yeah right ha hop ha hop ha.

Some others, though, over there.

Joseph drops down onto his hands and knees, crawls through the bracken fringe, settles himself with a view of the field. He can wait just here – man, has he got good at waiting! – and sooner or later one of the flock, herd, whatever, will stray over to him. All he has to do is keep an eye out. Will this thing work? He gives the sling a practice stretch, feeling pretty *probably not* if he's honest, and trying not to rue the fact he never bought Zac that air rifle, but Naomi put her foot down re that suggestion: 'You want to arm a ten-year-old? He hasn't even said he wants one!' Fair point. Joseph would never have been able to climb down the trellis with it anyway. Unless of course it was in a case, with a strap, et cetera, and this is what more waiting feels like, and look how long the shadows are over there, the sun sinking so midsummer-slowly, blood-orange through the treetops, but plenty of twilight left yet, bags of it, and yes, he knew it, look: there's a rabbit-shaped shape on the other side of that clump of bracken, now partly in view, now hopping a little nearer, looking pretty relaxed, stopping for a bit of a nibble, still too distant but yes, yes, coming closer, and pausing, and eating, and coming closer, and closer still, and when it reaches that bit of bare earth, if it does, well, that's when Joseph will have a pop at it, and Christ, excellent, it's nearly there.

Here it comes.

As in it's actually here.

Right, then.

Steady.

Joseph pinches a stone into the little leather sling and very slowly, careful to make no sudden movement at all, he draws the catapult rubber back, further, further, tighter, further still, right back, with the rabbit framed between the two stubby arms, and the elastic so taut now that the stone must surely fly hard and level and hit its mark.

Sadly, before he has the chance to find out, there is a sudden *crack* as the elastic, rubber, whatever, snaps.

Ow!

His hand is smarting.

And wow: the rabbit is exactly where it was. Stupid thing hasn't even looked up.

Joseph is still holding the little rock.

He stands and throws it at the rabbit, and of course misses, but at least that prompts the rabbit to bolt into the undergrowth.

Ha.

The slingshot rubber broke in the middle. As it would. There's not really enough either side to tie the thing back together again.

Hilarious.

As in he, Joseph Ashcroft, is a joke.

He's also, now that he's stopped focusing, utterly exhausted. Dizzy, sweating, aching, sick with tiredness, so spent he's tempted simply to lie down in the bracken exactly where he is, shut his eyes, and just give in.

But he can't.

He'll make it back to camp if he goes slowly. Might as well follow the edge of the field, noting the buttercups, the Jurassic Park-sized thistles, the – damn – rabbit-bitten grass. He knows this corner well because it's where he put the second . . . *snare*.

Joseph stops in his tracks.

Is he seeing things?

The trap has worked!

As in, it's occupied.

Hold on, though.

By a *squirrel*?

How on earth?

Squirrels generally avoid the ground, don't they, preferring to gambol about at tree level, making full use of their boastfully quick reactions and those grippy little claws. This one's are tight shut now. Possibly it got lost? Or is a baby? Some creatures – seagulls, for example – seem to be born pretty huge: possibly this is a large infant squirrel, young and therefore yet to master high-level travel from branch to fence post to bush and treetop, et cetera. Look at it, on its side, head canted back, grippy claws shut . . . opening.

Oh no: it's still alive.

Just about.

Joseph feels a surge of tenderness for the creature. How long has it been pegged here, kicking against his garden wire? Those black eyes are unblinking. Look at the soft white fur of its underbelly. And that ragged throat. It's definitely still breathing, poor thing.

If he had his boots on he could put it out of its misery that way, but in slippers, no thank you. Instead use the knife. Squat down, use the big blade, watch it disappear into the fur on the side of the squirrel's neck. This is not pleasant. Ignore the feeble kicking. Press hard. Harder.

Done.

Not much blood in a squirrel.

Or much meat on it, obviously.

A deer, chicken, rabbit even, this is not.

But Joseph is determined to follow through: he caught an animal to eat – the snare worked: take that, Lancaster! – and now he must eat it. All he has to do is remember what they taught him twenty years ago about skinning a rabbit. Just do that, plus of course gut it, prepare it properly, and cook it, and – karma-wise – all will be well.

May as well leave the head here.

And the tail.

It's just so squirrel, that tail.

In fact, let's have a go at preparing the corpse, carcass, whatever, here: that way he'll be returning home as from a trip to the shops, with a ready-to-go meal, sort of. It's easier to skin a just-dead – or was it just-bled? – animal; he remembers that, at least. You make a cut in the belly region, angling the knife tip up and not in, careful to avoid hitting the organs, guts and whatnot, and once there's a hole slash flap, do as much of the skinning as possible with the best tools known to a man, namely: fingers. That's right, peel it back, hear that sucking, soft rip. Messy, but yes, it's working, the skin is coming away like a sock off a bloody foot, all the way up to the forelegs, sort of sticking to the paws, though – so grippy! – but let's just cut those off here and now, like so, and do the same backwards to the hind legs, taking off its trousers so to speak, and again cutting off those feet.

Debagged, headless and tailless, the squirrel looks smaller still!

Also pretty marbly. Sort of glowing in the half-light.

But it's still full: he's yet to hook out the guts.

You jab the knife in under the breastbone, yes? And slit down towards the crotch, if a squirrel can be said to have one.

Now get your thumbs in there and prise the little body open, as if to read it like a book.

What have we here, then?

Mostly: grey, bubblesome, interesting.

Intestine.

Plus the darker heart and lungs and whatnot.

Just yank it all out, warm and slippery and smelling faintly of wet wood.

He could probably eat some of this offal, but not knowing what's what exactly means he'd be risking a mouthful of squirrel shit. So: just sling it all in that bush. Ditto the pelt, and other bits. Goodbye head, tail, et cetera.

Christ, what's left is about the size of a canapé!

Nonsense, it would fill a bap, if he had a bap to fill, which he sadly doesn't of course, but never mind that for a moment: he did it!

Yes, minutes beforehand Joseph was dead on his feet, a joke. Now he's borderline elated, triumphant. If sticky-fingered. Best return to camp via the stream. He can wash the meat, too. There it is, swishing back and forth underwater;

de-magnified it looks about the size of a child's hand. But he's damn well going to eat it.

96

After dark he starts a fire, waits for it to die down a little and, using a sharpened stick rammed through the ex-squirrel's middle, he roasts it over the flames. Not blackening the meat is tricky in the dark, but he does his best, and wow, as well as smoke, there's an actual smell of cooking in the den, which explains why his mouth is watering.

When all is said and done, this is all he is.

Hell, it's all anyone is.

Every one of us needs to eat.

And eat he will.

The squirrel – his squirrel! – is cooked.

Possibly overdone, in fact.

Never mind: this calls for a celebration.

Since he borrowed the whisky, he's not touched it for not-touching-another-drink-ever-again reasons, but now, as he takes the first hot bite of haunch – which tastes as much like tuna as it does sausage or chicken, or anything burned on a barbecue, in fact – he decides he needs to wash it down with something other than pre-boiled stream water, which, in any case, it seems he's out of. That was careless. But never mind! He pulls the bottle from its cardboard tube, peels the metal foil from around the lid and eases out the cork.

Oh, familiar squeak!

It almost makes him upend the bottle in the dirt.

But he doesn't. He sniffs the whisky instead, clocks the sharply different smokiness and immediately drinks, as in takes a gaspingly long pull on the bottle, flushing himself full of fire, thinking: there you are, and here I am.

Another gulp, and a bite of squirrel, and another gulp, and more of the stringy meat, and another, and the char-grilled squirrel is pretty much gone now, seen off with a few more gulps.

And . . .

He'd carry on but it seems his throat has swollen shut in protest for now.

Oh well.

The booze cannot have had time to work its chemical magic yet, but the brain – his brain! – is a funny old thing, meaning it's already relaxing at the prospect of its own relaxedness. Relaxing? Ha! From *relaxing* he'll advance swiftly through *carefree* to *couldn't-care-less* and beyond, towards the foothills of *don't-give-a-shit* and into the land of *who-gives-a-fuck* which, of course, borders the sparkling ocean of *oblivion*.

Great place to have a paddle, swim, little boat ride even. Once in a while. Not as often as he got used to during the 'you really have to confront this, Joseph; it's eating you up' year.

It being what, though?

As far as Naomi was concerned, though she didn't know the specifics: those kids in the oven, plus the baker with the triangular hole.

He takes a swig.

She was probably righter than his 'I've dealt with it' warranted.

But on top of that: the fearful disease, the state of things Big Beast-wise, the stupid costly shiny stuff.

All the ingredients very clear and obvious to him now, taking another gulp.

He settles back against the dirt wall of the den, pulls his woolly hat low over his ears, and hugs the bottle to his chest.

He's not about to drink all of it, is he?

No, because he's not an idiot.

Right now that would probably kill him.

There's a thought.

Ha.

He looks the other way, mind's eye-wise, and enjoys a mashed-up fuzzy collage comprised of things like Zac's hair lifting from his head as he bounces on the trampoline, the smell of Naomi's scarf, the word Gujarat, the idea of Lara on a horse, plus, weirdly, the glistening innards of splayed squirrel.

All good stuff.

Here they come round again: glistening scarves and the word trampoline and Gujarat opening its gates to let in Lara on a horse that smells of Zac's just-washed hair.

Once more: scarf-innard, Guja-squirrel, horse-smell, hair-gate, glist-oline.

Still lovely.

But what's this?

A dressing gown.

Ugh.

Joseph takes another killer gulp, but the image won't go away.

In fact, two more swigs down, eyes firmly shut, he sees the gown more clearly. Look at its stupid stripes, that monogram, the gold towelling belt loops and bulging pockets.

What's in them, then?

Of course: razor blades.

Gulp.

Hard to see the exact level of liquid in the bottle, the night being so dark above the roof-hatch, but when he swishes it about there seems to be more space than whisky.

No need to waste the torch battery: his hands know their way along the cot edge to the little recesses he's dug in the wall up at the head end of his bed. This one here has the knife in it, with the whetstone in the sheath pocket. Joseph clamps the whisky between his knees to free up both hands, so he can spend a pleasant few minutes sharpening an already sharp blade. That may sound a bit pointless, but if he's going to do the job he wants to do it properly, doesn't he?

What job?

Isn't it obvious?

The whisky alone might work, but this here knife tip would cut out the conditional, so to speak. Never mind that damn razor, Joseph tests the edge of his own blade – so sharp now it feels sort of sticky – against his fuzzy cheek.

That *Gujarat* headline looked promising: he can shut out the light knowing he's done something good, can't he?

He pulls up his left sleeve and lays the pale shape of his wrist across his knee. You're supposed to cut along as well as across it, aren't you, to be sure of bleeding out quickly?

Yes, well, that then.

He's already six feet under, give or take.

But possibly best close the grave-hatch first?

Good plan: actually inter himself . . .

He reaches to pull the little den-door shut and – oh damn – he forgot about the bottle, which flops over between his legs, whatever was left in it quickly emptying in the dirt.

Oh well.

He's shivering, and yet he feels so warm! He's very serious, very clear, and yet everything is also shades of stupid. He has to admit he's pretty sad, and yet, you know what, he's also quite happy.

They might not find him here for ages, years, aeons.

But what if they do?

And who might 'they' be anyway?

Some poor dog walker, in search of dog.

What have we here, then?

Oh my Lord.

Or, worse still, a child. One of the kids from the school. Imagine if he, Joseph himself, thirty-five years ago, when having a mooch around beyond the rusted iron boundary fence, had stumbled upon a desiccated man in the woods.

Is he sleeping?

No, dead!

Boom: nightmares, kid pretty much scarred for life, walk-in-the-woods-wise.

Although possibly it would also actually be quite exciting?

That's the wonderful contradiction of life!

Like now: this thinking, this feeling, first one thing, then the next, it's – still, even *now* – all so *impressive*.

The flat of the blade, pressed against Joseph's inner arm, has warmed up so that he can no longer tell where he ends and the knife begins, and while that's lovely it's also not good at all and, Christ, his head is swimming, meaning he has to concentrate hard to slot the blade back into its sheath without nicking a finger or slicing his palm, because, well, who was he ever kidding, that's where the damn knife belongs, obviously.

He doesn't bother putting it back on the elf . . .

Shelf

Or indeed climbing fully inside his sleeping bag, because he has no boots to take off, does he, just a gurgling belly and whirligig shed . . .

Head

So he can simply roll himself up on the rot . . .

Cot

Not minding that he's boinked said head quite hard against the dirt mall . . .

Wall

Because the head is in a hat, isn't it, and a hat is both protective and worn . . .

Warm

Just like the whisky smell bitch . . .

Which . . .

97

The hangover is not news.

It's as predictable as how he would have felt had he, say, run head-first into a wall, namely: an unconsciousness that smells somehow of petrol, plus a stiletto-tip of pain in the centre of his forehead.

When will it stop throbbing?

Also: peak thirst.

That desiccated version of himself he imagined last night? He's halfway there today, all husk, chaff, dustbowl, whatever. He has known proper thirst in the past month, but everything beforehand feels like nothing compared to his new, blotted, scirocco-wind self.

And sadly, for which read stupidly, his water containers are empty, because they just are.

It's still darkish.

Lighter when he opens the hatch, but – he checks his watch – only five fifteen.

Tap-shaped necessity propels him from the den. He doesn't even bother with the de-heeled moccasins, just grabs his bag and sets off at a half-jog, the occasional foot-shriek an almost-pleasant diversion from the metal-on-metal mashing of cogs in his head.

He takes the most direct route to Nine Pines.

And once there he cuts a clear diagonal across the big back lawn.

Because: fuck it.

Meaning, possibly, he's still stuck in the couldn't-care-less stage of drunkenness?

Ah, dewy grass, after all those bits of stick and stone-chip, so pleasant underfoot. Something about the lovely coolness of the lawn suggests that there's bound to be a new box of ice lollies in the freezer, and the thought of them immediately outflanks the tap. He must have a popsicle *now*. Knowing that it would be sensible to fill the water containers after raiding the freezer cements this decision, which turns out to have been wisely made, for lo, he's popping packs of tuna steak into his bag, staring all the while at the fresh box of Calippos, sitting just there, next to the salmon en croute.

Joseph shreds the box top, fumbles out a lolly and rips off its foil lid with trembling fingers. Only once he's bitten an ice chunk from the tube – Jesus Christ, that's beyond good! – and is squinting with lovely discomfort at the garage floor, does he see his neatly paired boots standing sentry next to the freezer.

Hold on.

Yes, they're definitely his.

He doesn't pick them up.

Just drops the freezer lid, sidesteps out of the garage, shuts the door, edges round to the tap.

With one eye on the house he trickles water into his bottle, breathing very quietly indeed. More quietly than that, in fact: sipping so noiselessly that when, from within

356

the kitchen Gordon starts up barking, the harshness of the sound has an industrial viciousness to it.

Joseph doesn't even turn off the tap properly: he just hobble-runs, barefoot and skeletal and hunched within his pack straps, scuttling across the lawn stripes for the cover of the beech hedge, a cockroach headed for the skirting-board gap.

Once through it, he keeps on all the way back to the wood.

That's where he's safe, after all.

And yet, safe enough?

Possibly not.

Therefore, take precautions.

Meaning: recce properly, tool up and dig in.

He skulks round the den a good hundred metres out, then again at fifty and twenty-five. Once he's sure nobody is nearby, he stows everything in the hole and works his way back around the zone with two things in mind, covering up all signs of habitation and cutting himself a few straight, thick sticks. What for? Sharpening, of course. He's going to ground for as long it takes, but he's not about to hide away defencelessly. Once he's harvested himself three poles, he scouts the den zone methodically, padding through the bracken and rhododendrons, scuffing over footprints and drawing the cover bushes in tight to the hole, paying attention to every fallen leaf and every bent stem. He even manages to pull a fresh clutch of brambles over the hatch as he lowers it from within.

98

All that day he stays put underground, each passing hour a congratulatory – still safe! – slap on the back. They're properly cumulative, these hours, for the longer nobody turns up, the less likely anyone will come. He doesn't venture outside at all, not even to relieve himself. The stench belongs to him. So do these sharpened sticks. Each of the three has a lovingly whittled pointy end, and all of them are laid with their noses up near the hatch. He drowns his hangover in tap water and time, not minding that he's not eating, unprepared to light a fire that first night for risk of sending up a smoke signal, preferring instead the burn of his hunger, its purifying, clarifying, monastic . . .

Pah, by nightfall, he's hungry as hell.

Also pretty tired: though he's intent on staying alert, listening out and so forth, his chin keeps dropping onto his chest, nodding-off-style. Here he is awake, listening to the trees creak, et cetera, but hell, he has to admit it, that hushing sound of the wind through the leaf canopy is somewhat lulling . . .

It's lovely when he lets his eyes shut.

But around one in the morning something makes them fly open. He sits blinking in the dark. What was that? Some new – snuffly? – noise. Did he hear it or dream it? The latter:

there it is again! And is that crackling to do with it as well? It's an animal sound, coming closer. Yes, something is moving above ground, ferreting through the undergrowth, but bigger than a ferret, louder: Christ, he can hear its this-way-and-that footsteps, paw-steps, whatever, very near by.

A sharp barking starts up, coming from directly above him, he's sure of it! Once, twice, three times.

Joseph wraps his hands tightly around one of his spear-sticks, crouching beneath the hatch. He's utterly awake, about to burst from the den, intent on scaring the thing – fox, dog, wolf?! – away, or even killing it when, as abruptly as the barking started, it stops.

Whatever's up there moves away.

Joseph stays very still indeed, listening intently, but the trees just shush to themselves for a long, long time and, as the hammering of his heart subsides, he convinces himself that the idea of a stray dog up there is as absurd as a wolf or polar bear: the big-sounding bark must have been his ears playing tricks on him, amplifying a fox yip or badger grunt through the drum-skin of the den.

The distraught mind: it's a tricky bastard.

Unfathomable, in fact. Not a quarter of an hour ago he was ready to kill, and now, again, his eyelids are heavy as hell, he's tired to the core, on the brink of falling asleep.

Just give in to it.

He'll have to rest eventually.

Blissful, to lie back, accept the inevitable, allow himself to drift off, up, away.

He sleeps too deeply for dreams.

99

And wakes – what the—? – to a strange smell.

Bacon?

Ha, ha, ha.

He doesn't bother lifting his head from the cot, much less sniffing deeply: why give his cruel imagination the pleasure? In a while he'll get up, build a fire, cook his own actual real three-dimensional tuna steaks. Still, he has to hand it to himself, the deep dark bit of his brain that's conjuring this full English breakfast is doing a pretty convincing job of it. As well as the smoked bacon smell he can just about hear the sizzling and spitting.

It can't be.

But it is.

He is not imagining anything at all: those are the real sounds and that is the actual smell of someone – close by – frying bacon in a pan.

His mouth is watering.

That, there, was the metallic rip of someone peeling the lid from a can. It says one thing as clearly as the speaking clock: baked beans.

And Jesus Christ, that's the chip and hiss of an egg being cracked open and slopped into the grease.

What next, the growling of a cappuccino machine?

Joseph does not know whether to laugh or ___.

Try.

No, *cry*.

He does neither, just gathers himself in the base of the pit, spear to hand, electrically confused.

What is going on?

Something cookery-related, that's for sure.

Yes, he's absolutely certain that his senses are not deceiving him, but why not do a sort of pre-flight check on them all the same, angling the point of his stick towards the hatch so that he can look hard at it wobbling there in the seam of morning light, to note that yes, the tip, having lain against the dirt wall, is greyly discoloured, but the rest of the whittled part is still a lemony yellow, which proves he can see clearly, and the solemn ache of hunger in his gut is no illusion either, it's just as real as the taste of his unclean teeth, and his nose and ears are likewise working perfectly, meaning everything is tuned up sense-wise, which in turn means what?

This: within thirty feet of where he's hiding, someone's cooking a fry-up.

Should he sit it out?

No, because whoever it is must know he's there; there's just no way this can be a coincidence.

Joseph levers up the roof-hatch.

There are stems and bracken shoots in the way, and a bit of the camouflaging bush kind of slumps forward off the half-raised door to block the view further, but through it all Joseph can still make out the shape of a man, and he's more like fifteen feet away than thirty, and he's sitting next to a larger gas-fuelled camping stove than the one Charlie bought Joseph, and there's a red pan on the stove, and the flame beneath it is sky-blue, and the man is pushing the bacon in the pan with a spatula.

Lancaster.

100

Lancaster doesn't seem to have spotted Joseph, who suffers an out-of-body experience, which runs as follows: he, Joseph Ashcroft of Airdeen Clore, is about to emerge from a hole in the woods, unless of course he lowers the lid again and retreats back into his hole in the woods.

Sadly, he doesn't have a chance to choose because without apparently looking up from his stirring Lancaster says, 'Morning, Joe.'

'Good morning.'

Lancaster waves at him: the gesture is clear despite the camouflage. 'Sorry to disturb you,' he says, 'but I thought a bite to eat might help?'

Joseph isn't actually out of the den yet: he could still drop the lid.

No.

He's climbing out and pushing through the foliage and Lancaster is turning towards him. Look at the muscles in those forearms, the bulk of the man's T-shirted shoulders as he shifts his weight. It's been a while since Joseph has seen him in anything but a suit. That bull-thick neck, the fuzz of red stubble running up to his freshly shaven head, the terrible competence with which he's still stirring that pan. It all distracts Joseph from Lancaster's expression –

eyes narrowed, mouth hanging open a little – what's the word for it? *Concerned.*

Lancaster drops his spatula.

The speed with which he rises makes Joseph do a whole-body flinch.

Joseph still has the spear in one hand: he kneel-slumps behind it, wobbly point raised, but Lancaster simply swats it aside on his way to raise Joseph gently by the elbows.

'My God; what have you done to yourself?'

101

There being no answer to that, Joseph tries to assert himself camp-wise, saying: 'You should turn off your stove,' because the smoke indicates that he should.

'Come here. Jesus. Slowly does it.'

'The eggs are burning.'

Lancaster guides Joseph to sit on a log he's pulled up, one arm around his shoulders, kind as a nurse. With the other hand he shuts off the gas flame.

'Never mind eggs and bacon; I should have brought a fucking stretcher,' he mutters.

Joseph finds this insulting. He can't look *that* bad. It's all very well for Lancaster to show up muscle-bound, smelling so . . . clean, and with a shiny stove, but he, Joseph, has put up with a great deal since they were last together. He's made do. He's kept going. He's endured.

So what if that came at a cost, appearance-wise?

'That's right. Sit there. Let's get a brew in you.'

Lancaster ducks off to pull a huge thermos from his waterproof-looking duffel, his every movement quick and precise and efficient, exactly like a man who knows exactly what he's doing, showing off by doing exactly that. His back is turned only for a moment, but it makes Joseph think: the game is not up, not yet, not quite, because it might still be possible to get away from Lancaster, mightn't it, were he to be distracted, or even incapacitated?

By whom?

Joseph!

Yeah right, plus whose army?

He's not about to try to run now, but he'll keep an eye out for an opportunity. In the meantime, Lancaster clearly thinks Joseph is at death's door, and that could be useful: Joseph decides not to disabuse him of that. Instead: listen to the sound of that tea sloshing out of the thermos! Typical Lancastrian foresight: it already has milk in it. Joseph's hand is doing some comedy shaking as he reaches out for the big mug. He slops a bit en route to his first sip.

'Thank you.'

'I can't quite believe this,' says Lancaster.

Joseph steadies himself. 'What?'

'Finding you here, like this.'

'How did you?'

'When your brother said you'd gone off camping we thought you'd pick somewhere nice. The Lakes, possibly, or the south of France. To begin with we imagined you'd just decided on taking some time out, that you'd be back to face the music in a week or two. Not this! At the very least I expected a tent.'

'A tent?'

'Bit selfish of you just to piss off without saying anything, then slope about the place like a burglar.'

'Burglar?'

'Everyone's been worried sick!'

Joseph is about to take another sip of tea when it occurs to him that Lancaster hasn't drunk any himself yet. What if the tea is drugged? How bloody stupid of him to go first. He's so cross with himself that his hand is shaking again, slopping more of the lovely tea. He should fling it all away. But just as he's getting ready Lancaster does two things, namely he puts a steadying hand on Joseph's wrist and takes a workmanlike gulp of his own tea.

Huh, outflanked again.

'Yes, but how did you find me?' Joseph asks.

'I didn't.'

'But . . .'

'Your dog did.'

'Gordon?'

'Yeah. We tried with him after Lara spotted your boots, but it didn't work the first time. Cold trail, possibly, or it could have been that she'd cleaned them up for you. Have to admit I was sceptical, but Naomi insisted we try again after yesterday and he got the idea, though I thought he might have woken you with that barking. Anyway, Naomi took him home, leaving me to cook up this surprise.'

'Did Naomi buy the bacon?'

'No, it was my idea. Would you like some?'

Joseph shrugs. *Like* doesn't quite cut it: Joseph wants a slice of bacon so ferociously badly he could weep. Of course he can't give Lancaster the pleasure of knowing that, but sadly, his traitorous tongue betrays him: 'If you've got some spare,' it says.

'Sure.'

Lancaster busies himself splitting the contents of both pans – beans, eggs, mushrooms, and bacon – onto two metal plates. He's pretty much whistling to himself.

Damn Gordon.

'There you go.'

'Thank you.'

Joseph looks down on the plate of food. The mushrooms, glistening with butter, sit on the left, next to a rich red island of baked beans. In the middle of the plate the scrambled eggs are pepper-flecked. And there, lying nonchalantly on top of them are three – no, four – rashers of crispy bacon.

He does not know where to begin.

102

'Take it slowly.'

One of the few films he took both kids to see at the cinema was *Fantastic Mr Fox*: sod Lancaster's instructions; Joseph has an urge to rip into the plate, starved-beast-style.

But he doesn't: it's a dignity thing, plus he needs all the time he can get.

Instead, he eats slowly, savouring every mouthful, even putting his fork (not spork) down now and then, casting around mind-wise for what?

An advantage?

Does he have one?

Only this: he knows these woods better than Lancaster does. If he can put some distance between the two of them, just enough to be out of sight – and he could do that within a hundred yards in any direction – he might be able to work himself further away, as in 'get away' entirely.

Ha.

Shoeless, penniless, husklike.

Yes well, this breakfast will help the old energy levels.

Lancaster has cleaned his plate and is leaning back. Look at those triceps. He's watching Joseph patiently. Is that in fact a kindly look in his eye?

'You knew the score, Joe,' he says at length. 'It's hardly like you're the first person it's happened to.'

'What score's that exactly?'

'You were lucky to survive the first bad year. Christ, it was you who explained the old "two in a row, the old heave-ho" thing to me! Why take it so personally?'

'This was a great breakfast. I owe you one.'

'You could say that.'

103

High up in the canopy a bird coos. It's a wood pigeon. Joseph has seen a few around. He looks up to see if he can spot any smudges of purply grey among the tangled greenness, but he can't. What does Lancaster mean by 'you could say that?' The cryptic bastard.

'Pretty stupid stunt to pull on your way out the door.'

'Stupid?'

'As in unrealistic, desperate. Some sort of cry for help, I assumed. But what were you trying to say?'

'I wasn't *saying* anything. I was redressing a balance.'

'Yeah, but . . .'

'But what?'

'You didn't seriously think you'd get away with it, did you?'

Noticing that his fingers are black with dirt, Joseph folds them into his lap. Beyond the spine, he thinks: that's the best direction making-a-run-for-it-wise. If he can get into the super thick rhododendron bank on the other side, there's a sort of tunnel he can work his way along, down towards the rabbit fields.

Lancaster goes on. 'I mean, the minute you started copying sensitive information beyond the bank's four walls – to a fucking liability in Leighton Buzzard! – a million red flags went up. Never mind my team, the gimps downstairs spotted it straight away. You wouldn't believe how hard I've had to spin this thing to make it look like a practical joke gone wrong.'

'He lives in Milton Keynes. And it's not a joke.'

'I can see that, believe me! The biggest clue? Pissing away your own money, or what was left of it, too. I tried, believe me, but beyond the bit your little friend wanted to keep for himself . . . well, the rest we couldn't undo. I reckon you've lost yourself two hundred and forty K.'

A fleck of bacon that had worked its way between two of Joseph's back teeth now comes loose. Damn, even that is tasty. And yes, it's a sign: it says that despite the horrible bereavement Lancaster is reporting, sounding as it does the death knell to Joseph's grand scheme, a little of the money – his money! – did get through. That, at least, is something. *Something*, and yet, in the $1.34 billion scheme of things, *nothing*. He swallows the bacon shard and – how embarrassing – finds himself fighting back tears.

'Christ, no need to look so glum about it. I'm telling you you're in the clear, more or less. Ben to the rescue. Obviously, you can kiss goodbye to your golden handshake, but they've bought my system-testing-moment-of-insanity bullshit. Smile, man. You're welcome.'

104

Even Lancaster's voice has grown more muscular, rich, convincing over the years; possibly because it's now powered by that deeper chest? Maybe he's been training his vocal cords? Is there a gym-based way of doing that? Whatever. It could just be put on. Yes, the confidence could all be an act designed to make Joseph go along quietly, so that Lancaster can turn him in. The bacon and so forth: it all seems very thoughtful, but possibly it's a smokescreen.

Eat this, have a cup of tea, you're in the clear! Now come with me . . .

Which, if a true lie, would in fact be good, because then there'd still be hope that he'd pulled it off, 'it' being sticking a hole in Airdeen Clore's money-coated side.

'Insanity,' Joseph says.

'Stress-related, momentary, a blip. I had a root around to try and find something to peg it on, but apart from the run-of-the-mill end-of-job, end-of-marriage, downsizing-shaped pressures I couldn't really find much.'

'No.'

'In fact, the opposite. It seemed you'd kicked the booze? Good effort there.'

'Thanks.'

'I thought about going with a catastrophic-falling-off-the-wagon theory, but really there was no evidence for that. The footage all showed you walking out of the building in a good straight line. And anyway, even when you were on the sauce, you seemed to manage to hold it together well enough at work. But maybe I was wrong about that?'

'No.'

'And of course there was the whole medical testing thing, but I'd have thought that would come as a huge relief after all these years with your head in the sand.'

Joseph feels a sudden and incredible stillness descend: the leaves in the treetops above him stop their flickering, there's not a breath of wind at bomb-hole level, the birds have fallen silent. He's a statue: more Mickey Mouse on the Disneyland ramparts than Churchill in Parliament Square, but still, it seems even the blood in his veins has come to a gentle halt.

How deep will Lancaster stoop?

Look at him there. What's he doing now? Digging something else out of his bag. It's a huge bar of chocolate. He's pinching the purple wrapper, tearing it open, pulling it off. Fruit & Nut. How assertively he's snapping the slab into two halves and holding one out. Even the gingery hairs on the back of his hand look vigorous, healthy, full of intent.

'Go on, Joe. You need feeding up.'

Everything inside says: no thanks, I'm all right for now, but Joseph's hand seems to be taking the chocolate and lifting it straight to his mouth. Give me that, it says. When he bites down his right canine feels wobbly, unsure of its toehold gum-wise, so Joseph impatiently snaps off a chunk

with his fingers, puts it straight in his mouth and lets it sit
there on his tongue, the taste rising like yeast left overnight,
bread in an oven, whatever.

It's nice.

Too nice!

Unbearable, in fact. Whichever bit of him is tasked with
processing taste is knotted in borderline pain right now.

Joseph's tongue quick-shifts the chocolate to his back
teeth.

They destroy it quickly.

He does a small grunt to mark the fact.

Take that.

Down it goes.

He finds he's grimacing.

'Medical all-clear aside, we need to get you checked out
by a doctor, mate. You're in a bit of a state.'

It's an insult: Lancaster clearly thinks he can lure him,
Joseph, Big Beast, from his lair, with half a bar of chocolate,
a cup of tea, and a lie-up.

Fry-up.

No! He's actually serving up lies! 'Medical all-clear' being
the most pernicious.

'The kids are desperate to see you, but you'll want to
sort yourself out first. The whole caveman thing might scare
them.'

His kids?

The bastard is going for a new, lower low.

'But I tell you what, before we head out, I'd love a look
at your little shelter.'

105

Lancaster levers himself upright in a boastful-triceps way and bounces on the balls of his feet, as if poised to work a piece of gym equipment. The laces in his Gore-Tex trail boot-shoes are very turquoise. Feeling somewhat loomed over, Joseph stands himself up, an Anglepoise lamp with weak springs, though he does his best to pull his shoulders back when upright.

Lancaster sidesteps his way through the undergrowth, pulling aside the brambles. 'Pretty good job you did here, Joe. Takes me back. Was there a reliving-your-youth element to all of this? Once was enough for me; I tell you that much!'

Joseph follows him. Look at the way Lancaster is yanking his camouflage left and right, stamping that fern down and kicking away the hawthorn offcut he so carefully placed to the right of the den entrance. Impotent twat.

Ha. Not that: *impudent*.

Funny how quickly the right word always arrives after the wrong one, isn't it? Funny-heartening. The word holes aren't so much emptinesses as puzzle gaps awaiting the right piece. He still has them all in the box.

What's this? Lancaster is complimenting Joseph on his concealment strategy, even as he ruins it. 'Without your dog,' he's saying, 'I really don't think I'd have found this. Mind if I have a look inside?'

'Help yourself.'

The gall of the man, squatting there to lift up the trap door, rocking forward on his bulging thighs, dipping his head down like a duck in a pond, all 'what have we here then beneath the lily pads?', et cetera. It's not his 'Christ, it smells a bit high in here,' that stings, more the fact of Lancaster's willingness to turn his back on Joseph, while on his knees! How fucking complacent is that? Without thinking the situation through, without hope, without a goddamn clue, Joseph nevertheless knows what he must do, and Lancaster's muted whistle of appreciation is the signal for him to do it. He bustles forward, plants a bare foot on Lancaster's raised arse, and shoves with all his might, so forcefully in fact that he falls over backwards himself even as Lancaster lurch-topples into-onto the den-hole-roof. It holds. Well built! That's something. Out of the corner of his eye Joseph can see that – damnit – Lancaster has managed to save himself from falling right in, but still, he's sort of lying twisted there, and his 'What the—?' betrays a hint of – yes! – panic.

106

Now, now, now.

Run for the spine.

He's light, he's spry, he's flying: look at him go.

Joseph makes it five, eight, thirteen, twenty-four crashing paces before . . .

How on earth?

Lancaster – striding, not running – has somehow cut him off, two big hands raised, arms wide, calling out rather than shouting: 'Joe, stop, Joe, there's no need for this, stop, Joe!'

Quite sing-song, that voice.

Infuriating!

How about this, then?

Joseph puts his head down and runs straight. Much like a noble beast, a bull, say, trapped in the ring! Who knows, he might be able to take down the matador with his last charge. Possibly stick him with a horn.

Knife!

Sadly it's back there, in his bag, in the den.

Two things happen at the same time: first, Joseph runs headlong into Lancaster; and second, exactly as he hits him, he realises he's glad he's not carrying six sharp inches of tempered steel.

Lancaster isn't on his knees, off balance, with his back

to Joseph this time; he's braced, arms out, leaning into the attack.

He catches Joseph like he, Joseph, used to catch the children when small.

Envelops him.

Wraps him up whole.

This can't be all he, Joseph, has got, can it? Do some kicking. Possibly a headbutt. Why is nothing connecting? It's like he's flailing against bedclothes. The harder he struggles the more enmeshed he becomes.

'Joe! It's me! Simmer down! Joe!'

Lancaster's chest feels like something carved. Also, it smells like something familiar . . .

Clinique For Men.

'That's right. Take it easy. I've got you.'

Joseph growls. At least he can do that.

'Come on, sit down, talk to me.'

Another growl.

'It's going to be okay, mate. Trust me.'

'Ha.'

'That's a start. "Ha". You'll laugh about this one day, I promise.'

'Are you fucking her?'

'What?'

'Are. You. Fucking. Her?'

'Who?!'

'Naomi.'

'Am I sleeping with your ex-wife?'

'Are you?'

379

'No!'

'You are.'

'Jesus, you really have lost the plot. What on earth makes you think that?'

'Your dressing gown.'

Lancaster is actually smiling at him. Joseph's fingertips feel bony rolled into fists.

'My dressing gown?'

'Yes.'

The smile broadens into an oh-I-get-it. 'Good spot. That is mine. But no, I haven't touched her. Honestly. No offence, but she's not even my type. She did ask for my help, though, and I did stop over, but only to keep an eye out for you, you daft bastard. Guilty as charged. She's been pretty worried, you know.'

'You're lying.' The words sound hollow.

'I'm not,' says Lancaster simply. 'I'm telling the truth and you know it. One day you'll look back on all this and laugh. Camping out in the woods. It will all seem funny. Christ, Joe, think of what we've got through before now. This is a joke compared.'

'No, I mean it. You're *lying*.'

'About what?'

'Everything.'

'Everything?'

'Nothing makes sense.'

'Yes it does. To me, anyway. I do actually get why you did it.'

'Why, then?'

'You were pissed off!'

'That's it?'

'You're a fighting man, Joe. Look at this: you are! You wanted to stick it to the bank on your way out. The fuckers chose Rafiq over you after all these years. You didn't think robbing them would work, not really; you just wanted to make a point. Things aren't going so well at home, but you get this new lease of life from the hospital and you think, you know what, if they're all showing me the door I'll show them how little I care.'

'No. I wanted to make amends.'

'Maybe. Either way I have to say I reckon you knew full well that I was still there, that I'd help cover it up.'

'You're going to take me in, hand me over, and they'll prosecute. You're sending me to prison.'

'For what?! Giving your own money away? Yeah, somebody should lock you up for that. But the rest is just a failed attempt. The bank isn't interested: do you think they want the press knowing one of their relatively senior guys tried to rob them? Of course not! That would be well embarrassing! No, they just want what they wanted before: you gone, without a fuss. And without your parting bonus, now: they're pretty happy about it!'

Relatively senior.

'Why did they have you hunt me down, then?'

'What? They didn't. Naomi called me, after she'd heard from your brother. She thought I might know where you were, or be able to help work it out, at least.'

'But the guy in London.'

'What guy?'

'You had Lara's phone tapped. He intercepted me after that.'

Lancaster does an I-know-nothing shrug, plus a smile laced with concern. 'Come on,' he says, 'let me pour you another cup of tea.'

'I don't want more tea.'

'Just rest a while, then. You look like you're about to fall over again. Perhaps you should put your head between your knees.'

107

Joseph allows Lancaster to guide him back to the little clearing with the camping stove, red pots, show-off-big thermos
and whatnot, and he half accepts the lowered-head suggestion, opting to drop his face, eyes shut, into his dirty palms.

He imagines a vase. A very valuable vase, possibly Ming.
He's no expert on vases! This one is his vase, either which
way. As well as being valuable money-wise, this vase is full of
hope. Plus it's beautiful. Or was. Now it is smashed. Smith-
ereens. That's the word! A thousand tiny hopeless pieces.
Also worthless? You'd think so, but: *not quite.*

Because of what?

That piece there. The little bit with the Ming crest on it, if
that's what they had, Ming vases.

Said crest represents what?

Something Lancaster said.

About?

The press.

The system won, as it always does. Joseph can't change
that because he never could. See that wall? Knock it down
– with your head! Not possible. That way lies a split skull
for him alone. But he can still give the bank a headache if he
goes to the papers. Confesses, et cetera. And not just about
what he tried and failed to do as he left, but about what he

did while he was there: the irregularities he helped the bank get away with deal-wise, the many governance-finessing regulatory piss-takes, the blind eyes turned, hell, the trading done on the back of confidential information, the bungs, the bribes, the . . . He has twenty years of proper insider knowledge about all this, and he can still make it count . . . for something.

Ha.

As in ah-ha.

But there's more to all of this, of course there is.

'What about Naomi?' he says.

'Naomi? She's worried for you, like I said. What did you expect?'

'Worried.'

'Yeah, beside herself. Reckons it's all because of Bosnia: the old PTSD.'

'She always wanted me to see someone.'

'Still does. You should.'

This makes Joseph laugh out loud.

Lancaster shrugs, marvelling at him. Eventually he says: 'I did.'

Joseph studies Lancaster's face. 'Seriously?'

'How could it hurt? Anything you say in the room stays in the room. The woman I saw was actually pretty good. I can give you her number. Look, at the very least, it will satisfy Naomi. Who'll be bloody relieved to see you, I tell you, mate.'

Naomi. The dressing gown, razor, et cetera. Even if she had been seeing someone: so what? It not as if he doesn't deserve it, and anyway, she's her own man. Woman. Till death us do part didn't quite work out but who knows, if he has the chance to explain all this to her, she of all people will understand. Her lovely arms. The way she walks. A cross between a strut and a waddle. Off to do something good. She'll see the point. Because unless Lancaster is out and out lying she's said she wants to see him again. That's more than a goddamn silver lining.

'She was kind of amazed at the whole Huntington's disease thing. That you'd kept it from her. Amazed, and pissed off, but finally relieved. Jesus, that could have gone the wrong way!'

Joseph, saying nothing, checks to see if he can feel the stillness descending again. The whole not-a-leaf-flickering thing happens again. The only movement is Lancaster wiping out the inside of a pan with a bit of paper towel he brought. So prepared!

'Ben,' says Joseph, 'please don't mess with me about that.'

Lancaster looks up.

'What do you mean?'

'Just don't.'

'You're the one who got himself tested.'

'I never saw the results.'

'You're kidding?'

'No.'

'Okay. Well. It didn't take much for me to find them out and I can tell you . . .' the slit of his mouth softens with – what is that? – *pity*? '. . . I can tell you're not going to believe me whatever I say.'

385

Joseph knits his fingers together to stop them shaking.

'But look, mate, you can do the test again. You'll see for yourself.'

This concerned we-go-way-back undertone is unbearable! Joseph gets up and turns around and walks off towards the den again. Without the camouflage: look at it. Now that is pitiful. In fact, Lancaster did do a bit of damage falling onto the roof. Damn him! This corner here is all broken in. Joseph can see the black strap of his rucksack on its side in the dirt. He reaches down, pulls the bag free, rummages through it to find – what? – the goddamn envelope, of course.

Are you an idiot? he asks himself.

Well, is he?

Quite possibly.

Only a fool would hand the unopened letter, treasured all this time, to Lancaster.

Joseph does that.

'I couldn't quite read it,' he says.

'My God, Joe.'

'The kids. I just . . .'

'You really haven't, have you.'

'So selfish of me.'

'Mate.'

'Could you open it?'

'Of course, but I already know what it says!'

'Please.'

108

Inevitably deft, Lancaster fillets the envelope, unfolds the single sheet of paper inside, looks it over cursorily and hands it up to Joseph.

There at the top: the St Thomas' logo and address.

Plus: Hospital Ref No. blah blah postcode, date, Dear Mr Ashcroft . . .

'*Further to the recent blood-screening tests undertaken to identify whether or not you have inherited the genes responsible for Huntington's chorea, I am pleased to inform you*' –

Pleased.

In the nanosecond before he reaches the next words: why not delighted?

– '*that the result was negative.*'

Joseph hears himself sigh, feels the descending coolness of a crisp new duvet unfurled over tired – so tired! – limbs.

The letter doesn't end there, but – Joseph scans the rest, just in case – it could have.

'*Negative.*'

What now? He's sort of slumping sideways again.

Oh well.

Lara.

He smiles to himself.

Zac.

There's a firmness to the duvet now. It's Lancaster. He's actually picking Joseph up, holding him, murmuring in his ear: 'You're okay, Joe, you're okay.'

'No, no, no.'

'Well, no more fucked than the rest of us, at least.'

Is that laughter percussing through Lancaster's deep chest?

'I've got your back, old friend. I really have.'

Old friend.

'What do you say we go and get you cleaned up?'

Joseph nods.

'Sit here, put these on while I break camp.'

From within his bag Lancaster retrieves Joseph's walking boots. The thought of Lara cleaning them for him raises a lump in his throat. As he pulls them on and does up the laces – so slowly – he watches Lancaster whizz this way and that, gathering up pans and stacking them inside one another and packing them into his duffel. He jumps down into the den as well: soon all Joseph's things are up over the hole rim, salted away, ready to move out. Well, nearly all of them. The cot he built, the handhold root, the mostly unbroken masterpiece roof; all that has to stay behind. Lancaster is saying something about how the kids might enjoy his bolthole; he could even help them repair it, though possibly once it's had a chance to air. And now the bags are bulging, full, ready to go. For a horrible moment Joseph fears that Lancaster is expecting him to carry his rucksack out of the woods – it looks heavyish again! – but of course he peremptorily shoulders both it and his own duffel and is even about to pick up the bin bag, half full of empty sausage plastics, bean tins, and popsicle wrappers, but since it's right next to his newly booted feet Joseph beats him to that. It's super light, this bin bag, but having bent quickly to pick it up, so is he: light-headed, at least. In that state he has a little wobble, as in he allows the actually-possibly-it's-still-best-to-run-for-it fear to rise in him again.

But of course he doesn't run.

He can't.

It's as much as he can do to imagine putting one foot in front of the other and following Lancaster from the woods.

He wavers there in the dappled morning light, dead on his feet, never more alive.

A wood pigeon coos. Another one answers. Or it could have been the same one cooing twice.

Doesn't matter: he, Joseph, has plans. Mostly they involve asking for help, plus filling in the holes with hope.

She wants to see him.

Take the first step.

You can do it.

So do!

He does.

It's just one step but it changes everything.

Acknowledgements

Thanks to Jonny Geller, Catherine Cho, and all at Curtis Brown; Walter Donohue, Sam Matthews, Claire Gatzen, Eleanor Crow, and all at Faber & Faber; Christopher Booth; and of course my family.

D